**Coming soon from Sandra Owens
and Carina Press
in the Operation K-9 Brothers series**

*Keeping Guard
Mountain Rescue*

**Also by Sandra Owens**

**Blue Ridge Valley series**

*Just Jenny
All Autumn
Still Savannah
Caitlyn's Christmas Wish*

**Dark Falls series**

*Dark Terror
Dark Memories*

**Aces & Eights series**

*Jack of Hearts
King of Clubs
Ace of Spades
Queen of Diamonds*

**K2 Team series**

*Crazy for Her
Someone Like Her
Falling for Her
Lost in Her
Only Her*

# OPERATION K-9 BROTHERS

---

## SANDRA OWENS

carina
press

**carina
press®**

Recycling programs
for this product may
not exist in your area.

ISBN-13: 978-1-335-40183-0

Operation K-9 Brothers

Copyright © 2021 by Sandra Owens

For questions and comments about the quality of this book,
please contact us at CustomerService@Harlequin.com.

Carina Press
22 Adelaide St. West, 40th Floor
Toronto, Ontario M5H 4E3, Canada
www.CarinaPress.com

**Printed in U.S.A.**

This book is dedicated to Sandra's Rowdies, who have been (not) so patiently waiting for Jack's story. Love you ladies!

# OPERATION K-9 BROTHERS

## Chapter One

"Stupid me. I trusted you," said the voice on the other end of the phone.

Jack Daniels, Whiskey to his SEAL teammates, blinked sleepy eyes at his bedside clock. Three in the morning sucked for getting angry calls from women. What the hell had he done to this one?

"Who's this?" That was the wrong thing to say. Jack held the phone away from his ear in an effort to save his hearing. He didn't recognize the number on the screen. Her voice wasn't familiar either.

"Sweetheart," he said, interrupting her tirade. "You sure you have the right number?" Even though her voice and phone number didn't ring any bells, he couldn't say for sure he wasn't the douchebag—along with some other impressively creative names she was calling him—in question.

Ah hell, now she was crying.

"How could you?" she said, her words slightly slurred. She hung up on him.

After thirty minutes of trying to go back to sleep, Jack let out a long sigh. How could he what? That question was going to bug him until he got an answer. Although her voice hadn't been at all familiar, he'd liked it, even when she'd been calling him names. He grinned. Sewer-sucking slimeball and twatwaffle were good, but his favorite was doggy doo. That one had a nice ring to it.

He got out of bed and padded to the living room where he'd left his laptop. Dakota sighed in resignation before hoisting herself up from her dog bed, her nails clicking on the wood floor as she followed him. She liked her sleep, something he interrupted too often for her taste because of his nightmares. At least they weren't occurring every night anymore. She sat near his leg and peered up at him with worried eyes.

"Not a nightmare this time, girl. We got a mystery on our hands. What do you think of that?"

She knew him inside and out, knew from the tone of his voice that he wasn't weighed down by his memories this time. Once she determined he didn't need her comfort, she made two circles, got her damaged leg under her, then curled up on the floor at his feet, apparently liking her sleep more than mysteries. Jack was intrigued, though, his interest in something flaring for the first time since coming home.

It only took a few minutes to find a name and address attached to her phone number. Nichole Masters, currently living in Asheville. Nope, not ringing even one little bell in his memory bank of female acquaintances or hookups. It was possible he'd forgotten one but not likely. He had a good memory, especially for women, and she had a sexy voice he was sure he wouldn't have forgotten.

Jack stared absently at the half moon framed by the window. Coming to a decision, he nodded. "All right, Nikki girl, you have me curious." As his teammates would tell anyone who asked, get on Whiskey's radar and all bets were off.

He showered, and after staring at himself for a minute in the mirror, he shaved off his beard, seeing his face for the first time in months. He felt naked.

At sunrise Jack made a recon run on one Nichole Masters. Her house was a cute little bungalow near the River Arts District of Asheville, North Carolina. As soon as he downloaded her Facebook profile picture to his phone, he knew that he'd never met her. There was no way he'd forget that face.

He should let it go, but she'd fucking cried, believing he was the cause. That couldn't stand. And yeah, he recognized that his reasoning was skewed. She'd thought he was some other douchebag, but Jack couldn't get her voice out of his head. Then there were her eyes, a warm golden brown. Were they as beautiful in person as they were in the photo? But it was her smile that drew him. It was an honest smile, and he sensed that Nichole Masters was a happy person. That some faceless man had made her cry didn't sit well.

It creeped him out a little that he was stalking her—and it sure as hell would her if she knew—but he needed to learn where she worked. Once he knew that, he'd come up with a plan to meet her in a way that wouldn't freak her out. Besides, he had nothing better to do.

He was on medical leave after getting too up close and personal with an IED. Dakota had saved his life by putting herself in front of him and pushing him back, in all likelihood preventing him from being blown to bits. She'd been severely injured, had almost lost a hind leg. Thank God she had survived, though, and was now recuperating, along with him. He would be returning to his team. She would not. She'd served her time, had saved the lives of many of his brothers, along with his, and had earned her retirement.

But it was preying on his mind. Dakota needed him, but he'd have to leave her behind when he was healed enough to go back. The problem was that he didn't know who to give her to. It had to be someone both he and Dakota trusted, and the only names that came to mind were his teammates. Because he'd given himself a deadline—two more months to get his arm and shoulder in shape—he was running out of time to make a decision.

Since there was a VA hospital in Asheville, he'd come home as soon as he'd been released from Walter Reed Bethesda Medical Center. After a month in the hospital—first in Germany and then at Walter Reed—he'd been ecstatic to leave that place behind. Physical therapy on his arm and shoulder was a bitch, but the sooner he was healed, the sooner he could get back to his team.

The first thing he'd done after getting out of the hospital was to track down Dakota. He almost hadn't recognized her. She'd been curled up in a corner of the kennel, rib bones showing, eyes dull, and fur lackluster. At the sight of him, she'd tried to stand, only to fall over when she put weight on her damaged leg. Since she belonged to the military, he'd had to call in some favors to get her released to him, but he'd been relentless in making that happen. When he'd first brought her home, she had been depressed and lethargic, and Jack thought she'd as much as given up. Thankfully she'd come a long way, and except for her leg, she was back to the dog she'd been before the bomb.

At precisely eight, Nichole Masters appeared, wearing a blue-and-white striped dress and white sandals. Jack blew out a breath as she walked down the steps of her little porch, a mug in one hand and the end of a leash in the other.

She was gorgeous. Her shoulder-length hair was a riot of curls in a fascinating mix of colors—reds, golds, and browns. A man could happily get lost in all that hair. She was tall, which he liked, and a little on the thin side, which he didn't like. Made him want to feed her.

He wasn't close enough to hear what she was saying to the puppy straining at the other end of the leash, but the dog was completely ignoring her. Jack could have told her that the little beast was going to keep winning their test of wills unless and until she positioned herself as the alpha dog in their relationship.

The puppy finally lifted a leg and watered a bush. The woman disappeared back inside with her little friend, and then a few minutes later walked out with a purse over her shoulder and the dog still on his leash.

Jack followed her to the River Arts District. After she parked and exited her car with her dog, he waited a few minutes before heading for the renovated warehouse she'd entered. As soon as he walked in, the aroma of coffee caught his attention and he headed for the small concession stand. While he waited for his order, he scanned the area. Artists on both sides of the aisle were setting up their tables and booths for the day.

It was a mix of arts and crafts. Next to the coffee stand, an older couple had a display of landscape paintings: waterfalls, mountain sunsets, and a few of downtown Asheville. Directly across the aisle was a booth filled with stained-glass pieces.

It was a cool place, one he'd have to come back and investigate when he wasn't on a mission. A puppy bark caught his attention, and coffee in hand, he headed for it. In the middle of the building, he found his target standing in front of a long table loaded with pottery, tangled up in the leash her puppy had wrapped around her legs.

"He taking you prisoner?" Jack said.

She glanced over at him with laughter in those golden-brown eyes, and his heart thump-skipped in his chest. That had never, ever happened before, and he almost turned and walked away. A female-induced twitchy heart wasn't his thing.

Then she leaned precariously, looking like a tree about to topple over. Jack dropped his coffee onto the table next to her and was at her side in time to catch her before she landed face-first on the cement floor. Damn, she smelled good, like vanilla and maybe almonds. Whatever it was, it made his mouth water.

"Um, you can let me go now."

And there was that throaty voice that had kept him awake last night. "Do I have to?" He winked to let her know he was teasing—not really—and then he made sure she was steady on her feet before crouching down in front of the puppy.

"Hey, buddy," he said, putting one hand on the dog's rear end. Jack lifted his gaze to his new fantasy. "What's his name?"

"Rambo."

"Here's the deal, Rambo. When I say sit, you're going to plant your butt on the ground." He pushed down on

Rambo's rear end while pressing the palm of his other hand to the puppy's nose. "Sit." Still keeping his hands on the dog, he had to repeat the command a second time when the little guy tried to climb onto his lap.

Rambo wasn't stupid. He recognized Jack was the alpha and kept his butt glued to the ground this time, although he did wiggle his rear end, all that puppy energy making it impossible to sit completely still. But he kept his gaze on Jack, as if waiting for his next instructions.

"Good boy." Jack gave him a chin scratch as a reward.

"Wow, how did you do that?"

As soon as the puppy heard her voice, he tried to jump up her legs, his tail furiously wagging. She laughed, a musical sound that Jack liked a lot.

"A combination of things. Using my hands to signal what he needs to do for one, but mostly the tone of my voice."

"Can you show me?"

*That would be an affirmative.* Jack took a moment to rein in his lust before lifting his eyes to hers. "I could help you train him."

He took the end of the leash from her hand and unwound it, freeing her legs. Wasn't his fault if the leash was so tight that his fingers brushed across her skin as he performed his chore. Not that it was a chore in any way, shape, or form. The goose bumps that rose where he touched her pleased him. She wasn't immune to him.

"Are you a professional dog trainer?"

How much truth to tell her? Most of it, just not the stalking part. That was entirely too creepy. He stood, keeping the leash and tightening it so that Rambo had to stay by his legs.

"Jack Daniels," he said, holding out his hand.

She raised a finely arched brow. "For real?"

"Yeah. My parents had a weird sense of humor. My SEAL teammates call me Whiskey, if that works better for you." A lot of people thought SEALs weren't allowed to reveal their identity, but that wasn't true. They just didn't go around advertising the fact. He hoped knowing would make her feel more comfortable with him.

He smiled—impressed that he remembered how— and waited to hear her answer.

Nichole eyed the blond-haired, blue-eyed man who was apparently a dog whisperer. Wow, an honest-to-God SEAL, and he was as hot as the SEAL heroes in her romance books. Maybe even hotter. Definitely hotter.

"Nice to meet you, Jack. I'm Nichole Masters." She held out her hand, and it disappeared inside his massive one. His touch was gentle, but she was sure he could crush her bones if he wanted. His voice sounded vaguely familiar, but she was positive she'd never met him before. Jack Daniels was not a man a girl would forget.

"And you, Nichole." Rambo barked, and Jack let go of her hand. He smiled down at her puppy. "Yes, we haven't forgotten about you, Rambo." He glanced up at her. "That's a big name for the little man to live up to."

"I'm hoping he'll grow into his name. He's a rescue, part German shepherd, part anyone's guess. The vet said maybe some sheltie." Her hand was warm from being in his, her fingers tingling a little from his touch. The last time she'd had tingly anything from touching a man had been with Lane, before he had shown her his true self. But she wasn't going there, not when a hotter-than-hot hero was sharing her breathing space.

He handed her the leash. "Two intelligent dog combinations and very trainable. He'll test you, but he'll also want to please you."

She blinked, trying to catch up with their conversation. She ran his last words through her mind. Right. They were talking about Rambo. "Believe me, he's doing a great job of testing me." She'd never had a dog before, and honestly hadn't had a clue how rambunctious or destructive a puppy could be.

He glanced around. "Maybe this isn't the best place for him. At least not until he's trained."

As if to prove his point, Rambo tangled his leash around her legs again, then stuck his nose under her dress, lifting the hem halfway up her thighs. She bent over to grab the skirt before she flashed not only a hot SEAL but all the strangers around them, whose attention suddenly seemed to be on her.

Rambo dropped to his feet, gave a happy bark, and then tried to run in the opposite direction. With her legs bound together by the leash, preventing her from getting her balance, she toppled forward, her face heading directly for Jack's crotch.

She put her hands out to keep her mouth from landing on the most private part of him, but when she realized that would result in her groping him, she panicked and ended up windmilling her arms. A mere inch before her mouth got entirely too up close and personal with a man she'd only met minutes ago, a pair of hands slid under her arms and lifted her back to her feet. That would have been great if her new position wasn't breast to SEAL chest. An extremely hard chest. Desire spiked through her, adding to her embarrassment. Her cheeks and the back of her neck felt like they were on fire.

"Ah…ah." She realized her arms were sticking out in a pretty good imitation of a scarecrow, so she dropped them to her sides. He kept his hands on her arms, trailed his fingers over her skin, down to her wrists, leaving goose bumps in his wake. She lifted her gaze to his. Lord have mercy, his eyes were a hundred times darker than they had been before she'd smashed her breasts into his chest. She wondered if he would mind if she climbed him like a tree.

A slow—sexy as all get-out—smile curved his lips. "Hello," he murmured.

"Hi," she chirped. *Really, Nichole, you've taken to chirping?* He let go of her and stepped back, then dropped to his knees. Her heart slammed into her rib cage at seeing him in that position while her mind was stuck on the breasts-to-chest thing and her skin tingling from his touch.

As if he could read her thoughts, he lifted his eyes—still a darker blue—and gave her that sexy smile again. "I'm just going to free you."

"Oh." That came out sounding disappointed, and he chuckled. What in the world was wrong with her? She'd never reacted to a man like this before, not this fast and this…well, tingly.

"There, all better," he said once he had her unwrapped from the leash. He tapped the puppy's nose. "You're a handful of trouble, aren't you?" Rambo tried to lick him. Jack stood and handed her the end of the leash.

"This is the first time I've brought him here with me. I guess I jumped the gun, but he's learned to recognize when I'm leaving and starts to cry. I felt guilty for sticking him in his crate all day. Eventually I want to be able to bring him, but obviously I need to wait until he loses some of his puppy energy."

"That will happen, even faster if he gets some training, but yeah, this isn't a good place for him right now. Too many interesting things and people to check out."

"Live and learn, right?" A couple walked up to her booth. "Um, I need to get to work."

"You have your phone on you?"

"Yes. Do you need to make a call?" Heaven help her, the man really did have a killer smile.

"No. I was going to put my number in it. You know, in case you decide to take me up on my offer to help you train Rambo."

"Oh. Right." He probably thought she was a scatterbrain, but it was entirely his fault for being so sexy that it was hard to think around him.

As if to prove he needed training, her dog was straining at the end of his leash, trying to get the couple's attention with begging yips, hoping for a little petting. "Rambo, no." She pulled him back toward her, and of course, he planted his paws so that she ended up dragging him.

She glanced at Jack, expecting to see disapproval, but the only thing in his eyes was amusement. "Here." She unlocked her phone and handed it to him. "You'll definitely be hearing from me if you can teach him some manners."

"I can."

When he handed her phone back, their fingers brushed against each other, and there was that tingling again.

"Take care, Nichole." He squatted in front of Rambo. "I know you have a lot of energy, buddy, but try to behave for your mistress." Rambo tossed himself onto his back, his tail scraping across the floor.

"I don't think *behave* is in his vocabulary."

Jack glanced up at her as he gave her dog a belly rub. "Part of teaching him that word will be to teach you how to master him."

There was something in the way he said that, in the flash of heat in his eyes, that had her almost fanning her face. "Um, master him, right." *Jeez, Nichole, get your mind out of the gutter.*

That was easier said than done with this man, and when the heat returned to his eyes and one side of his mouth curved up, she knew he knew right where her mind had gone. Again.

She glanced at the couple, who were still browsing. The woman picked up a mug. "I love how you embedded a maple leaf in these. I'll take the set."

"I'll be right with you." She glanced at Jack. "Gotta go." Before something else came out of her mouth… Like *my bed is only a few minutes from here. Want to go play?*

He rose in a slow unfolding of his body that had her eyes tracking every movement and flex of his muscles. Oh, yeah. Sex. On. A. Freakin'. Stick. She'd been burned so badly by her last boyfriend that she'd gone through an I-hate-men stage. That phase might have just ended.

"Hope to hear from you, Nichole," he said before picking up his coffee.

"I think you will," she murmured as she watched him walk away. "And real nice butt, Whiskey," she added.

Her morning had started off as one of the crappiest ever. She'd woken up tired and out of sorts after drinking enough wine to get up the nerve to call Trevor the Bastard Allen at three in the morning and tell him what she thought of him for sabotaging her commission. She'd figured that if she was up at that time of night, stewing over what he'd done, that it was only right for his sleep to be disturbed. The jerk had pretended not to know who she was.

Rambo hadn't helped her mood when she'd found her favorite running shoes chewed up. Her fault for leaving them out, but weren't all the toys she'd showered him with enough? Considering everything the world had rained down on her recently, she deserved a hot SEAL to play with, right? But she refused to appear too eager—because, really, the man probably had eager-to-get-into-his-pants women at his beck and call—so she'd wait a bit to contact him.

## Chapter Two

*There were two seasons in Afghanistan: freeze-your-ass-off cold and heatstroke fucking hot. At the moment Jack was positive he'd sweated off a good fifteen pounds under his uniform, flak jacket, and gear. He spit the dust out of his mouth and swiped his sleeve across his forehead. If he took off his helmet, a gallon of perspiration would probably fall down his face. He closed his eyes and tried to imagine that the warm water he was chugging was a beer so cold that it had turned into an icy slush. Didn't work.*

*After giving Dakota some water, he nodded at his team. Time to move out. They were doing a reconnaissance run, looking for an Afghan official who'd been kidnapped. Intel had come in that the man was being held in the small village two klicks ahead. Since the information had come from an unreliable source, their orders were to find a place where they could observe. If they could confirm the official's presence, they'd mount a rescue.*

*He was point with Dakota, and he made a useless wish that they could find a location to set up that had a damn shade tree. Useless because there wasn't a single tree between him and the horizon. Dakota was a few steps ahead, her tongue flopping out the side of her mouth as she panted in an attempt to cool down. She was his third dog, and a good one.*

*A klick out from the village, Jack removed his sunglasses to wipe the sweat from his forehead again. Dakota came to a sudden stop, then pushed her sixty pounds of muscled body against his legs, forcing him back.*

Jack lurched up, the sound of the explosion roaring in his ears and the smell of burning flesh in his nose. A wet tongue licked his face, the stench of cooked skin replaced with dog breath. Dakota's whimpers penetrated his brain, bringing him back to the present.

He sucked in a lungful of air. "It's okay, girl." More air inhaled. "I'm awake." This was their routine each time the nightmare came. It was always the same, the thunderous boom of the explosion sending him straight up in bed, his heart jackhammering in his chest, and his lungs searching for air. Dakota was always there to bring him out of it.

A week passed, and Jack still hadn't heard from Nichole. He'd been sure he'd get a call from her after they talked about Rambo's training. Had he lost the ability to read women? Maybe the bomb had stolen that particular talent.

He continued with Dakota's daily therapy treatments on her leg and stuck to his morning ten-mile runs. Although he was scarred all the way down the left side of his body except where his flak jacket had protected him, his legs worked just fine. And Dakota was making good progress, which was great.

What he wasn't good with was his damaged shoulder and arm refusing to heal as fast as he wanted. His team needed him, and between worrying about them and having nightmares, he was fighting bouts of depression. But he was a SEAL and SEALs sucked it up. So that was what he was doing, or trying to.

His house had belonged to his parents, and at their deaths five years ago, ownership had come to him, no mortgage attached. He'd considered selling it, but it was full of memories of his mom and dad, and he'd decided to hang on to it. For a while anyway. Now he was glad he had. He'd had a place to come home to after getting hurt. Besides, the mountain views off his back deck were amazing. It was a good place to heal.

Unable to fall back asleep after his latest nightmare, he made a pot of coffee and went out to the deck to watch the sun come up. Dakota put her head on his knee, her dark-chocolate eyes peering up at him.

"Time for our run, huh?"

Dakota barked her agreement.

"Let's go then."

She was a Belgian Malinois, a working dog. A dog that needed to be active and useful. With her damaged leg, she couldn't manage his ten-mile runs, so he'd go a half-mile one way and back with her, then put her in the house before doing another nine miles. She was never happy about getting left behind. She still believed it was her job to protect his six, and how could she watch his back if she wasn't with him?

His thoughts returned to Nichole as he ran. How had he been so wrong, certain he would hear from her? And what to do about it? Although he should forget about her, he was finding that impossible.

Maybe he'd give her another week, then drop by her

booth at the River Arts District. Tell her he was in the neighborhood—or something stupid like that—and was curious to see how Rambo was doing.

Or maybe not. If she didn't call, then she wasn't interested in seeing him. Truthfully, it was irritating that he couldn't get her out of his head.

Hot and sweaty after returning home, he jumped in the shower. He had a physical therapy session in the afternoon, but what to do with himself until then? The hours when he had nothing to do but think were killing him. He was out of the loop—didn't know what was going on with his team—so he worried. Were they out on an op right now? He should be with them, and although it wouldn't be Dakota, he'd have a new dog sniffing out bad guys and IEDs, helping to keep them safe.

Ants crawled under his skin, something that was happening more and more lately. He snatched up the keys to his Ford 150 pickup. Dakota loved to go for rides, and it made him happy to see her hanging her head out the window, tongue lolling out the side of her mouth, a silly dog grin on her face. Yes, his dog smiled, and although she looked ridiculous doing it, he never could resist smiling back at her.

He was in dire need of a buddy to go out and have a beer or two with, if the highlight of his days was a grinning dog. A certain woman who seemed to be ignoring him would be even better.

"Want to—" His phone rang before he could say the words *go for a ride*, which would have brought his sleeping dog instantly to her feet. Even so, she jumped up from her nap on the floor and glared at the phone.

"Disturbing your precious sleep, are we?"

She shifted her glare to him, as if he'd purposely made the contraption make noise.

The screen displayed Caller Unknown, and he almost didn't answer. But it was an Asheville area code, and his heart skipped a beat. No, it wasn't Nichole. She would have called him by now. He answered anyway.

Nichole managed to wait an entire week to call Jack Daniels, and that wasn't an easy thing to do. She wanted to call him minutes after he left to tell him she would take him up on his offer to train Rambo. Each time her fingers crept to his number on her phone, she chanted, *Don't be easy. Don't be easy. Don't be easy.* Because seriously, what woman wouldn't throw herself at his feet and beg him to take her, however, wherever, and whenever he wanted? She wasn't going to be one of those girls.

So she made herself wait. It didn't stop her from watching the entrance to the artisans' mall, half expecting to see him walk in. He didn't. Not only was that disappointing, but it made her wonder if she was wrong in thinking she'd seen interest in his eyes. And because she let seven days go by, and because he hadn't made an appearance, she was now hesitant to call him. Maybe he was relieved she hadn't taken him up on his offer to train Rambo.

She sighed when her dog put his paws on a customer's legs, begging for attention. "No, Rambo." He ignored her. "I'm sorry," she said to the woman as she tugged on his leash, dragging him back to her. He was such a friendly dog, and she didn't want to curb his enthusiasm for life, but he couldn't keep jumping on people.

"Perhaps he would be happier left at home," the woman said before walking away.

Nichole resisted the urge to stick out her tongue. No, he needed to learn how to behave. This was the first time since last week she'd brought him with her. A colony of ants had taken up residence in her kitchen, and the exterminator had sprayed this morning. Worried that Rambo might have a reaction, she hadn't wanted to leave him in a closed-up house all day.

She not only wanted a companion but also hoped Rambo would be protective of her when he grew older. She was a single woman, sometimes leaving the Arts District after dark, and she felt safer having a dog…or she would if he ever learned how to guard her.

Her dog was a sweetheart, and she loved him dearly, but if some guy tried to get in the car with her, Rambo would probably open the door for him and then shower him with kisses. She didn't expect Rambo to be a puppy guard dog, but she would sure like to see him grow into the role. It was doubtful that was going to happen without some kind of training.

It was time to call Jack. A customer walked up, one who thankfully seemed to like rambunctious puppies, and after playing with him for a few minutes, the woman bought a complete ten-piece set of dishes. After agreeing on the date Nichole could deliver them and paying for half the commission, the woman moved on to the next booth.

It was a good sale, although not a record. During the past year she'd been making a name for herself, and clients were seeking her out. Her biggest sale would have been a commission to supply a local three-star Michelin-rated restaurant with dishes designed solely for them—the commission that Trevor the Snake Allen had sabotaged. That she'd thought he was an amazingly talented potter, had thought he was a friend, and had made the mistake of telling him about the commission had her wishing Rambo was trained to kill. Maybe her puppy could lick him to death.

Trevor had gone behind her back and somehow convinced the restaurant owner that Nichole wasn't capable of delivering such a big order in the agreed-on time frame, but that he could for five thousand less than she'd quoted, and deliver two weeks sooner. Even worse, the owner had given Trevor her samples so he could duplicate them.

She wasn't happy with the restaurant owner, but she was livid with Trevor. Unfortunately, she hadn't had a signed contract. After showing her samples and agreeing on a price and deadline, she'd told the owner that she'd return the next afternoon with a contract. She'd left the samples with him, another mistake, but it never occurred to her that a snake would slither in and bite her on the butt.

There was no recourse, as she hadn't copyrighted the design. Most potters didn't, as it was expensive to file a copyright for each design they created. If she'd had an inkling that Trevor would steal her commission, she sure would have.

Rambo circled her legs, tying her up again. She sighed as she bent over and untangled herself. "You're a stinker, you know that?" He licked her hand.

She picked up her phone, found Jack's name, and hit Call.

"Daniels here," he said.

"Um, hi. It's Nichole Masters. Rambo's owner."

"Hello, Nichole. This is a nice surprise."

He sounded pleased to hear from her, and that had her smiling. "Were you serious about training Rambo?"

"No."

Her heart tumbled, feeling like it landed in her stomach. "Oh—"

"I was, however, serious about helping you train him. It won't do any good if you don't know what you're doing. He'll just forget anything he learns if you don't know how to reinforce what we teach him. That means you're included in the sessions, otherwise it's a no-go. Are you good with that?"

*So good!* "Sure. That makes sense, and I do want to know how to handle him. I want him to be happy, but he also needs to behave. Right now, he's not so good at that."

"Most puppies aren't. What is he, four or five months old?"

"I'm not sure of his birthday, but about that."

"In people years he's a preteen. Lots of energy and testing the boundaries. When do you want to start?"

She glanced down at Rambo to see he was gnawing on the table leg. "As soon as possible."

"What about this evening?"

Her heart gave a little lurch. That soon? "Yeah, sure. I usually get home around six. Give me a little time to change and grab something to eat. Say six-thirtyish?"

"Why don't I make it easy on you and bring a pizza?"

She was liking this guy more and more. "That would be great."

"What do you like on your pie?"

"Anything but green peppers, olives, and anchovies."

"Already we have something in common." He chuckled. "Text me your address, and I'll see you this evening."

Before she could respond, Trevor Allen walked up, and the rage she'd managed to stifle the past few days surged. "What are you doing here?"

"Nichole?" Jack said. "Is everything okay?"

"I have an offer for you." Trevor lifted his chin toward the phone at her ear. "When you finish your call, we'll talk."

"I have nothing to say to you."

"Finish your call, Nichole."

"Go to hell." She turned her back to him.

"Nichole?" Jack said again.

"Gotta go, Jack. See you tonight." She disconnected before he could ask what was going on. Her hands were shaking as she shoved the phone into the back pocket of her jeans. How dare Trevor the Bastard come here, much less want to make her an offer. There was nothing he could say that would make her want to be anywhere near him or connected to him.

Rambo yipped, and she glanced over to see he was bouncing around Trevor's feet. "Rambo, no!" She snatched him up. "We don't speak to him. Ever."

"Ah, come on, Nichole. It was just business, and you should be thanking me. I taught you a valuable lesson. I do feel a tad sorry that you lost the contract, so to make it up to you, I'm offering you five thousand to work with me on getting the commission finished on time." He smiled.

For a very short time she'd thought his smile was boyishly cute. She'd even been a little in awe that such a talented potter was interested in her. Wanting him to see her as a peer had prompted her to brag about the commission she'd been offered. A big mistake that.

Now she wanted to slap that stupid smile right off his face. He was a good-looking man, his appearance artsy with his black hair a little too long and scraggly, dark eyelashes that she envied, and hazel eyes that had fascinating gold rings around them. His style of dress was grunge, and he embraced it with enthusiasm with his oversize shirts, torn jeans, and scuffed combat boots, the very picture of a serious artist…or so she was sure he believed.

She called bull on his idea of her helping him being a favor he was offering from the goodness of his thieving heart. More like he either realized he couldn't duplicate her design or that he couldn't meet the deadline he'd given. Maybe both, and that thought pleased her to no end. "You can take your offer and stick it where the sun don't shine."

His eyes narrowed and his lips thinned. "Classy." He glanced away, and when his gaze returned to her, the pinched look on his face was gone and the smile was back. "Look, I scratch your back, you scratch mine. Win, win." He held his hands out, palms up. "I'll even let you put your name on the back of the plates under mine."

The nerve! She strode to him, getting in his space. "The only thing I'm going to scratch are your eyes out if you don't go away." Rambo whined, apparently picking up on the tension. Either that or she was about to squeeze him to death. She eased her grip on him.

"We'll talk after you calm down." He walked farther into the mall.

*Calm down? Calm down?* She planted her feet to keep from chasing him and tackling him to the floor so she could beat the crap out of him. It disturbed her that she had these hateful feelings. She was not a violent person, and she detested Trevor for bringing out something inside her that she'd never known existed.

"You're getting heavy, kiddo." She set Rambo on the floor and shook a finger at him. "You are not to cozy up to him, you hear? He's the enemy." Rambo licked her face.

It was interesting that Trevor hadn't said a word about her calling him in the middle of the night. She'd been sure that he'd have something to say about that.

In an attempt to get her mind back to a peaceful state, she grabbed the soft cloth she used to dust her pottery. Pottery—making it, touching it, even dusting it—made her happy. She dusted her heart out. It was working, the tension easing as she shined each plate, bowl, saucer, mug, and decorative item. She particularly loved the collection of fairies that were popular with customers.

"Are you calm enough to talk now?"

At hearing Trevor's voice, she took a deep breath and counted to ten before turning to face him. She'd thought he'd left. "I'll never be calm enough to talk to you."

He shook his head as if she were a naughty child. "Nichole, get over your sulk. I'm making you a great offer here."

"Seriously? You jackass, you're offering me a sliver of my own commission back?" She headed for him, fully intending to follow through on her threat to scratch his eyes out.

"There a problem here?"

The deep voice speaking behind her had her spinning her head like a possessed person who needed an exorcist. "Jack? Where did you come from?"

## Chapter Three

"Here and there." Jack stepped next to Nichole. "He bothering you?"

The man's gaze swung to him. "Who the hell are you?"

"Depends on her answer. Either someone you don't need to worry about or your worst nightmare." He'd always wanted to say that, the worst nightmare part, and he had trouble keeping a straight face.

She glared at the man. "He's not bothering me because he's leaving."

Deny it all she wanted, but it was obvious the man was bothering her, and Jack didn't like that one bit. But until he knew the problem, the last thing he needed to do was overstep, making the situation bigger than it was.

Toward the end of their phone conversation, she'd sounded agitated, and he'd heard a man talking to her. It didn't take a rocket scientist to decipher her "What are you doing here?" and the tension in her voice to figure out the dude was upsetting her. It wasn't any of his business, but he hadn't been able to stay away.

Jack eyed the lean man, not impressed. He supposed the tears in the knees of the jeans was a thing these days, but he thought it was pretty stupid to pay good money for damaged goods. And the guy's combat boots? No way they'd ever set their soles on desert sand.

"Correct me if I'm wrong, but I believe the lady said you were leaving." Jack raised a brow when the man didn't move.

"I need to talk to Nichole…alone."

"Not happening unless that's what she wants." He shifted his gaze to Nichole. "Is that what you want, darlin'?" Okay, he was laying it on a bit thick, but the dude was rubbing him wrong.

"No, sweet cheeks, he has nothing to say that I want to hear."

*Sweet cheeks?* He couldn't hold back his snort, then tried to cover it up with a cough. Nichole's elbow in his ribs said he hadn't done a good job of that. Damn, he liked this girl. Rambo was trying to climb up his legs, so he picked up the puppy, holding him in his good arm while he draped the other one over Nichole's shoulders, creating a picture of a happy little family. "You heard the lady. Now scram."

"This doesn't concern you, Neanderthal. It's between me and Nichole."

Jack sighed. He'd hoped the guy would respect Nichole's wishes. That wasn't happening, unfortunately. He didn't know what the problem between them was and didn't care. His parents had taught him that women were to be respected and treated equally. Maybe he needed to teach this man that lesson.

"What's his name?" he asked Nichole.

"Trevor."

He set Rambo down, and then handed Nichole the leash. Stepping into Trevor's space, he bumped his chest against the man's. Whatever he wanted from Nichole was making the dude desperate. Desperate men tended to get stupid. No man was going to get stupid around Nichole on his watch. If that meant he was a Neanderthal, so be it. She might give him hell for interfering later, but he could take it.

"Here's the thing, Trevor. She doesn't want to talk to you, so I'll give you three seconds to walk away."

"Or what? You're going to beat the shit out of me, then pound on your chest and say, 'Me Tarzan'? Go ahead, make my day."

Jack couldn't help it, he laughed. "You're a funny dude. But your three seconds are up, and I'm going to do this." He put his hand on the back of Trevor's neck, spread his fingers, dug his thumb and index finger into his neck's pressure points, and walked Trevor and his never-seen-combat combat boots through the mall and out the door.

"Take my well-intentioned advice, Trevor. Leave Nichole alone." He dropped his hand from the man's neck. "Do we understand each other?"

"You're a beast, a…a bully."

"Yep, that's me." He turned his back on the man and headed inside. As he returned to Nichole, it occurred to him that she might not appreciate his little stunt. He was forming his apology as he reached her.

"Thank you," she quietly said. "You got him out of here without making a scene."

Okay, no apology necessary. That was good. He hadn't blown it with her right out of the gate. He tipped an imaginary hat. "I aim to please, ma'am."

"I thought you were going to get in a fight with him. Thank you for not doing that."

"I'm averse to beating up anyone weaker than me.

You want to clue me in on what that was about? If it's none of my business, feel free to tell me to butt out." What he wanted to know was if Trevor was or had been her boyfriend.

"It's a business thing. I'll tell you over pizza." She glanced up at him. "We're still on for that, right? Unless you think I'm too much trouble."

He grinned. "I'm thinking you just might be my kind of trouble, Nichole Masters."

"Oh…"

He liked how her cheeks turned pink. A customer approached her table, reminding him that she was working. "I'm gonna walk around the place. I've noticed some neat stuff I want to check out." He was also going to make sure Trevor didn't come back. "What time do you close up?"

"Anytime I want to after five."

"Great. I'll be back by then. How about I take Rambo with me? Give you a break for a while." He could get some training in while he waited for Nichole to finish her day.

"Sure. If he gets too rambunctious, feel free to bring him back."

"He won't. My little buddy and I understand each other." Or would soon.

With Rambo at his side, he spent an hour or so wandering from booth to booth. There were all kinds of merchandise in the mall: jewelry, stained glass, more pottery, paintings, carved wood, and metal art. There was even a woman sewing a quilt as people watched. He particularly liked the metal art and stopped to check the items out.

"Saw you escort Trevor Allen out," the artist said. "Forest Ellers."

"Jack Daniels." When that got a smirk, he said, "I can see there are dozens of responses to that rumbling around in your head. Trust me, I've heard them all."

Forest laughed. "I just bet you have."

"So you know Allen?" Maybe he could get some intel on the man.

"Yeah. Great potter but lazy. He used to have a booth here before he decided he was too good for the likes of us and opened a studio downtown. His space was always a mess, and he had a bad habit of encroaching on his neighboring booths. Whenever one of the artists complained, he would cajole one of the women around here to tidy up for him."

Had Nichole been one of those women? He wanted to ask if she'd ever dated the man but didn't. That was information that needed to come from her. Jack picked up a really cool dog made from various kinds of metals. He waited for more intel, but Forest seemed to have reached his limit of what he was willing to say. That was okay. Jack was getting a bead on Allen, and his impression of the man wasn't improving.

"I'll take this," he said, setting aside the foot-tall metal dog. When he pulled out his wallet, Forest put a hand up.

"It's yours. Consider it my token of appreciation for this afternoon's entertainment. You walking Trevor out like he was a puppet was the best thing I've seen in a long time."

"Thanks, man. I have a thing for dogs, and this is damn cool."

With another hour before Nichole could get away, he

decided to take his first ever piece of art to his truck, then work a little with Rambo. The dog had caught on pretty fast to walking with him. Each time Rambo had tried to take off, he'd given the leash a gentle tug, bringing Rambo back to him. After the fifth time of doing that, Rambo had given up trying to escape.

The puppy was sired by working dogs, and even though he was too young yet to know it, working was in his DNA. He just needed direction to find his place in the world. Jack knew how to give that to him.

After putting his art piece in his truck, Jack took Rambo over to a square of grass alongside the parking lot. He crouched down. "Here's the deal, little man. You need to help me impress your mistress. I know you have a lot of energy, and we'll curb that while still keeping you happy. That work for you?"

Rambo licked his cheek, making Jack laugh. Man, he loved dogs. As he began the dog's first lesson, it hit him that he'd laughed more since Nichole had mistakenly dialed his number and called him doggy doo than he had…well, since before he'd gotten up close and personal with a bomb. Someday when the timing was right, he was going to enjoy giving her an earful about drunk dialing him.

For now, though, he had a pizza date to look forward to.


"The first rule to remember is that you're the pack leader."

"Okay. How do I do that?" Nichole asked. Jack was standing next to her in her backyard, and his masculine, woodsy scent was a distraction to the point it was hard to pay attention.

He'd followed her home, and they had ordered a pizza. While eating, she'd told him what Trevor had done, and she had the feeling Jack regretted letting Trevor off so easily. She'd never expected to have a real-life warrior on her side, but here one was in the flesh. And what nice flesh it was.

What impressed her the most was that Jack hadn't used his fists to get his point across to Trevor. If it had been Lane there today, her ex-boyfriend wouldn't have been satisfied until Trevor was bleeding and begging for mercy. Because of Lane's violent tendencies, she had grown to despise any kind of fighting. But Lane was history that she had no wish to revisit, so she pushed thoughts of him away. If only the man himself would stay away.

"I'll teach you that as we go along."

"Teach me?" What were they talking about?

A smile curved his lips and amusement lit his blue eyes. "Where's your mind, Nichole?"

*On how good you smell. Those blue eyes of yours. Kind of wondering just what things you could teach me.* She gave herself a mental shake. "Um, my mind wandered a bit. Sorry."

"Mmm-hmm," he murmured, his smile morphing into a sexy smirk.

"Ah, you were saying?" She was sure she was blushing, which only confirmed that he was right as to where her thoughts had wandered to.

"Since my mama taught me it's impolite to embarrass a lady, I won't ask what's going on in that beautiful head of yours."

*Oh boy.* Another sexy smirk like that and her panties were going to melt off without any help from her.

Jack Daniels was lady-parts-lethal, something she'd best remember.

"But back to what I was saying. A few tricks you can start doing to establish your role as the alpha dog is be the first out the door and the first back in the house when he's with you. That's signaling him that you're the boss. You do that instead of letting him run out ahead of you and dragging you along behind him."

"I can do that."

He smiled, and not immune to that sexy curve of his lips, her heart fluttered. She wondered if she was in over her head with this man.

"Also, when you're out walking him, keep the leash tight so he has to walk next to you. A step or two behind you is even better."

"Okay." That would sure make walking him more enjoyable. He was already getting big enough to be able to pull her along behind him.

"Being a preteen, he has a short attention span, so stop working him when his attention strays away from you. That's usually about five or ten minutes at first. Before you start a training session, have a playtime to work off some of his energy. He'll be more attentive then. Always be consistent in his training and go overboard in your praise. Lots of *good boys* and petting. Do that and he'll show up for his next class with his tail wagging, ready to go to work."

"That makes sense." Although everything he was telling her seemed like common sense, it was all stuff she hadn't considered.

"The first thing he needs to learn is to come when he's called. That's important if he ever gets free of his leash while you're out with him. For a reward, we'll start with treats, but pretty quickly we'll wean him off them. I like to use clickers and balls as a reward."

"Clickers?"

He pulled something out of his pocket that resembled a car remote and pressed a button, letting her hear the clicking noise. "It makes a distinct sound that he'll learn to associate as praise. Eventually we'll also use a ball. My dog thinks getting a ball is the best thing in the world."

"You have a dog?"

"Dakota. She's a working military dog. Or was. She was hurt, so she's been retired."

"Oh, I'm sorry."

"So am I." He walked to where Rambo was pulling the leaves from a bush. "Rambo." When her puppy ignored him, he said the dog's name again, but sharper this time, getting Rambo's attention.

Nichole wanted to ask about Dakota and how she'd been hurt, but she had the impression that Jack didn't want to talk about it. He showed her how to start teaching Rambo to come when called and how to praise him, and for the next five minutes she worked with her dog. When Jack said it was time to stop, she grinned. She knew it would take more sessions, but already Rambo had made more progress than in the month she'd had him.

"Thank you. That was incredible." She kneeled and combed her fingers through Rambo's fur. Jack had told her to always end each lesson on a positive note, so she said, "Good boy. You're such a good boy." With his tail swishing like crazy, he flopped over on his back for a tummy rub.

"He catches on pretty fast, so if you can keep on a schedule of three or four short sessions a day, you'll be happy with his progress. Remember to stay consistent. That's important."

"Got it." She stood. "When can you come back?" Or was she presuming too much? "I mean, if you want to."

Blue eyes snared hers. "I do want to. Just let me know when you're free."

She was free every night, but that sounded too pathetic to say. "Friday. Late afternoon if that's good for you. That will give me two days to work with Rambo on what we learned today."

"Works for me." He glanced down at Rambo. "Well, I guess I better go."

"Um, okay." She was tempted to ask if he wanted to watch a movie or something, but it would be embarrassing if he said no. "I'll walk you to your truck." Keeping the leash tight so Rambo would have to stay next to her, she strolled alongside Jack.

"Do you have any days off?" he asked.

"I work my booth at the mall Wednesday through Saturday. The rest of my time is spent in my pottery studio." In the beginning she'd covered all the hours herself, and then came home and made her pottery at night. That had been grueling, so as soon as she could afford it, she'd hired someone to cover her booth on Sundays, Mondays, and Tuesdays.

"Yeah? Where's that?"

"My garage. I'll show you next time you're here if you want."

"Sure. I'd like to see it." He grinned. "You can teach me how to make an ashtray. Isn't that what beginners always make?"

"First thing I made was a cereal bowl. It was awful,

but my mother still has it. She eats her oatmeal out of it every morning."

"That's cool." He stopped at the door to his truck and leaned against it. "Back to your schedule. I was thinking about taking Dakota for a short hike on Sunday. Would you and Rambo like to tag along?"

Her heart thumped. Was he thinking of it as a date, or did tag along just mean hanging out for a few hours with a friend? Her vote was on it being a date. "Sure. That sounds like fun."

"Great. In the meantime, I guess I'll see you on Friday for Rambo's second lesson. Give me a call when you get home, and I'll head over."

"I will." An awkward silence fell between them when he made no move to get in his truck. Was there more he wanted to say, or was he waiting for her to say something?

"So…" She trailed off. *What? You're the most interesting man I've met in a long time, maybe ever. Or, I love your eyes. They remind me of the sky on a beautiful spring day, and as soon as I get to my studio, I'm going to try to duplicate their color. Even better, would you like to kiss me?*

Rambo jumped up on his legs, and she tore her gaze away from Jack's face to look down at her dog. "It's so embarrassing when he does that to people."

"It's a behavior you want to curb. For now, ignore him, and he'll give up. If you react, even to scold him, he's getting the attention he wants. Once he learns to sit on command, you can tell him to do that when he jumps on someone."

"Then sitting needs to be his next lesson."

"Noted." He grinned. "I know it's hard, but just keep reminding yourself that patience is a virtue."

"Not one of my strengths."

"Another thing we have in common." He opened the truck door. "Enjoy the rest of your evening, Nichole."

"You, too." Was it her imagination, or had his voice turned softer when he'd said her name? Probably her mind working overtime because that was what she wanted to believe. She watched him drive away until his taillights faded from view.

"Rambo, I think I'm toast."

## Chapter Four

The pain was intense. Jack had hoped that by now his arm and shoulder would feel like they were healing, but it wasn't happening. Sweat dotted his forehead from the exercises his physical therapist put him through. He *would* get full use of his arm back, and he *would* return to his team. He just had to work harder.

"Three times a week isn't cutting it, Heather. Start booking me in for Tuesdays and Thursdays, too."

"You're already pushing yourself too hard, Jack. You run the risk of doing even more damage."

"Then make sure that doesn't happen." She didn't get it. His team needed him. He knew no other life outside of the military.

"No additional sessions." She sighed. "Look, I know how badly you want back with your team, but risking further injury isn't the way to go about it. Have you made an appointment to see a doctor yet since coming home?" She shook her head when he didn't answer. "You haven't, have you?"

He didn't need to see another doctor. He knew his body, and all he needed to be able to do was hold an assault rifle in his shooting hand without trembling. A little girl could hold seven pounds without shaking, and that he couldn't made him want to put his fist through a wall.

"Five days a week, Heather. Either with you supervising or two days on my own." He was already doing some of that anyway.

Heather Matthews was a ballbuster physical therapist, and he liked her for that. She worked him until he came close to begging for mercy. Not that he ever would, but she was exactly what he needed. Except when she didn't fall in line with his plans. Her husband had been Delta Force, so military dudes pushing their weight around didn't faze her.

"No to both. Not five days a week, or you going off on your own except for the exercises I gave you to do at home." She glanced at her watch. "Wait here. I'll be right back."

While she was gone, Jack tried to lift his arm above his head. It refused to cooperate. "Damn," he muttered as he rubbed the offending appendage.

Heather returned and handed him a card. "You have an appointment with Dr. Patel next Thursday. Be there."

When he glared at her, she laughed. Not the reaction he was going for.

"Give it up, Jack. If a Delta Force guy can't intimidate me, a SEAL doesn't stand a chance."

He snorted. "If I didn't know I was badass, my feelings would be hurt."

"Uh-huh. Just badass yourself to that appointment if you don't want to see my mean side."

"Yes, ma'am." Maybe.

They walked out together, and her eyes lit up when she saw her husband in the lobby. "Hey, babe. This is a nice surprise."

Jack had met Deke before when the man had been waiting for Heather to get off work. As he watched Deke slip his arm around his wife's back and give her a quick kiss, the envy he felt surprised him.

What was that about? He'd be leaving soon and wasn't looking for a relationship. An image of him on deployment, a smile on his face as he read a letter from Nichole, flashed through his mind. With his parents gone and no siblings, the only mail he got was from his grandmother. That hadn't bothered him before, so why did the thought of getting letters from her please him? A lot.

He shook his head, getting that picture out of his mind. They wouldn't be writing letters to each other. When he was gone, she'd forget about him. He frowned, not liking the idea of that. What was with all these stray thoughts going on in his head? He barely knew the woman, shouldn't be thinking past the day he would leave, after which he'd never see her again.

"Jack, good to see you," Deke said, offering his hand.

"You, too. How's it going?" Jack wondered if he'd adjusted to life outside of the military. He wasn't sure what the man did for a living. He thought he remembered Heather mentioning something about law enforcement, a cop maybe?

"Great. Just dropped by to say hi to my girl and bring her a treat." He reached behind him and picked up an iced coffee from an end table, handing it to Heather.

"Aww, aren't you sweet?"

"There's not a sweet bone in my body, but you just keep on believing that, sweetheart."

Jack took his leave. It was Friday, which meant that he would get to see Nichole. He had three hours before he could knock on her door, more than enough time to go home, take Dakota for a walk, and then jump in the shower. Maybe he'd take Dakota for a ride to use up more time.

"Jack, wait up." Deke jogged toward him. "I got an hour to kill before Heather gets off. Want to go for a beer?"

Perfect, but... "Did your evil wife send you on a mission to get my promise to keep the doctor's appointment she made for me? Without my permission I should add."

Deke laughed as he slapped Jack on the back. "She is evil, isn't she? But no, she didn't send me on a mission, and I know nothing about her plans for you." He held up a hand. "Swear. In your place, though, I'd be very afraid. Which is why you should let me buy you a beer."

"Why not?" He liked the man, and because Deke had been Delta Force, he would know better than to pry into things Jack didn't want to talk about.

They were soon sitting on stools at the bar in a hole-in-the-wall place near the physical therapy center. As soon as they each had a beer in front of them, Deke's gaze fell to the arm Jack was absently massaging. "You tried shooting with that arm yet?"

Or maybe Deke wouldn't have any problem prying. Yes, Jack had been to the gun range. It hadn't been pretty. His arm had trembled so much that he'd missed the target completely. He hadn't been back.

"Not sure I'm ready for that yet." It wasn't a lie, and yes, he was avoiding the question, but he couldn't bring himself to admit that a baby could shoot better than him right now.

Deke tapped his fingers on the bar, his gaze studying the contents of his mug, and Jack had the impression he was debating his next words. Whatever was coming, Jack was sure he wasn't going to like it.

"I never thought I'd retire from the military. Delta Force was my life." He glanced over at Jack. "I know you get that. Then I was shot in the leg. Messed up my knee pretty bad. Had to have a few operations. I didn't handle it well. The idea of not being able to return to my team was hard to swallow. I didn't know anything else."

Jack could sure relate to that.

"I arrived for my first appointment with Heather depressed and carrying a lot of attitude." He grinned when Jack widened his eyes. "Yeah, she was my therapist. That girl didn't put up with any of my shit. She was exactly what I needed, someone who got in my face and told me like it was."

"She does do that." And he'd never admit it to her, but he kind of liked that. Mostly.

"To make a long story short, my knee will never be like it was, but with Heather's help I got it fit enough to pass the physical requirements to join the police force."

"And you got the girl."

Deke grinned. "That I did, making me one lucky son of a bitch."

"So why are you telling me all this?" Jack frowned. "Did Heather tell you that I needed a pep talk?"

"Lord no. She doesn't talk about her patients with me. Ever. I don't even know what you're in therapy for. Assumed it was your arm since you were rubbing it. I just needed a beer buddy for an hour. But I will say this. I see that haunted look in your eyes that used to be in mine. So, if you ever need to unload, give me a call. I'm always up for a beer."

"A man can never have too many beer buddies. What's your number?"

He didn't need a sympathetic ear because he had nothing to be depressed about. He *was* going to heal, and he *was* returning to his team.

Jack stepped out of the shower. In less than an hour he would be knocking on Nichole's door. Hearing Deke's voice go soft every time he said Heather's name had put crazy thoughts in his mind. What would it be like to have someone like that whose eyes lit up at seeing him the way Heather's had when she'd spied Deke? An image of Nichole flashed through his mind, of the laughter in her eyes as she'd looked up at him when tangled up in Rambo's leash.

Did he even want someone like that in his life? He'd always thought he would in the distant future, after he was out of the military. That had been his plan. So why did seeing Deke and Heather together have him picturing Nichole looking at him like that? Would she even want to after seeing his scars?

Shortly after arriving home, he'd gone to a downtown nightclub. He hadn't been with a woman since leaving on his deployment eight months earlier. All he'd wanted was to lose himself in the soft feel of a woman. He'd wanted a few hours of forgetting about the pain he'd endured, some time out from worrying about his future and how long it would take before he was healed so he could return to his team.

The woman he met that night—danced with, flirted with—had invited him home with her. The moment he'd stood in her bedroom and taken off his shirt was ingrained in his memory. She'd gasped as her gaze locked on his arm. "Oh my God. What happened to you?" She'd backed away as if his arm was a contagious disease-ridden thing. "I'm sorry, but I... I just can't." Her cheeks had turned red from embarrassment as she apologized.

He'd put his shirt back on and hadn't tried to hook up since. He turned and studied his right side in the mirror. His arm did look slightly better than it had that night, but it was still an ugly mess, the reason he always wore a long-sleeve shirt. Angry-looking red welts and puckered white skin stretched from his shoulder to below his elbow. He ran his palm over his arm, something he did each day, checking to see if feeling had returned. It was still mostly numb.

He eyed his leg. That wasn't so bad. The burns there had only been first and second degree, and eventually the scars would fade to almost unnoticeable. But there was an ugly hole where a piece of shrapnel had gouged his thigh. Fortunately, it hadn't damaged any muscles or nerves in his leg.

After shaving and brushing his teeth, he walked into the bedroom to dress. Stretched out on the floor, Dakota watched with interest as he pulled on jeans. "Don't get excited, girl. You're not going anywhere." As if she understood him—and he often thought she did—she lowered her chin to rest on her paws and peered up at him with sad eyes.

He picked up the blue button-down shirt he'd planned to wear, stared at it a moment, then made a decision. It was time to find out if Nichole was going to have a problem with his arm. He hadn't worn a short-sleeve T-shirt in public since getting hurt, and after slipping one on, he went back into the bathroom to look in the mirror. The worst of it—his shoulder and upper arm—

was hidden under the shirt, but there was no mistaking that he'd been burned.

Dakota followed him, and he glanced at her. "Does this gross you out?" he asked, turning so his bad arm was facing her. She grinned. "You're a dog. If sniffing another dog's ass doesn't disgust you, I doubt my arm bothers you." But would it Nichole?

Jack hadn't said anything about dinner, but Nichole decided to have something on hand just in case. Other than pizza, she didn't know what he liked, but a variety of lunchmeats, cheeses, and bread seemed safe. She'd also added a bag of chips and assorted cookies from the grocery store bakery to her cart. That should be enough food for a man with a good appetite.

She still wasn't sure if he was interested in her or just being a nice guy willing to help her train her dog. Hopefully she'd get an answer to that question tonight. Also hopefully, the answer was a definitive yes. And maybe a kiss. A girl could dream, right?

Instead of one of her preferred sundresses, she opted for capris and one of her favorite potter T-shirts since the purpose of Jack's visit was to work with Rambo. She pulled her hair up into a ponytail and then applied some cherry-flavored lip gloss. The doorbell rang, and she glanced at the clock. Jack was early.

Rambo barked as he scrambled to the door. He loved doorbells. They meant people, and people meant attention and belly rubs. She'd played with him before showering to drain some of his energy, but he was giddily bouncing like a lunatic as he stared at the door, willing it to open.

"One of your favorite persons is here to see you."

Only it wasn't Jack. As soon as she opened the door to find Lane standing on her porch, she mentally cursed herself for not checking through the peephole to make sure it wasn't an unwanted visitor on the other side.

To keep her ex from coming inside, she pushed Rambo back with her foot before stepping out and closing the door behind her. "What are you doing here?"

She'd told Lane more than once she didn't want to see him. She glanced at the chromed-out motorcycle parked on her driveway. Why hadn't she heard it when he'd arrived? Had he coasted up so she wouldn't know he was here? Probably, since he would have guessed that she wouldn't open the door to him.

"Still playing hard to get, babe?" He smirked.

"There's no playing about it, Lane. And I'm not your babe. I want you to leave." She didn't want him here when Jack arrived. Lane was unpredictable, and he considered her his property. Jack would be a trespasser, and Lane would act first and ask questions later. That typically meant fists would be involved.

Lane wore "bad boy" well, from the messy mop of dark brown hair down to the motorcycle boots. The tribal tattoo covering one arm used to fascinate her, more so the dragon on his back. He knew that, which was probably why he put his hand on the doorframe, strategically positioning his arm so the tat was near her face.

There had been a time when she'd been drawn to men like Lane Gregory, the ones who thumbed their noses at the rules, who had a dangerous edge. She hadn't needed therapy sessions to know that Tate had left her with unfinished business. Tate had been her first bad boy, and she'd fallen hard for the always-dressed-in-black, motorcycle-riding boy her senior year of high school. It had been a surprise when he showed an interest in her, the overachiever good girl.

At first she'd ignored him when he would say hi to her in the halls, but she couldn't deny that he was cute. Over time she got to know him, and beneath the swagger and bravado was a boy with a gentle heart, and she'd loved him as much as a teenage girl could love a boy. He had broken her heart, although unintentionally. He'd left this world doing what he loved best, riding his motorcycle.

Looking back, she could honestly say that Lane had been an attempt to recreate those few months during high school when she'd felt like she was floating on a cloud. At first, she had thought she'd found another Tate, because Lane had hidden his true nature well. But he hadn't been able to sustain it. His anger and aggression began to show in small ways. Hard grips on her arm, flashes of temper when she didn't please him. When his treatment of her and others escalated into violence, she ended things with him. That hadn't gone over well, and he'd showed his displeasure by hitting her.

Problem was, he refused, even now, a year later, to accept that they were done. "Go away, Lane." She reached behind her for the doorknob. "And stay away."

He put his hand over hers, stopping her from opening the door. "Look, I know you're still pissed about me hitting you. That was wrong and won't happen again. Besides, I didn't hit you that hard. I'd never hurt you, Nichole."

That he could say that with a straight face didn't surprise her. He really believed that he hadn't hurt her. From experience, she knew there was no reasoning with him, and it disturbed her that she wanted to slap him. He was the reason she hated violence with a passion.

"Move your hand. In fact, remove yourself from my property." Jack would arrive any minute now, and a confrontation between the two of them was the last thing she wanted.

"I'm meeting some friends downtown for a few beers. Thought you'd want to go."

"No, thanks."

He sighed. "Come on. It'll be like old times."

Exactly.

"You love riding behind me," he said when she didn't respond.

Correction. She used to. She still enjoyed riding on a motorcycle. Just not with him. When he dropped his arm to his side, she ducked inside and pushed the door closed, locking it.

"Damn it, Nichole." He banged his fist on the wood.

She leaned against the door and closed her eyes, willing him to go away. A few minutes later, after getting another *damn it*, she heard the rumble of his bike. She went to the window, letting out a relieved sigh when he backed out of her driveway. Seconds later Jack drove up. That had been close.

"Hey," she said, stepping out to the porch as he walked up.

He smiled. "Hey yourself." His gaze shifted to the road. "Who was that?"

Drat, he'd seen Lane leaving her house. "No one."

# *Chapter Five*

"Mmm," Jack murmured. He didn't believe her. There had been tension in her voice, and she'd looked at the floor when she'd answered. The motorcycle had been backing out of Nichole's driveway as he was coming down her street, and the rider had looked angry. That had Jack on alert.

Unfortunately, he didn't have any claim on her and couldn't push the issue. Didn't mean he wouldn't keep a watch out for the dude. He smiled at her T-shirt. "Is that true?"

Her eyebrows scrunched together. "What?"

"This." He tapped a finger over the words on her shirt. "You have magic hands?" The words My Hands Are Magic were printed over a picture of hands wrapped around a pottery bowl.

The tension on her face eased, and she grinned. "Absolutely."

"I might need proof of that at some point."

"We'll see."

He sure hoped so. "Your boy ready for his next lesson?"

It was either that or kiss her, and he wasn't sure she'd welcome his mouth on hers. Her gaze fell on his arm, and she gasped. That was it then. His scars repulsed her. He was disappointed. Had thought she might be different.

"What happened?" She slipped her hand around his and pulled his arm toward her. "I can't imagine how much this had to hurt."

Maybe she was different, and a warm feeling the likes of which he'd never felt before was there, somewhere deep inside him. He wasn't sure what to do with that. When she gently traced a finger over the scars that were visible, he closed his eyes. It was the first time a woman had touched his arm since the bomb. Well, except for nurses and Heather, but they didn't count, didn't make him long for something more, didn't make him realize how much he'd missed a woman's touch.

"What happened, Jack?"

Her voice was gentle and caring, and he swallowed past the lump in his throat. *Suck it up, SEAL.* He opened his eyes, his gaze falling on her. All he saw on her face was compassion, the disgust he'd expected missing.

"Your hands really are magic," he said, almost whispering, afraid if he talked she'd stop touching him. His gaze followed the path of her fingers over the puckered skin.

She lifted her eyes to his and smiled before returning her attention to his arm. When she slid her fingers under his sleeve to lift it, he put his hand over hers.

"Don't. It's not pretty to look at."

She brushed his hand away. "Will you tell me what happened?" she said as she lifted his sleeve.

"Got in the way of a bomb." He watched her face for any sign of revulsion, but it didn't come.

"Well, that sucks. Is that how your dog got hurt, too?"

"Yeah."

She feathered her fingers over the scars, and the sensation was kind of weird. Parts of his arm felt her touch on his skin, but the most damaged parts didn't feel a thing. The thought of wishing for something more crept back into his mind. She was the first woman since his high school girlfriend—the one who hadn't lasted past his first deployment—who had him wishing for more than a few tumbles between the sheets. That was dangerous thinking.

Until he was out of the military, forever was not in his vocabulary. The way Nichole made him feel, even though he barely knew her, had him thinking he should walk away right now. Before he really developed feelings for her. But his feet refused to move.

"Ah…" He had no idea what he intended to say.

A whine sounded from behind the door. She tugged his sleeve back down. "He knows you're out here, and he's getting impatient to see you."

When she dropped her hand away from his arm, he wanted to snatch it back. *Danger. Danger. Danger.* He ignored the voice in his head as he followed Nichole and Rambo to the yard. It was a simple matter of control, something he had in spades as a SEAL. If he didn't want to fall in love, he wouldn't.

In all fairness, though, he needed to make sure she was clear on the fact that he would be returning to his team. If they were on the same page, then all systems were a go. They'd have a bit of fun, enjoy each other's company, and then he would leave.

If she wanted more, now was the time to bow out before any feelings were involved. The last thing he wanted to do was hurt her.

They spent ten minutes on Rambo's training, and

Jack was impressed with the puppy's progress on coming when called. He couldn't help smiling at Nichole's laughter each time Rambo raced to her when she called his name. Although he'd planned to have that little talk when they finished, he put it off, not wanting to have a serious discussion when she was so happy. She'd agreed to go hiking with him on Sunday. He'd do it then.

Saturday morning, he visited his grandmother. "Morning, Ursula," Jack said to the retirement home's receptionist as he signed in. "My grandmother in the craft room?" It was where she usually waited for him.

"She is."

"Dare I ask what she's made for me this time?"

"Now, Jack, you know I never ruin her surprises." She grinned. "I will say this one's a doozy."

"God help me." He headed to the craft room, shuddering at the sound of Ursula's laughter.

Last week his grandmother had painted a picture of what was supposed to be him without a shirt, telling him that he should give it to his girlfriend. She knew damn well that he didn't have a girlfriend, at least not one he'd told her about.

He wasn't sure what category to put Nichole in, but she wasn't girlfriend status. *Not yet.* Where the devil had that thought come from?

The picture was a hint that he needed to get busy finding and marrying a woman so he could give her great-grandbabies while she was still alive to see them. She was also positive that as soon as he had said wife and babies that he'd stay home where he belonged and not go traipsing off to dangerous places where people blew you up.

He'd downplayed how badly he'd been hurt and always wore a long-sleeve shirt when visiting her, so she'd never seen his scars. He also kept to himself his determination to return to his team. She was his only surviving relative, his father's mother, and she meant the world to him. If only she'd stop making him embarrassing things.

When he reached the craft room, he paused at the door. His grandmother was sitting at a table with Harold Robinson, her boyfriend. He grinned and shook his head. Harold couldn't weigh more than a hundred pounds sopping wet—about forty pounds less than his grandmother—and didn't have a hair on his head. He was beyond proud of his white handlebar mustache.

"Hey, Grammie." Jack kissed his grandmother's cheek. "How's my favorite girl today?"

"Who the hell are you?" Her gaze slid over him. "You look vaguely familiar, but I could be mistaking you for my grandson, who seems to think he can pop in occasionally and I'll remember him."

Jack laughed. "I was here last Saturday morning, as you well know." Whenever he was home on leave, they had a standing Saturday morning date for pancake breakfast.

"I'm old. I don't remember yesterday, much less what happened a week ago."

"Such a little liar. You remember in detail my every misdeed." He glanced at Harold. "Morning, Harold. You making her behave?"

"Never tried to, son. She's perfect just like she is." He stood. "I'll leave you two to it. Time for my morning bowl of oatmeal and lousy cup of decaf."

Jack had invited Harold to breakfast with them a few

times, but the man always refused, saying it was Lizzy's special time with her grandson. It really was, and Jack appreciated that Harold understood.

He perched on the edge of the table, glanced down at the knitting bag next to her chair, and stifled a groan. When the purple bag was present, it meant she'd knitted him something. That was never good. "You look very pretty this morning, Grammie."

She was the quintessential picture of what a grandmother should look like. Short white hair that curled around her ears, kind eyes behind her wire-rimmed glasses, an easy smile, age lines that gave her face character, and the ever-present string of pearls around her neck.

She smiled up at him. "Thank you, Jackie. A woman has to look her best to keep her man." Her eyes—not as bright a blue as they used to be, but eyes that never missed a thing—danced with laughter as she glanced behind him. "Incoming."

He groaned. That could only mean one thing. A pinch on his ass from Dirty Mary, his grandmother's name for Mary Keselowski, her eighty-three-year-old friend who had the filthy mouth of a sailor. She also had a massive crush on Jack, much to his grandmother's amusement.

"Look who's here, Mary. Your favorite hottie."

"You don't have to encourage her," he muttered.

"Where would be the fun in that?"

"Hot damn." The second Mary reached him, her fingers landed on his butt. "Looking good, McHottie."

He eased off the table to get away from her questing fingers.

She lifted her phone. "Smile, handsome. I need a picture for my spank bank."

Jack choked. Where did little old ladies learn stuff like that? When his grandmother chuckled, he glared at her.

Mary studied the photo she'd taken. "Not bad. Would be better if you'd take off your shirt."

"Not happening."

"Oh, I almost forgot your present." His grandmother pulled something red out of her knitting bag and handed it to him.

He stared at the cucumber-size thing, then lifted puzzled eyes to her.

"It keeps the family jewels warm."

"Oh, just say it, Lizzy. It's a cock sock," Mary said. "It was my idea."

Of course, it was.

Mary's gaze fell to the zipper of his jeans. "Do you think we made it big enough?"

Aaannd, he was outta here. He stuffed the thing into his pocket, then put his hand on his grandmother's elbow. "Breakfast. Now."

"At least someone thinks it's funny," Jack said when Nichole laughed.

"Oh, it is. Hilarious, actually." She held up the family jewels warmer, dangling it in front of him. "I think I'd really like your grandmother. I would have given anything to have seen your face when Mary—"

"Dirty Mary. Grammie's name for her, not mine."

She grinned at hearing his growly voice. "Right. When Dirty Mary told you it was a cock sock. How old did you say they were?" There was something adorable about a badass SEAL calling his grandmother Grammie.

"In their eighties. How the hell does a little old lady

know what a spank bank is?" He shuddered. "I went home and poured a gallon of bleach over my head to get that image out of my mind." He rolled his eyes when she lost it, but she caught the twitch of his lips. "Give me that." He snatched it away, stuffing it in his pocket.

She hadn't laughed this hard in a long time, and it felt good. They were sitting on a boulder at the edge of the falls on a beautiful Sunday morning. The hike to get here had taken an hour down a sometimes-slippery trail, and unused to hiking, Nichole was dreading the trek back up. But it had been worth it. The sky was a brilliant blue, the air was blessedly cool from the icy water cascading into the crystal-clear pool, and the man beside her was downright fine.

After playing in the water for a bit, Rambo was stretched out in the sunshine, enjoying a nap. Dakota sat in front of Jack's feet, her gaze sweeping the area.

"She seems very aware of her surroundings."

Jack leaned over and peered down at his dog. "To her, everything's a job, even a Sunday morning hike. She's keeping an eye out for bad guys, watching our six."

"Our six?"

"Our backs. Comes from a clock. If you were standing in the center of a clock face looking at the twelve, the six would be at your back."

"Ah, I see."

When Jack had arrived to pick her up, he'd introduced Dakota to Rambo. Rambo had jumped all around her, trying to get her to play. Dakota had lifted her gaze to Jack, as if to say, "Can't you do something about this pesky thing?"

Nichole had been afraid Dakota would bite Rambo, but Jack had assured her his dog only attacked on command. She'd never seen a dog so well behaved. Maybe Dakota could teach Rambo some manners.

"It's beautiful here." She leaned back on her elbows and lifted her face to the sun.

"You're beautiful."

She glanced at him to see him watching her. Everything around her stilled, the only sound that of the water as it splashed into the pool, and the only thing she saw was Jack's blue eyes studying her. Not once had Lane said she was beautiful and looked at her as if she really was to him.

"Thank you." She wasn't used to getting compliments from a man and wasn't sure what to say other than that.

He glanced away. "We need to talk, but I don't quite know how to say it without sounding like an ass."

"Just spit it out, whatever it is." His nervousness put her on alert, and she sat up, steeling herself for…well, what, she wasn't sure, but she didn't think she was going to like it.

"Okay, here's the thing. I really like you, Nichole."

"But?"

"Yeah, there's a but. As soon as my arm is healed, I'm returning to my team."

Ah, so that was where this was going. "And you're not looking for anything serious?"

He nodded. "I'm not. I learned the hard way through experience and watching my teammates try to keep relationships going that they just don't work for men like me. I want to keep seeing you as long as I'm here, but I don't want you to expect something I can't give you." His gaze shifted to the waterfall, then back to her. "That sounds really selfish, doesn't it?"

She shrugged. "Maybe a little, but I'd rather know where you stand than to find that out later." When it was too late because she'd fallen for him. Because it was be an easy thing to do with this man if she didn't guard her heart.

"If you want me to take you home, I'll understand."

"No." She put her hand on his arm. "I've been warned. So we'll agree that we'll have fun while you're here, and when it's time for you to leave, the fun will be over."

She already knew it was going to be hard to walk away from him, yet she wasn't going to be smart. She had a history of falling for bad boys. Jack was nothing like any of her previous boyfriends. He was a nice guy, an honorable man, and a hero to his country. She could only respect him for being honest with her.

"Are you sure about this? Because the last thing I want to do is hurt you."

"I'm sure." She ignored the voice in her head that questioned her sanity.

"Then give me your mouth, Nichole," he said as he leaned toward her.

It was both a command and asking for permission. She knew that if she refused, he would respect that. Yet—oh God, yet—it was the command in his voice that snared her, that sent heat spiraling through her. That had her ready to offer whatever he asked for.

"My mouth is yours," she whispered.

"There is a God." He closed the distance between them.

His lips touched hers, his mouth covered hers, and his scent wrapped around her. She'd been kissed more times than she could remember. Some had been great, some okay, and some forgettable. Never had she been kissed like this. Like she was being consumed, devoured.

He slid his tongue across the seam of her lips, and all she could do—wanted to do—was open to him. So she did. He leaned closer, placed his hand on her hip, and spanned his fingers over her shorts.

There was nothing innocent about his kiss. His mouth was a carnal thing, hot and demanding, his taste intoxicating. The heat from his body seeped into her. If she had a white flag, she'd happily wave it. She put her hand on his arm, wanting to touch him. When he tensed, she realized she'd placed her fingers on his scars. He was just going to have to get used to that.

"You didn't have to stop," she said when he pulled away.

"Yeah, I did." His gaze shifted away from her, the heat that had been in his eyes fading.

"Jack?"

He darted her a glance, then returned his attention to the crystal-clear pool. "Not long after I got home from the hospital, I went out one night. I was lon…" He shook his head. "Sorry, this isn't something I should be telling you."

"Why not? So you went out. I'm guessing hoping to hook up?" Had he been about to say he was lonely?

"Yeah, that, so it would be bad manners for me to talk about that to you."

"Why would it bother me? We didn't know each other then." She moved her hand higher on his arm to where the scars began. "Tell me about that night." Not that she really wanted to hear about him hooking up with someone, but she believed there was something he needed to get off his chest.

He shrugged. "Nothing happened."

"And why was that?"

"Because when I took off my shirt, she gasped when she saw my arm. Her exact words were, 'I'm sorry, but I just can't.' That was a mood killer if there ever was one."

Nichole would like to have a few words with the woman. He'd gotten those scars being a hero in the service of his country, but she didn't think he saw himself as a hero. Probably none of them did, those men and women who put their life on the line to protect and serve.

"Will you do me a favor?"

"What's that?"

"Take off your shirt."

He gave her a look that said she was crazy. "No."

As if sensing her master's distress, Dakota shifted to face him, peering up at him with worried eyes, and quietly whined. He reached down and scratched her head. "It's okay, girl."

"How else are you going to find out if your scars disgust me? Better to know now if I'm like that stupid woman, don't you think?" He seemed to have forgotten that she'd already seen most of his arm, that she had even touched his wounds without recoiling.

His lips twitched. "She was stupid, eh?"

"That's my opinion, yes."

He glanced at his arm, at the scars showing below the sleeve of his shirt. "You haven't seen the worst of them."

"Well then. Go for it. I'm totally prepared to be grossed out."

Another lip twitch. "This is only the second time since getting hurt that I've worn a short-sleeve shirt."

The first time had been the other night at her house. He'd wanted her to see his scars, had expected her to be repulsed like that stupid woman. That he'd worn one today told her that he trusted her or was trying to. She was pretty sure her heart had just melted.

"Quit stalling, Jack."

## Chapter Six

Was he really going to do this? Bare his ugliness to the prettiest girl? How did that even work, ugly with pretty?

As Jack slipped his fingers under the hem of his T-shirt, he didn't think his heart had ever pounded this hard, even in the middle of a firefight. Maybe Nichole was right, and the woman had been stupid, but her words had been seared into his brain. Thinking about it now, it was surprising that he'd hunted down Nichole when he expected the same reaction from any woman.

From the time he'd heard Nichole's voice on the phone he'd been drawn to her, forgetting that he was damaged and not once considering that she probably wouldn't want anything to do with him. But she was full of surprises, good ones so far.

He drew his shirt up and off, dropping it next to him on the rock. *Suck it up, SEAL.* His stomach lurched as her gaze clinically roamed over him, much like the way his doctors had every time they'd examined him. He watched for that moment when her eyes would prove her disgust. It didn't come.

Instead. Fuck. Instead, she kissed his arm, from the bottom of the scar that had almost disappeared, up to the top, to the worst ones on his shoulder, where the bomb had done the most damage, and then where the infection had set in. The ugliest part of him. What was he supposed to do with that? With her kissing places he wasn't even sure he would?

"You called me. Drunk. You drunk dialed me." Had those words come out of his mouth? They apparently had since she jerked away, making him wish he had a time machine so he could back up a good ten seconds.

She blinked, then narrowed her eyes at the same time as that delicious mouth of hers showed her displeasure by giving him the coldest frown he'd ever seen. Cool trick, all that.

"What?" she said.

That one word was a loaded one. "About three in the morning. You were crying and called me a bunch of names." He hated how she was looking at him, as if he were something that had crawled out from under a rock. He'd always meant to tell her, but he hadn't intended to just blurt it out like that. "You said, 'How could you?' and I had to know what I'd done to you. I thought maybe it was a wrong number, but I wasn't sure, so I looked you up."

"You stalked me?"

"I don't know if I'd exactly call it stalking." He sighed when she raised her brows. "Yeah, okay, I stalked you, but only long enough to find out where you worked. I'm an ass."

"An ass and a toad," she said as she slid off the rock, landing next to Dakota. "Is he always a toadstool?" she asked his dog. Dakota huffed, sounding way too agreeable. "You're donkey doo, you know that?"

Jack couldn't help it. He laughed. That got him a glare from Nichole. Even Dakota, the traitorous thing, gave him a dirty look. "You have a talent for name calling. Donkey doo just replaced doggie doo as my favorite one."

She pushed up, crossed her arms over her chest, and scowled. He wondered if he should tell her that her attempt to glare him into next week wasn't working, mostly because her arms were pushing her breasts up. He was a man. Breasts trumped all else, and hers were ten times better than perfect.

"Eyes up here, soldier!"

He could tell her that a SEAL was never referred to as a soldier, but she could call him soldier all night if she let him anywhere near those sweet girls. As difficult as it was, he managed to drag his gaze up to her face.

"Sorry," he said. Or not. Now that he knew his scars didn't disgust her, like a broken record, his male brain was stuck on one word. *Sex. Now.* Okay, that was two words, so he wasn't as boneheaded as he was acting.

*Sex now with her.*

There. A complete sentence. He could think again. That was good.

He tried a smile but didn't get one back. He sighed. It was time to grovel. "You're right. I'm donkey doo, doggie doo, a toad, and all those other things you called me. I knew it was creepy to stalk you, but—" She narrowed her eyes. "Right, no buts. I'll take you home, then I'll disappear from your life."

"Probably a good idea."

He was glad she thought so because he sure didn't. Although it was undoubtedly for the best, considering the way his chest hurt at the thought of never seeing her again. Better to put a stop to those kinds of feelings while he still could.

"I'm sorry, Nichole. Really." He tugged his shirt back on, then picked up his pack from where he'd dropped it on the rock.

"So that's it? You're not going to try to change my mind?"

Was that what she wanted him to do? Women were confusing. He glanced at the dogs. Rambo had woken from his nap and was sitting quietly—a minor miracle that—next to Dakota, both of them staring at him, as if waiting to see if he'd manage to screw this up. He tried to think of the right words, but his mind was a complete blank.

To hell with it. Didn't actions speak louder than words? He strode to Nichole, cupped her cheeks, lifted her face, and lowered his mouth to hers. When she didn't slap him, he took that as a positive sign. On a soft sigh, she melted against him.

He raised his head. "This is me doing my best to change your mind. Is it working?"

"Yes, you creepy stalker, it is. Now shut up and kiss me again."

"Yes, ma'am." He was trained to follow orders, and this was one he was definitely on board with. Her breath quickened, matching his own as their tongues tangled. Drunk on endorphins, his worries about his arm, his future, about anything melted away. He'd found his oasis, and he never wanted to stop kissing her.

Wild need raged through him, and he wanted to devour her right here. Right now. He wasn't sure he would ever get enough of her, of her taste, of the feel of her body pressed to his. He wanted to consume her and be consumed by her.

"You taste like cherries," he murmured against her mouth.

"Lip gloss."

How could he resist a woman who smelled like vanilla and tasted like cherries? He broke away from her mouth and peppered kisses across her cheek until he reached her neck. He pressed his tongue over her pulse point, feeling the rapid beat of her heart. She purred, sounding like a kitten. He smiled against her skin, gave serious consideration to taking her down to the ground with him.

This wasn't the place—and maybe even not yet the time—for giving free rein to what he wanted, what he was practically dying for. He reluctantly pulled away, then rested his forehead against hers. She scared him. The timing was all wrong for the connection and chemistry they had between them.

Yet he knew he wouldn't walk away from her, even though he should.

"I'm seconds away from forgetting we're in a public place," he said. "If I told you what I'm feeling inside right now, you'd have too much power over me, Nichole." He leaned back and looked into her eyes. "So I won't."

Her gaze fell to the zipper in his jeans, then she lifted mischief-filled eyes to his. "I think I can make an educated guess. But more research might be in order before I'm positive."

He laughed. "Research is good as long as I'm the subject matter." He slipped his hand around hers. "You have a grill?"

"Doesn't everyone?"

"If not, they should. How would you feel about picking up a couple of steaks for dinner? I'll cook." They could go to his house, but he'd never brought a woman there before. It was his sanctuary, and although he liked the idea of seeing Nichole in his home, in his mind that was stepping their relationship up another level. He didn't think he was ready for that. Wasn't sure he ever would be.

"Sounds great."

"You could also show me your studio and teach me how to make a bowl or something."

"Only if you agree to reenact the scene from *Ghost*. I've always wanted to do that. I just haven't found the right man before."

"I have no idea what that is."

She stared up at him as if he had two heads. "Seriously? That is only one of the most erotic movie scenes ever. I have the DVD. We'll watch it first so you'll know what to do."

"If it involves you and erotic in the same sentence, then I'm your man."

"We'll see if you're up to the challenge."

"Nichole, a little advice. Never challenge a SEAL unless you're prepared for the consequences."

She laughed. "I'm not afraid of you, big guy."

*This girl.* How did she do it, make him feel like the luckiest man in the world that she liked him?

Nichole glanced at the man sitting on her sofa. Her house was small—a two-bedroom, one bath—and with him in it, it seemed as if the place had shrunk. Dakota sat next to his legs, ever watchful.

"Does she even know how to relax?" she asked. The fascinating thing was Rambo. He sat close to her, mimicking her, his eyes alert. Maybe instead of spending the time to teach him to behave, she should just turn him over to Dakota for training.

"At home, after she hears the click of the door lock."

Nichole marched to her door and turned the lock. Sure enough, at the sound, the dog visibly relaxed. Dakota glanced up at Jack, some kind of message seemed to pass between them, and then she made a few circles before curling up at his feet with her chin on his shoes. Rambo watched with interest, then copied her.

"You two are spooky," she said. But cool spooky. "It's like you mind-talk with each other."

He grinned. "We actually do. She wanted to know if I liked you."

"Did she? And what did you say?"

His gaze snared hers. "Yes, very much."

*Be still my heart.* "Well, it's only fair since I like you very much, too." If he had any clue how lethal that smile of his was, he'd keep it on his face at all times. Before she melted into a puddle in the middle of her living room, she grabbed her box of DVDs.

When she found *Ghost*, she held it up. "Ready?" At his nod, she slid the disk into the slot. "This is a great movie, so pay attention."

"My eyes are glued to the screen."

"Ouch. That must hurt." She laughed when he rolled his eyes.

When she sat on the sofa, he pointedly looked at the foot of space between them, then lifted his gaze to hers and raised his eyebrows. Without a word, he had her moving to him until their bodies were aligned from arms down to legs. It was where she wanted to be.

"Better," he said, then put his arm around her and

pulled her closer, until her shoulder rested against his chest. "Even better. What's this movie about?"

"Demi Moore is in love with Patrick Swayze, and he's murdered. He comes back as a ghost. That's all I'm going to say."

"Really, Nichole, we're going to watch a ghost movie?"

"Yes, Jack, really. Now shut up and watch."

He glanced at her and smirked. "You're bossy, you know that?"

"So I've been told."

"Are you this bossy in bed? Because if you are, you should know I'm good with that." He waggled his eyebrows.

"Maybe you'll find out someday. Or maybe not." He totally would.

He leaned over, putting his mouth next to her ear. "Oh, I will, I promise you."

A delicious shiver raced through her, and he chuckled, letting her know he'd felt it. The opening credits finished, and as the movie began, she blinked. She'd watched this movie many times, and knowing what was coming, tears stung her eyes.

It didn't take long to learn that Jack liked to make commentary. "Dude, open your eyes. You just walked by a bad guy hiding in the doorway." Then, "So that's the answer to life after death. You turn into a lightning bug," he said when the twinkling white lights swooped toward Patrick Swayze.

And so it went. She tried not to encourage him by laughing, but whenever a laugh or chuckle at one of his asides did escape, his expression was entirely too smug. He was funny, and for her, there was nothing more appealing than a man with a sense of humor. Good looking, a really nice man, a drool-worthy body, and funny meant she was in so much trouble!

But whatever.

There was no way she could resist Jack Daniels. Her salvation was that he'd be leaving in a month or two, and that would be that. All she had to do was program her mind to not fall for the sweetest, hottest man she'd ever met.

"I'd totally do her," he said when a close-up of fat tears from luminous green eyes meandered down Demi Moore's cheeks.

Nichole snorted. "I don't know one straight man who wouldn't. Heck, I'd almost do her."

He groaned. "Don't be putting pictures like that in my mind."

"Am I torturing you?" She peered up at him. His blue eyes, darker than they had been minutes earlier, answered her question. She hid her smug smile. She'd surprised him with her comment, and she had a feeling he wasn't a man who surprised easily.

"Yes, but in the best kind of way."

Before she could think of a response, the scene she especially wanted him to see came on. "Hush. This is where you need to be quiet and pay attention."

"I'm yours to command."

That was all he said as he stared at the TV screen. If he had any idea of all the ways she'd like to command him, he'd instantly forget they were watching a movie. Nichole had wanted to recreate the pottery scene since the first time she'd seen it. She just hadn't had the right man before to do it with, and now she had. When the scene ended, she held her breath, waiting to hear what he would say.

## Chapter Seven

Nichole was practically bouncing in her seat, waiting for his reaction, and Jack couldn't resist teasing her. He wrinkled his nose. "Looked pretty messy to me." Fact was, it really was a sensual scene, and he was definitely going to reenact it with her.

"Oh. Well, I guess—"

"That we are so going to do that." He chuckled at her puzzled expression. "I was messing with you."

She punched his arm. "Ha-ha. Funny man."

"That's me, baby." He glanced at the TV. "That was one hot scene. Back it up and play it again. I need to memorize it so I'll get it right when we do it."

The pleased smile she gave him went straight to his gut. He inwardly snorted. Who was he kidding? That smile was an arrow to his heart, and *that* he did not want to admit to himself or anyone else. So she had burrowed her way into his head more than any other woman ever had. Didn't mean anything. Not one damn thing.

"You're going to have to do it without a shirt on," she said as they watched the scene a second time.

"Uh-huh. I've figured you out. You're just fishing for an excuse to see my manly chest." He winked as he rubbed his hand over his T-shirt.

"Maybe, but you're going up against Patrick Swayze, and those are some big shoes to fill."

He lifted his leg, putting his foot in her line of sight. "Size thirteen, baby. You know what they say about that."

She laughed, then slapped a hand over her mouth. "Sorry. I didn't mean to imply that you're exaggerating the size of your..." She dramatically paused, then said, "Shoes."

Damn this girl for making him like her so much. "You're not paying attention to the movie." He put his hand under her chin and directed her eyes back to the TV. "Does that thing she's making look like a phallus?"

"Oh my God, it does. I never noticed that before."

"If we're going to make one of those, do you think my cock sock will fit it, or do I need to ask Grammie to make a bigger one?"

The girl he wanted out of his head before she took it over completely rolled onto her side, wrapping her arms around her middle as she snorted laughter through her nose.

He grinned. His work here was done.

Dinner had been filled with tension of the sexual kind. He'd cooked the steaks on her grill, and she'd bustled about, making a salad and a crusty French bread loaf. He'd taken every opportunity to brush up against her, soaking up her shivers and sighs. And now they were in her pottery studio.

"So, this is it," she said as his gaze swept around the one-car garage that had been made over for a pottery artist.

Shelves along the wall were filled with inventory,

and he walked over to take a closer look at all the things she'd made with her clever hands. A figurine of a dog sitting at a young woman's feet caught his eyes. He picked it up. "How much is this one?" It reminded him of her and Rambo, and he wondered if the two of them had been her inspiration.

"It's yours."

He glanced over his shoulder. "It absolutely is, but what did you plan to sell it for?" He wasn't going to leave here without it, but he wasn't going to take food out of her mouth either. This piece of art created by her would go with him back to Afghanistan, and every time he looked at it, he would think of the time he'd had with her.

"A dollar."

He snorted. "Such a little liar. If you charged anything less than fifty for this one, I'd call you a fool. Since I know you're not, sold for fifty bucks, and I consider myself lucky to have it at that price."

When she only stared back at him as if he were a man she'd never understand, he stalked to her. "Does your pottery wheel need time to warm up? I'm only asking because I feel the need for…" He lowered his mouth until it was an inch from hers, and satisfaction rolled through him when her breath hitched. "Getting messy. With you."

"You have to take off your shirt."

Her words came out breathless, and he brushed his lips over hers. Feeling breathless himself, he stepped back before he forgot why they were in her studio. He hooked his fingers under his T-shirt, then paused. She'd seen his scars, but he was still worried that they repulsed her.

"I'm not that other woman, Jack," she said as if she could read his mind.

No, she wasn't. Together they pulled the shirt over his head. She took it from him, dropping it on her worktable. He stilled as she walked behind him, and like she had at the waterfall, she glided her fingers gently over his shoulder. He wished he had the words to tell her what her touch meant to him, how incredible her hand felt sliding over his skin. Then she pressed her lips on the worst part, the ugliest, where he'd suffered third degree burns.

"Nichole," he said, his voice no more than a whisper. Although he couldn't feel much, knowing her mouth was on him *there* sent a shiver down his spine. She stepped in front of him, palmed his cheeks as she lifted to her toes, and then kissed him. He tangled his fingers in her hair, but before he could deepen the kiss, she backed away.

"If we keep that up, we're going to forget why we're here. We need the song." She messed with her phone for a moment, and then "Unchained Melody" sounded from a Bluetooth speaker on her worktable. "I have it looped, so it'll play as long as we want it to."

"That's good."

She stared at him for a few seconds as her cheeks turned pink. She was blushing, and it was adorable.

He smiled as he trailed his fingers over the pink. "I'm nervous, too," he said. Not really, but he wanted to put her at ease.

"So…" She glanced around. "Um, I'll sit at my pottery wheel, and you can come in behind me. Just wait until—"

"I got this, Nichole." He brushed his lips over hers.

"You know what? We don't have to do this. I know you must think it's silly."

"We are so doing it." At seeing the uncertainty in her eyes that he wasn't just humoring her, he said, "Surprises me, too, that I want to go up against that Swayze dude in your fantasy, but he has smaller feet than I do, so I'm not worried." She repaid him with the laugh he was going for to put her at ease.

"Big shoes to fill," she said through her laughter.

"Those I got." He brushed his fingers over her cheek. "Do your thing."

He positioned himself at the door, then waited a few minutes, and when she had a lump of clay on the wheel formed into an impressive duplication of the thing that had looked like a phallus in the movie, he moved behind her. Pulling a nearby stool over, he sat behind her.

"Couldn't sleep?" he murmured, remembering that line or something close to it.

She tilted her head, looking up at him with the hint of a smile. "No. I didn't mean to wake you."

"Can't sleep without your warm body next to mine." He was adlibbing now, but the words felt right. He slid his hand under her hair, lifting it, then put his mouth on her neck, smiling when she shivered. "Your skin is so soft. And you smell so damn good, like vanilla and almonds. Makes me want to lick you."

"Jack."

That was it. One word. His name spoken on an exhale of breath, enough that he was the one shivering now. As he peppered kisses over her neck and shoulder, he trailed his hands down her arms until they covered hers.

"Messy," he said as clay and water turned their skin gray.

She grinned up at him, and the happy light in her eyes was his undoing. He was making this woman's fantasy come true, and in return she was breathing new life into his troubled soul. It wasn't an equal exchange, what she was giving him compared to his only acting out a movie scene. But when she looked at him like that…

"I need to kiss you long and hard," he said as he brought his messy hand to her face.

Unfortunately, he hit her giant phallus, causing it to bend over in a perfect replica of a limp penis. They both stared at it, and he could feel her shaking as she tried not to laugh.

"That's not me, I swear." That did it. She laughed so hard that she fell back on him. "Ah, now I have you where I want you." He pulled her from her stool onto his lap.

She laughed so easily, something he'd noticed from the first when she'd been tangled up in Rambo's leash. Instead of losing her temper with the puppy, she'd stood there, her eyes alight with amusement as she'd laughed. He wanted to soak up this joy of life she seemed to have.

As she stared up at him, he lost himself in her eyes, in the desire he saw in them, in her intoxicating scent, in the soft smile curving her lips. He felt like he was falling under a spell, that some kind of magic was swirling in the air around them.

"Nichole," he said, his voice as rough and raspy as that of a lifelong smoker.

She softly smiled. "I know."

How could she know what was in his mind, but he saw in her eyes that she did, that maybe she felt the magic, too. He closed the space separating their mouths, and when his lips touched hers, he moaned from the pure pleasure streaking through him. Wanting her closer, he wrapped his arms around her back, holding her tight against him.

She slid her hands around his neck, then up into his hair. She was probably smearing clay all over him, but he didn't care. As the passion between them grew, she met every one of his demands, gave back as good as she got. Their tongues tangled, tasted, and explored.

Jack thought he was either having an out-of-body experience or perhaps a heart attack. The damn organ was beating so fast and hard that it sounded in his ears like a jackhammer hard at work tearing up the asphalt of a street.

He didn't want to stop, but he forced himself to pull away. Any other woman, and he'd go for what could happen next between them, but Nichole wasn't a one and done. He wanted something more with her, and despite his earlier declaration to himself, he wondered if they could sustain a relationship after he returned to his team if they worked at it.

How he was even thinking that so soon was surprising to say the least, but he felt a connection with her that he'd never experienced with another woman. The thought of walking away from her when it was time to return to his team… No, maybe somehow they could make things work.

"I think I should probably go." Before he couldn't.

She pushed away, scooting back onto her stool. "Why?"

There was hurt and wariness in her eyes, and he regretted putting it there. But he was determined to do things right with her. "Believe me, I don't want to."

"Then don't."

"Yeah, I am." Was this even him saying these things? He'd never hesitated before when it was obvious a woman wanted him, but then he'd never before wanted things to go past a night or two.

"Sure, whatever." She turned her back to him, picked up the broken phallus-looking thing and smashed it flat.

"Ouch," he said, getting the message. Amused, he swallowed a chuckle. He was messing this up, though, and if he wanted to be welcome back, he needed to make her understand. He moved until his chest was to her back, putting his arms around her.

"Nichole, this thing between us, whatever it is, is different for me. I've only had one serious girlfriend from high school. I thought we had something, but within a month into my first deployment she cheated on me."

She stilled in his arms, telling him she was listening. "When I found out, I decided then and there that I'd never have another serious relationship as long as I was in the navy. And I haven't, not in the eleven years since. For me, it's been one-offs with women who were only interested in the same thing."

"Is there a *but* coming?"

"Yes, and that *but* is Nichole Masters. I don't know what's happening between us, but something is. We have about two months before I leave to figure it out. If that's what you want."

"And when you leave, what then?"

"I don't know. I guess we'll decide that when the time comes."

When she didn't say anything, he knew he was bungling this. "You're not a one and done. You haven't been from the start. I want to…" He searched for the right word. "I want to romance you. If you don't want the same thing, tell me now because if not, I don't think I can do this with you."

He'd rather walk away now while there was still time to protect his heart. He'd explained it in the best way he knew how. His damn heart beat erratically as he waited for her answer. Maybe he shouldn't have been honest with her, should have just let things play out.

Nichole squeezed her eyes shut. After his talk at the waterfall, she'd settled her mind on this being a fun fling until it was time for him to return to active duty. And truthfully, wasn't that for the best?

After Lane, she'd said no more relationships, no more letting a man control her. That was never going to happen again. Her judgment was questionable, though. Lane hadn't given any hint of his true personality in the beginning, and look where that had gotten her.

Yet the thought of Jack walking out of her life made her want to grab his hands and hold on to him. She turned to face him. The vulnerability and hope she saw in his eyes were things she'd never seen in Lane's. Her ex-boyfriend believed he was entitled to take what he wanted, when he wanted, heedless of others' wishes. She'd told him repeatedly that she didn't want to see him, but he refused to listen. Didn't care what she wanted.

Jack wasn't like Lane. She knew if she told Jack that she didn't want the same thing as him, he'd respect her decision and walk away, never bothering her again.

He would be leaving, returning to active duty. He'd said things would end then. Now, even though he wasn't promising anything past his leave date, he was changing the rules, and she couldn't turn her back on the chance that there could be something deeper between them. She could fall in love with this man, and that scared her. And if she did…well, she'd just stock up on wine and ice cream and wallow in her misery when he left.

"I do want to see where this goes." Oh, that smile on his face was a beautiful thing to see. As much as she was determined to protect her heart, she wasn't sure she'd be able to manage that trick.

"And you'll let me do it right and romance you?"

She laughed. "Yes, Jack, I'd be honored to be romanced by you. That doesn't mean you have to leave now, though."

"Yes, it does." He leaned forward and kissed her, long and hard. "I don't trust myself around you, sweetheart."

"Fine, be like that."

He tapped her nose. "You're adorable when you pout."

"Ha! You ain't seen nothing yet, baby."

"Bring it on." He grinned as he patted his chest. "I'm man enough to take it."

She suspected he was man enough to take a lot of things. He also confused her. There wasn't a man in her experience who would be walking away after she'd invited him to stay, and he clearly wanted her. Although it was sweet that he wanted to romance her.

"There's a sink over there." She pointed to her left. "You might want to wash your hands before the clay dries."

As he headed that way, her gaze roamed over him. The scars, especially the ones on his shoulder, were horrific, and she couldn't imagine the pain and suffering he must have endured. They didn't disgust her, but what did was the woman who'd made him feel like he had to hide them. She'd like to have a word or two with the witch.

The rest of him was perfection. She couldn't wait to roam her hands over his strong back, broad shoulders, narrow waist, and lean hips. In fact, why wait? She stood and walked up behind him. She should probably wash her hands first, so she nudged in next to him.

Before she could grab the soap, Jack did, then he wrapped soapy hands around hers. He slowly caressed each finger. From there, he moved over her palms, then up her wrists to her arms. Their gazes locked and held. How could a man make washing her hands such a sensual thing?

"Hi," he said, staring down at her, his attention on her mouth.

"Are you sure you want to leave?"

"Want to? No." He turned off the water, then grabbed the towel hanging on a hook. "But I'm still going to." He dried her hands and arms, then his. "Have dinner with me tomorrow night."

"Or I could cook you dinner."

"Nope. I want to take you out. You like to dance?"

"I do." She hadn't been dancing in…well, like forever.

"Great. I'll pick you up at six. Let me collect Dakota, then I'll get out of your hair."

She put her hand on his arm. "You can get in my hair all you want, Jack."

"Stop saying things like that. I'm having enough trouble leaving you as it is."

Stubborn man. She walked him out and stood on her porch as he loaded Dakota into his truck. He looked back, then strode to her like a man on a mission, put his hand behind her neck and pulled her to him. He kissed her as if he were a drowning man and she was his air.

"See you tomorrow night," he said after almost turning her knees to jelly.

Long after his taillights disappeared from view, she stared at the empty road. Never had a man so consumed her with want before, not even Lane when she'd thought she loved him. She was very much afraid Jack Daniels was going to break her heart.

## Chapter Eight

The last time Jack dated was when he'd been with Tori. They'd been their high school's cool couple, the star quarterback and the cheerleader. He thought she was the one, and asked her to marry him the day before he left for boot camp. She said yes, and he slipped an engagement ring on her finger. They lasted through his first months in the navy, through his BUD/S training but not past his first deployment. She decided a doctor would make a better husband than a military man would.

Truthfully, he was glad she'd realized that before they married, although he hadn't appreciated her Dear John letter at the time, especially since she admitted in the letter that she'd been seeing a doctor while Jack was dodging bullets in Afghanistan. She'd not only broken his heart but taught him a lesson. Girlfriends got lonely when their man wasn't around, or so Tori had claimed.

After that he adopted the one-and-done motto of many of his teammates. That way he didn't have to wonder if his girl was cheating on him when he wasn't around. With hindsight matured by age, he realized he and Tori had been too young for a serious commitment. He would have never screwed around on her, but he doubted a marriage between them would have lasted.

As he shaved, getting ready for his date with Nichole, Jack studied his reflection in the mirror. It was still his face, but someone else had possessed his body. How else to explain walking away from Nichole when she'd clearly wanted him to stay the night? "Idiot," he muttered, chuckling. But he was glad he had.

He was older now, as was Nichole, and maybe it could be different with her. The hope was growing that it could. And that was why he decided to slow things down. He didn't want their relationship to feel like it was only about sex. He wanted them to get to know each other, to explore the possibilities, see where things could go. And just maybe…

Dakota put her paw on his leg, and he glanced down at her. "To answer your question, yes, I'm going out, and no, you can't come this time." Her nose dropped, pointing down at the floor. "Don't give me that poor-pitiful-me look." Her head lowered and her shoulders slumped. Ah hell, his dog could put a guilt trip on him like no one's business.

He picked up his phone and called Nichole. "Hey," he said when she answered. "I'm leaving shortly, but, well, this is probably going to sound stupid. Can Dakota stay with Rambo while we're out? She'll behave, I promise." Dakota's ears perked up at hearing her name.

Nichole laughed. "Are you asking if Rambo can babysit your dog?"

"Yeah, I guess I am. She's giving me one of her dejected looks because I'm going out, and believe me, she's perfected that expression."

"That's probably because it works on you. Of course you can bring her."

"Thanks. See you soon."

He set the phone back on the counter. "There you go, you shameless beggar. You got an invite."

Dakota barked.

The words Jack had planned to say at seeing Nichole were lost the moment she opened the door.

"Are you okay?" she said when he just stood in front of her, mute.

He shook his head.

She put her hand on his forehead. "You don't have a fever."

"Yeah, I do. It's called a Nichole Fever. I'm burning up." His gaze roamed over her. "Give me a minute."

The black dress showed off every delicious curve, but it was the cutout above the swell of her left breast that snagged his eyes. About three inches long and an inch wide, it was outlined in red, and sexy as hell. A tantalizing glimpse of skin in an otherwise simple dress. It was sleeveless, the bodice reaching the bottom of her neck, and the hem stopping just above her knees. On her feet were strappy red heels that buckled around her ankles.

"If I start drooling, I'm blaming you," he said.

She smiled, her eyes filled with delight. "Then I probably shouldn't show you the back."

"You probably shouldn't but do it anyway." He made a circle with his index finger. "Sweet baby Jesus," he rasped when she turned.

The dress was backless right down to just above the curve of her ass where a small red bow perched. He exhaled a long breath as his gaze traveled back up to her hair. She'd pulled it up on one side, securing it with a red clasp. The other half of her hair curled around her shoulders.

When his team was downrange, they alternated between heart-stopping battles and times of pure boredom. During those boring days, they'd pass around books and magazines. He remembered an article he'd read a year or so ago that men associated the color red with sex. He could now swear to the truth of that, even with only splashes of red in strategic places—her feet, over her breast, at the lowest part of her spine, and in her beautiful hair.

"Nichole."

"Hmm?" She glanced over her shoulder at him.

"You're a very dangerous woman." He stepped up to her before she could turn to face him and put his hands on her upper arms. Sliding them down, he threaded their fingers. "To me," he whispered into her ear.

"Thank you, I think."

"No, thank you. Before I forget I'm supposed to take you out, let's get the dogs settled so we can be on our way. We have dinner reservations in thirty minutes."

"Rambo's already in his crate." She glanced down at Dakota, sitting quietly at their feet. "Hello, pretty girl. How about you have a serious talk with Rambo about chewing up my shoes."

"One way to avoid that is to remove temptation."

She sighed. "I know. I'm used to kicking off my running shoes right inside my back door, a habit I need to break. He chewed up a second pair today, so he's not been a good boy."

They left Dakota inside, and as Jack walked out with Nichole, he put his hand on her back, her skin warm under his palm. "Have I told you how much I like this dress?"

"I think you might have mentioned it." She paused at seeing the car. "Oh, I was expecting to have to climb into your truck."

"This was my dad's." His father had been a car nut, and the silver 2004 Thunderbird Roadster had been his last car. It was a good memory of his dad, so he'd kept it.

"It's super cool."

He opened the door for her. "I think so, too." After she was seated, he walked around to the driver's side. He slid into his seat and glanced at Nichole. She smiled at him, and there went his heart, doing that twitchy thing again. It was disturbing, but not quite as alarming as the first time it happened.

Her gaze roamed over him. "You clean up pretty nice, too."

"Thank you." If she knew how much time he'd spent debating what to wear, she'd laugh. He'd ended up with a pile of clothes on his bed before settling on the dark gray pants, a light blue button-down, and the gray sport coat. The surprise had been that he even owned the coat he'd found in his closet. He tried to remember why he had it, but nothing came to him.

As he turned out of her driveway, a motorcycle approached, and Jack recognized the man as the one he'd seen before, the one she'd said was nobody. The motorcycle slowed, the man staring hard at him.

"Keep going," she said, glancing behind her as they drove away. "Damn it, why can't he just go away?"

"Who is he?"

"My ex-boyfriend. He refuses to believe we're over."

Jack pressed down on the pedal. Personally, he'd like

to have a few words with the asshole who was bothering her, but that probably wasn't the best way to start their first date. "Is he stalking you?"

"Not really. He just keeps coming by, expecting me to get over my snit and fall back into his arms."

"Is there a chance of that happening?" He braced for her answer, not liking how much he wanted to hear a no. If she had any feelings for the guy, though, he wanted to know now, before he got comfortable with having a twitchy heart.

"Not a snowball's chance in hell." She glanced behind her again. "Is he following us?"

Jack was wondering the same thing. He turned at the next corner, his gaze on the rearview mirror. The motorcycle followed them. Turning on his blinker, he pulled onto the shoulder. Her ex wasn't going to ruin his first date with Nichole.

"Jack." She put her hand on his arm. "Please just go."

"And what? Have him follow us into the restaurant?" Her face paled, which only made him more determined that the asshole was going to leave her alone. "No man should harass a woman who doesn't want his attention. He needs to understand that." He opened his door. "Stay here."

She grabbed his arm. "Please don't fight him."

He couldn't promise that. It depended on her ex. He wouldn't start a fight, but he wouldn't run away from one. "Just stay in the car, okay?"

Without waiting for an answer, he strode to the motorcycle stopped behind them. He straddled the front wheel and put his hands on the handlebar, curling his fingers around the steel. "You're upsetting Nichole. That doesn't make me happy. How about you get lost."

The man lifted the black-tinted visor of his helmet. "You gonna fucking make me?"

"Not me. The cops. I already called them. Told them some asshole was following me." He had a feeling this man wouldn't want the police nosing around.

Mean brown eyes slitted. "There's one thing you need to know, dude. Nichole's mine, and I don't like you sniffing around her."

"Some valuable intel, *dude*. Nichole isn't anyone's property." He glanced at his watch. "I figure a police cruiser should be pulling up in about three minutes. I'll be more than happy to let them sort this out."

"You'd be wise to watch your back. I got friends who can make you disappear." He snapped his fingers. "Just like that."

This was like watching a bad B movie, and Jack considered laughing in the man's face. Instead, he let his eyes go ice-cold. "You don't know me, so you have no reason to believe me, but you should. I'm not a man you want to mess with." He let go of the handlebars and stepped to the side. "Pretty sure I hear a siren headed this way."

The man revved the engine, then burned rubber as he took off. Jack memorized the license plate. He'd call his new friend, Deke, tomorrow, see if the cops had anything on the douchebag. When he returned to the car, he said, "You need to take out a restraining order on that guy."

Nichole wanted to scream. Why couldn't Lane leave her alone? "I know. I was just hoping it wouldn't come to that. What did he say?"

"Oh, he just warned me that I was encroaching on his property."

"Jerk. I'm not anybody's property."

"Told him that. I said I'd called the cops, so he decided he didn't want to stick around." He put a hand over hers. "Are you okay? We don't have to go out if you don't want to."

"No way am I letting him ruin my evening. You promised dinner and dancing, and I'm collecting." Jack was right, though. It was time to get a restraining order.

"That's my girl." He shot her a panty-melting smile. "I should probably warn you. I'm a dancing fool."

"But are you any good?"

He grinned. "Oh, baby, just try to keep up."

The man hadn't lied, he could dance. Nichole considered herself a good dancer, but Jack could flat-out move. She grinned as he spun her under his good arm. They'd been on the dance floor for three songs, and she was going to need oxygen soon. He wasn't even breathing hard.

The song ended, and before she could tell him she needed to sit this one out, the band segued into a slow song. He pulled her to him, and since there was nowhere else she wanted to be, she slid her hands around his neck. His arms wrapped around her back so that they were pressed together from chests to hips.

"Where'd you learn to dance like that?" she said.

"My mom owned a dance studio. She'd recruit me to partner up when there was a shortage of boys in a class. She made me learn it all. Foxtrot, the waltz, the tango, you name it."

"I'm impressed. What's your favorite dance?"

"The tango." His eyes heated as he peered down

at her. "It's making love on a dance floor with your clothes on."

Oh yeah, sign her up. "That's a great way to describe it. It is a sensual dance."

"I'll teach you, and then we can come back and show off."

She might not survive dancing a tango with him. "I'm afraid my clothes would fall off without any help from me if we did that. They're already wanting to, and we're not even tangoing."

"Yeah?" He slid his hands to her hips, pressed his fingers into her skin, and put his mouth to her ear. "In that case, we'll dance it in private." His hands left her hips, and he pressed a warm palm against her spine. "Did I tell you how much I love this dress, Nichole?" He slowly glided his fingers up her back, then back down again, sending shivers spiraling in all directions. "You like me to touch you, don't you?"

Was he kidding? She felt like she was going to end up in a gooey puddle at his feet when he said her name in that raspy way. Never mind that his touching her was making her body sing. Several more of his touches on her bare skin, and she was going to find herself begging.

He chuckled when she didn't answer. "If I wasn't determined to romance you, I'd throw you over my shoulder right now and haul your sexy ass back to my cave."

She almost whimpered. "You have a cave?"

"No, but I'd find one." The slow song ended, and he led her off the dance floor. "You want to stay or go?"

"I'm ready to go if you are." After all the dancing, her feet were killing her, and she didn't think she could dance another step.

"I'm hungry. Why don't we find a Huddle House and have some pancakes or something?"

"Seriously, after that amazing dinner you're hungry?" He'd taken her to one of the downtown restaurants, and she'd watched in amazement as he'd devoured a huge steak and all the trimmings.

He grinned. "Growing boy and all that." His gaze darted to the left, and he pulled her to a stop. "But first there's some people I want you to meet."

The couple he led her to were in a corner, their attention so focused on each other's mouths that they didn't even realize they had company.

"Hit the road, Jack," the man said, his lips still glued to the woman's.

Okay, maybe the guy was not so unaware, and Nichole tugged on Jack's hand. They obviously weren't welcome.

Jack laughed. "Dude, let go of your wife long enough for me to introduce you two to someone."

"Is he still here?" the man said.

His wife chuckled. "He's a stubborn one. You might as well talk to him." She pushed her husband away and smiled at them.

Jack slid onto the chair across from them, pulling her down next to him. "Deke, Heather, this is Nichole. Nichole, Heather's my physical therapist, and this ugly thing is her husband. Deke's a cop, so don't tell him about that joint you have in your purse."

"I *do not* have a joint in my purse." She raised her hand. "I swear, Officer."

"Mmm, maybe I should frisk you to make sure," Jack said, his gaze traveling over her.

Deke snorted. "Nichole, what's a nice girl like you doing with a bonehead like Jack?"

"Hey." Jack slapped a hand over his heart. "You wound me, bro."

"Ignore these two clowns," Heather said. "It's nice to meet you, Nichole, but you look familiar. Are you sure we've never met?"

"Have you ever been to the River Arts District? I have a pottery booth there where you might have seen me."

Heather squealed. "Yes! I even have some of your pottery." She grabbed Deke's arm. "She made that beautiful bowl on our coffee table."

"You made that?" At her nod, Deke said, "I think my wife loves that bowl more than me."

Jack laughed. "Understandable."

"Harsh, man," Deke said.

They talked and joked for another thirty minutes, and Nichole really liked Jack's friends. She was pleased when they made plans to get together for dinner on Saturday night. She and Jack stood to leave.

"I'll give you a call tomorrow," Jack said to Deke. "There's something I want to talk to you about." He glanced at Heather. "And I'll see you Wednesday for my torture session."

"It was great meeting you both," Nichole said.

As they walked out, Jack put his hand on her back and smiled down at her as he stroked his fingers up her bare spine. *Can we have his baby?* her ovaries pleaded. The place was crowded, and he shifted so that he was a little in front of her, clearing a path to the exit. He didn't push anyone out of the way. It was more that his presence radiated some kind of power that had people moving aside, and that was just hot.

He'd left her wanting on the night they'd enacted the scene from *Ghost*, but tonight he was hers, even if she had to tie him up so he couldn't get away.

"What's that smile for?" he said as he opened the car door for her.

"Just wondering if I have any rope at home."

"Huh?"

She patted his arm. "Nothing for you to worry about."

"Not sure that's a comfort, darlin'." He slipped his hand to the back of her neck and lowered his mouth to hers. After kissing her senseless, he said, "But you won't have to tie me up tonight to have your way with me." He winked.

Not only was he sexy as all get-out, but he was a mind reader, too. "Are you sure you want to stop for pancakes?"

"That craving has passed. Now all I want is a taste of you." He tuned the radio to a station playing love songs, and then held her hand on the ride home. Her body hummed with anticipation in a way it never had for another man. Then they turned onto her street, and her gaze narrowed on the car parked in her driveway.

"Crap. Not tonight," she said at seeing her brother sitting on her porch steps.

## Chapter Nine

"Who's that?" Jack parked his car next to the one in Nichole's driveway. The man sitting on her steps wasn't her ex-boyfriend, at least not the one he'd met.

"My brother." She let out a weary sigh. "He's supposed to be in Florida at my parents'."

Okay, a brother he could deal with. Before he could get to her side of the car to open her door, she was out and marching toward her brother. Jack caught up with her, and her brother scowled.

"Who the hell is this, Nic?"

Jack held out his hand. "Jack Daniels."

Ignoring him, the man kept his gaze on Nichole.

"Jack, this is my brother, Mark, who is supposed to be in Florida right now."

"Yeah, well, Lane called."

"And of course you came running. What happened to the new job you just started?"

"Florida's hot as hell." He shot Jack a glance. "Besides, the 'rents were all up in my business."

"The word is parents. Have some respect for the people who gave you life and still put up with your bullshit," Nichole said.

Mark sighed. "Can we not do this with an audience?"

"Sure. Come back tomorrow and we'll talk."

Jack had noticed the carry-on bag sitting next to the door, meaning her brother intended to stay with Nichole. He didn't like the man's attitude with Nichole, so it was difficult to keep his mouth shut.

"Thought I'd bunk here tonight," Mark said.

"I should go." Jack put his hand on Nichole's back. Her muscles were tense, and the last thing he wanted to do was leave her, but he needed to before he said something to her brother. She might be unhappy with Mark at the moment, but Jack doubted she wanted him inserting himself in the middle of whatever was going on between them.

She glared at her brother before turning a soft smile on him. "Probably for the best. I'll walk you to your car."

"You going to be okay?" he asked when they reached his door.

"Yeah. My brother's a jerk, but he's harmless."

Jack wasn't so sure about that. "Call me later, just so I know you're okay."

"I will." She pressed her mouth to his. When she finished assaulting him—and God knew, he was more than fine with that—she lifted her gaze to his. "I had plans for you tonight, Mr. Daniels."

He grinned. "I know. Something involving ropes, and believe me, I was all for whatever your plans were." He brushed his thumb across her bottom lip. "Don't forget to call me later."

"I will. Promise."

Damn, he didn't want to leave. He had a bad feeling about her brother and his reason for showing up without telling her he was coming. Not his circus, though.

Unable to help it, he shot her brother a warning look before getting in his car. One word from Nichole and he'd do what he was hardwired to do. Protect.

As he drove away, he fought the urge to turn around and go back, to go all caveman on Nichole, and after snarling *mine* and beating on his chest, he'd take her back to his barbarian cave and let her tie him up.

He chuckled. He'd known exactly what she'd been thinking when she had muttered something about ropes. There wasn't a rope he couldn't get out of, but he wasn't about to tell her that.

Acting out the scene from *Ghost* the other night had been the hottest thing he'd ever done. Walking away from her that same night had been the hardest thing. But he had because he wanted more with her. A big surprise, that. She didn't know it, but Nichole Masters had him second-guessing himself. That was not something he knew how to deal with.

Back home, he realized he'd forgotten Dakota was at Nichole's. Since he wasn't about to leave his dog anywhere near Mark Masters, he got back into his car. As he drove to Nichole's, he wondered if he'd subconsciously left Dakota there, giving him the excuse to return. Make sure she was okay.

"Lane said you were screwing around on him. Guess it's true."

Nichole glared at her brother. "My private life is none of Lane's business. Or yours. You can stay here tonight, but I want you gone tomorrow."

When he was six, Mark had been diagnosed with leukemia. Both she and her parents had catered to him from that time on, even after he'd been declared cancer free a few years later. That had been a mistake. Not during the time he was sick, but their continuing to baby him once he was well hadn't done Mark any favors. The brother she'd once adored had grown up to be a selfish, weak man. He couldn't keep a job and blamed everyone but himself for that.

What he couldn't see, wouldn't believe, was that Lane played him like a fiddle. He also refused to believe that Lane had gotten violent with her because Lane swore he never had. It made her angry that her brother would take Lane's word over hers.

"He loves you, Nic."

"No, he doesn't. Lane doesn't know how to love. He only wants what he can't have. And if you think he's been celibate since we broke up, then you're stupider than I thought."

Mark shrugged. "He's a man. It doesn't mean anything."

"I'm not even going to dignify that with a response." She stared at him as sadness filled her heart. Her parents refused to admit it, but they really had lost him. The little boy who used to idolize his big sister was gone, replaced by a brother she could barely tolerate. She couldn't blame Lane for that. Mark had been well on his way to being a poor excuse for a man before Lane entered the picture.

Lane, a master manipulator, recognized a puppet when he saw one, and hadn't wasted any time getting his hooks in Mark. When Lane pulled Mark's strings now, Mark danced.

"I'm going to bed. When I get up in the morning, I don't want to see you here."

"And where am I supposed to go?"

"I assume you left a good job because Lane beckoned. Go stay with him." She walked past him, heading for her bedroom.

He grabbed her arm. "Stop being a bitch. You—"

A low growl had both of them swinging their heads toward the sound. Dakota sat in front of Rambo's kennel, her attention on Mark. Nichole hadn't even realized that Jack had left without his dog. She wouldn't attack, would she? Jack had said she only attacked on command, but with the way she was looking at Mark with cold, alert eyes and her ears pinned back, Nichole wasn't so sure about that. Mark was being an ass, but she didn't want him mauled by a dog.

"You should let go of my arm," she quietly told her brother.

As soon as he dropped his hand, Dakota relaxed, but kept her intense focus on Mark. Rambo stuck his nose between the slats and whined, apparently picking up on the tension in the air.

"I'll take the dogs to my room with me." She was leery of Dakota for the first time, so she approached slowly. "It's okay, girl. He's not going to hurt me." She opened the kennel door and let Rambo out. "Come on, guys."

Both dogs followed her down the hallway and into her room. Nichole closed the door, locking it behind her. Rambo licked her legs, ran in a few circles, and then headed for Dakota, who'd parked herself at the door, putting in mind a sentry on guard.

The evening sure hadn't turned out the way she'd expected or wanted, and what a disappointment that was. She needed to call Jack and see what he wanted to do about Dakota. Both dogs probably had to go out, but first she needed to change into something more comfortable.

She groaned in pleasure after taking off her heels. They were definitely not shoes to spend the night dancing in, but the pain had been worth it with the way Jack's eyes had devoured her from head to shoes. She slipped on leggings and a T-shirt, then slid her feet into a pair of flip-flops. When she reached the door, she heard voices. She put her ear against the wood.

The hell! Furious at hearing Lane talking to Mark, she jerked open the door, forgetting about Dakota. The dog raced out in front of her. "Dakota, stop. Sit." Surprising her, the dog dropped her butt to the floor at the end of the hallway. Rambo barreled past, but came to a stop next to Dakota, mimicking her. Nichole stood behind them.

"You're not welcome here, Lane." She glanced at her brother. "You had no right to let him in."

"He just wants to talk to you, Nic."

"There's not a thing he can say that I want to hear." When Lane took a step toward her, Dakota growled. "You'd be smart to leave." She put her hand on Dakota's head. "This is my guard dog, specifically trained to keep you away from me."

Rage flashed in Lane's eyes before he hid it. "Baby, put the damn dogs away."

"No. Get out of my house. Both of you."

When Jack reached Nichole's house, he scowled at seeing the motorcycle parked behind her car. Stealth was the best plan when one didn't have intel. He parked on the street in front of the neighbor's, then eased up to Nichole's door. Whoever had come in last hadn't closed it completely, leaving about three inches of space to look through.

The only thing he could see was Nichole's brother, but the voice speaking was that of her ex. At hearing him call her *baby*, Jack forgot his stealth plan. He stormed inside, all warrior as he locked eyes on the enemy.

"The lady wants you out of her house."

Dakota, recognizing they were working a mission, rose from her sitting position, her teeth bared.

Jack let his voice go hard and cold. "My dog wants to sink her teeth into you real bad. You have exactly three seconds to disappear before I give her the command to attack."

Hatred filled the man's eyes as he stared back at Jack for a moment, but at least he wasn't entirely stupid. He backed out of the room. "This ain't over, Nichole," he snarled before slamming the door behind him.

Jack doubted that the man was going to go quietly away. He glanced at her brother. "You want him gone, too, Nichole?" He'd like to give Mark benefit of the doubt since he was Nichole's family, but Jack didn't trust him.

She studied her brother, her expression showing her disappointment in him. "No, he can stay tonight. But one more trick like that, Mark, and you'll never be welcome in my house again."

Jack took that to mean that Mark had let her ex into the house. He was relieved that it hadn't been Nichole who'd let him in.

"Seriously, Nic, you're gonna let this asshole—"

"Careful," Jack said. "My bad side isn't a good place to be." He hated the hurt he saw in Nichole's eyes. A brother should have his sister's back, should be the one protecting her. She was not getting that from him, and knowing that only fed Jack's protective instincts. It also made him want to knock some sense into the boy-man's head. "I don't get it, dude. She's your sister, and the man who just left is bad news. Why would you want him anywhere near her?"

"You don't know nothing. He's never mistreated her. He loves her, and you're messing things up."

Nichole marched up to her brother. "I've told you repeatedly that he has mistreated me." She bent over and pulled up the leggings on her right leg. "See that scar? That's a burn mark from when Lane got mad and pushed me against the hot tailpipe of his motorcycle." She pointed to a small scar on her upper arm. "That one happened when he hit me, and his skull ring cut me."

Jack saw red. It was a good thing he hadn't known about those while her ex had still been here.

"He didn't mean to hurt you," Mark said, but his voice lacked its earlier conviction.

"So he claims." She sighed. "Go to bed, Mark. I'm tired of talking to you."

The boy-man—that was how Jack saw him, a boy in a man's body, not sure of his place in the world—dropped his head, his shoulders sagging. "I'm sorry. He said he'd never hurt you, and I believed him."

Rambo was turning in circles, sniffing the floor. "Why don't you take the dogs out before Rambo gifts you with a puddle to clean up," Jack said to Nichole. "Give me a minute with your brother."

Her gaze darted between the two of them. "Just don't kill him, okay?"

He grinned at her. "I'll do my best not to."

She glanced at the door. "What if Lane comes back?"

"Dakota won't let him near you, but it would still be best to stick close to the house."

"I will."

After she was gone, he crossed his arms over his chest and looked straight into Mark's eyes. "This can go one of two ways. One, I'll beat some sense into that stupid head of yours, or two, you can swear here and now that you'll start treating your sister the way a brother should. Your choice. I'm good with either."

At least the man-child had the grace to blush. "I just thought she was being dramatic...you know, like women tend to be."

"I don't know what women you're used to being around, but Nichole doesn't have a dramatic bone in her body." Well, except for playacting out sexy movie scenes, but he wasn't about to go there with her brother. "I can see that after only knowing her for a few weeks. You've known her all her life. You should be the one telling me that."

"You really like her?"

A bit of avoidance there in admitting he'd been wrong, but Jack let it go. Mark Masters needed a role model, and much to Jack's chagrin, he was apparently taking on that responsibility. "Yeah, I really like her. And unlike Lane... What's his last name, anyway?"

"Gregory."

Jack filed that intel away. Later tonight, he'd start compiling a dossier on the man. "Unlike Lane Gregory, I'll never leave a scar on her body. Any man who does that to a woman isn't fit to live."

Based on how Mark's eyes widened, Jack figured he probably shouldn't have said that last part. He had no intention of killing anyone, but there were people in this world who needed to be taught a lesson, and he was the man to do it. In the meantime, it seemed he had made some kind of deal without any prior agreement with himself that he was going to take Nichole's brother in hand. He was an idiot.

"I'm busy tomorrow, and Wednesday morning I have time booked at the firing range. After that, I'll stop by if you want to hang out for a couple of hours. Maybe grab some lunch before I have to go to my physical therapy appointment."

"Can I go with you to the range?"

"Ah…" Hell, why had he mentioned that?

# Chapter Ten

Nichole fumed as she walked the dogs. Lane was an ass. Her brother was an ass. And the man who thought he could step in and solve all her problems? He was an ass, too. From the time her brother had gotten sick, she'd been pretty much on her own. Her parents' attention had been focused on Mark, and rightly so. She'd learned to take care of herself at an early age, and she didn't need anyone to do it for her.

"Hey," said the voice that sent shivers down to her toes. Damn him. "Nichole?" Jack said when she kept walking, keeping her back to him. She wasn't sure why she was feeling so bitchy toward him. He'd done nothing but show her respect and had dispatched Lane with little more than a spoken threat.

She stopped, and then turned to face him. "I can fight my own battles, thank you very much." She really was a bitch. But Lane showing up tended to do that to her.

He stuffed his hands into his pockets. "I don't doubt that for a minute." He lowered his gaze to the ground. "My mom taught me that women are to be respected. My dad taught me that you protect your woman. The navy taught me how to do that. I'm sorry if I stepped out of line, but when it comes to you, I guess I don't think straight."

Her irritation fizzled at his admission, and she sighed. "No, I'm the one who's sorry. I'm not mad at you. At Lane, yes, and I'm tired of Mark disappointing me. I could really use a hug."

"Then I'm your man."

He held out his arms and she walked into his embrace. If only she could just live here, next to his body. And truthfully, if Jack hadn't shown up, she wasn't sure what would have happened with Lane. He'd pretty much left her alone until Jack was in the picture, and now he was acting like a peeing dog marking his territory.

Rambo tried to jump up her legs, and she peered down at him. "He wants in on the hug."

"I'd rather just keep hugging you." He leaned away and smiled down at her. "You smell better."

"I sure hope so. Really, though, thanks for coming back. Tonight didn't go at all like I wanted."

"Same, but we'll have other nights. I'm going to head home, but I'm leaving Dakota with you in case your ex comes back. She won't let him mess with you."

"I doubt he'll be back tonight, but thanks."

"If he does, you call me."

"Okay."

She walked him to his car, got another kiss, and then watched him drive away again while wishing the evening had gone a lot differently.

"Are you still mad at me?" Mark said the next morning.

"I'm less mad than I was last night, but if you ever bring Lane here again, I'm going to have to hurt you." After putting bowls of food down for Dakota and

Rambo, she stirred cream into her coffee, then buttered two slices of wheat toast. Taking her plate and cup to the small kitchen table, she sat across from her brother.

"I won't, but he said he just wanted to talk to you, and that you'd been blowing him off." He shrugged. "I didn't see the harm in it."

"The harm in it is that it's not up to you to decide who I talk to."

"Got it." He finished his bowl of oatmeal with sliced strawberries.

When he'd been sick, he'd learned to eat healthy, and he still did. He exercised daily and had routine check-ups. Even though it had been over ten years since he'd been declared cancer free, she knew the fear of it happening again was a black cloud hanging over his head.

Her problem with him was his immaturity, and for that, she blamed both herself and their parents for babying him. It was as if he believed he was living on borrowed time, so he should get what he wanted when he wanted it. A steady job wasn't one of those things he wanted.

"Do you think Jack was serious about taking me shooting with him?"

"Shooting?"

"Yeah, he said I could go to the firing range with him."

"I don't think that's a good idea." What was Jack thinking? Her brother had no business shooting guns.

The stubborn expression on his face was one she'd seen many times when he was determined to get something he wanted. "I'm past the age of having to ask permission, Nic. I just wanted to know if you thought he meant it."

"I think Jack doesn't say something he doesn't mean, so yes. When are you going back to Florida?" She wouldn't mind at all if he transferred his idolization from Lane to Jack, and if bonding at a firing range achieved that, so be it. Even better if he learned to be his own man, but she wasn't sure he knew how.

Golden brown eyes—the same color as hers—shifted away. Crap, he wasn't going back, which meant he would be her responsibility.

"Mark, Dad found you a good job. You need—"

"Yeah, yeah. I heard it all already from Mom and Dad. I need to grow up, keep a job, take care of myself, and not mooch off you and them." He picked up his spoon and clanged it around in the empty oatmeal bowl. "I can do that here."

"You didn't when you lived here before." He'd bounced from one job to the next because he was bored, or they didn't treat him right, or just pick a reason. He'd used them all. Her brother was a good-looking man, almost pretty. His hair was darker than hers, and he was a head taller. Girls loved him, and he flirted shamelessly, but he didn't have the attention span for a serious relationship.

It was time to stop catering to him. "I'll give you two weeks to find a job and a place of your own." He'd lived with her off and on, and he was far from the ideal roommate. He was a slob, he figured if she was already going to make her own dinner, she might as well make enough for him, and she'd sat up too many nights waiting for him to come home so she'd know he made it back safely. She wasn't going to do it again. Besides, with Mark here, she and Jack would have no privacy, and that wasn't going to work for her. "Since the clock is ticking, you should start on that job search."

"I thought I'd catch up with my friends today."

"Mark…" She huffed a breath. "Fine. Do whatever you want, but two weeks from today your butt is on the street, job or no job. I mean it." And that was all she had to say about it. She was done with taking care of him.

After he left, she took the dogs for a long walk. She'd expected to hear from Jack by now since she had Dakota. When she got back to the house, knowing Jack would be by at some point to pick up his dog, she changed into a yellow sundress. She needed to work in her studio today, but that required ratty clothes, and she wanted to look nice when she saw him.

While she waited to hear from Jack, she glanced at the clock. Her best friend should be up by now. She'd met Rachel Denning in third grade when she'd overheard Tiffney Carlyle making fun of Rachel's hair. Nichole had pushed Tiffney, Tiffney had pushed back, and the two of them had ended up in the principal's office. It was Nichole's one and only physical fight—thankfully—but she and Rachel had ended up best friends, the friendship lasting through high school, college, and adulthood.

"Rach, when are you going to get your skinny butt back home?" she said when Rachel answered her phone. Her friend was in LA, working a stunt double job for a famous actress.

"Nic! I was thinking about you this morning, so I knew you were going to call."

"Stop it," Nichole said, and they both laughed because it was something Nichole often said to her. Rachel sometimes knew things, which was just weird and freaked Nichole out while at the same time she thought it was cool.

"Who is he?"

Nichole blinked. "Who is who?"

"The man you want to talk to me about."

"I swear, you should bottle that magic shit you do. You'd make a fortune."

Rachel laughed. "If I really had magic, believe me, I would, but nothing magic about it. I just know you."

"God, I miss you." No one got her like Rachel did.

"Miss you, too, babe. Talk to me. What's his name?"

Nichole told her everything about Jack, about Lane pulling another of his stupid stunts—Rachel hated Lane—and about Mark showing up.

"Let's slide back to Jack," Rachel said. "First tell me what he looks like so I can imagine him."

"He's tall, blond, blue-eyed, and is seriously ripped. He's a SEAL, and—"

"An honest-to-God freaking SEAL?"

"Yeah. Crazy, huh? But, Rach, he's the sweetest man I've ever met."

"A keeper?"

"I wish, but he'll be returning to his team as soon as his shoulder's healed. I don't see this being a long-term thing, so I'm just going to have fun with him while it lasts." Even though he'd hinted that there could *maybe* be something more than that, and as much as she wanted to believe he wouldn't forget about her after he left, she just couldn't. Call it protecting her heart, because…out of sight, out of mind, and all that.

"Uh-oh. I know you. You're going to fall for him, and then he's going to break your heart when he leaves."

"Nope. I'm going into this with my eyes wide open. So, what about you? Meet any hot actors yet?"

"Lots. This town is crawling with hotties, but I avoid them like the plague. Talk about broken hearts, they leave them in their wake. I have had a few dates with a cameraman on the set. Nothing serious, but who knows? I really like him and wouldn't mind if it turned into something."

"No! If you fall in love with him, you'll never come home. Text me a picture of him."

"Same. Send me one of your sexy SEAL."

Nichole went to the window when she heard a car engine. "He's here, so I'm going to go."

"Love you, babe. And watch your back. I don't trust Lane not to pull something stupid."

"Sexy SEAL's doing a good job of keeping him away, but I will. Love you, too."

Jack arrived at Nichole's, satisfied with his morning's work. He'd met Deke for breakfast, and his cop friend was going to see what he could find out about Lane Gregory. Deke agreed that Nichole should take out a restraining order, and Jack was going to push her to do that.

She opened the door before he reached it, and all he could think when she stepped outside was how beautiful she was. She was a vision in her yellow dress with her hair loose and curling around her shoulders.

All he knew at that moment was that he had to kiss her. He strode up the steps to the porch, stopped in front of her, and without a word of warning, he slipped his hand around her neck, and pulled her to him. She tasted like sunshine and sin. It was a potent combination. Innocent and naughty at the same time. He wasn't sure he'd ever get enough of her.

"Well, good morning to you, too," she said when he released her.

He liked how husky her voice was. "Morning, sweet girl. I assume you didn't have any more trouble since I didn't hear from you?"

"You assume correctly." She pulled the door open, and Rambo bounced out.

When the puppy jumped against his legs, begging for attention, he ignored the little rascal. They walked inside, and as soon as Rambo gave up trying to get noticed, Jack squatted in front of him.

"See, when you behave yourself, good things happen." He gave Rambo a head scratch, then transferred his attention to his best girl. "And how is Dakota this morning?" He glanced at Rambo as he scratched under Dakota's chin, her favorite place. "You see how well she behaved, sitting quietly until it was her turn? You should try it sometime."

He'd missed his dog last night, especially when she hadn't been there to calm him after his nightmare. He hadn't realized how much he relied on her to quiet his demons. But she'd served a higher purpose by staying to guard Nichole.

"Today's one of your studio days?" he asked Nichole as he stood.

"It is, and I have some items to finish that I need to take with me tomorrow."

"I'll get out of your hair, then." Today was an off day, no physical therapy or anything else on his agenda, and he'd planned to ask if she wanted to go out to lunch. He let the question slide since she had work to do.

"By the way, Mark wanted to know if you were serious about taking him shooting."

"If I said it, I meant it. Is he here?" That would give him something to do.

"No, he's out catching up with his friends."

She seemed annoyed by that. "Where's he staying?"

"With me." She sighed. "I gave in and said he could stay here for two weeks while he found a job. You'd think he'd get right on that."

He decided it was best to keep his opinion on her brother to himself. "You up for some Rambo training this evening?"

She smiled as she walked to him. "If it means spending time with you, then yes." She lifted to her toes and kissed him.

Her taste and scent invaded his senses, leaving nothing but desire in its wake, consuming him. He groaned as he pulled her against him. She dug her fingers into his shoulders when he slid his tongue into her mouth. He briefly considered picking her up and carrying her to her bedroom, but he didn't want any interruptions of the brother kind.

Last night hadn't ended the way either one of them wanted. He wasn't going to let that happen again.

"Why don't we have Rambo's training session at my house? I'll make you dinner after." He waited for panic to strike at asking her to come to his home. It didn't. In fact, he wanted to see her there.

She grinned mischievously. "Ah, I get to see where a sexy SEAL lives? You know, you can tell a lot about a person by their stuff."

"Is that so?"

"Yep, so don't hide your whips and handcuffs."

He grinned. "Don't have any of those, darlin', but I'm damn good at improvising if that's your kink."

"I'm not sure I have a kink, but we could have fun finding out." She dramatically blinked her eyes.

He glanced at his watch. "Is it time to pick you up yet?" He loved how easily she laughed. "No, huh?"

"Anticipation is half the fun."

"Not sure about that. Instant gratification sounds like a whole lot more fun."

Laughing again, she punched his arm. "Go on. Get out of here so I can get to work."

He gave her a sad face. "Fine, I'll go as soon as you give me a kiss to get me through the day."

"Poor thing. Come here."

What was a man to do but obey a lady's command? When she sucked his bottom lip into her mouth and clamped her teeth down on it, he thought he was going to embarrass himself. He might have been this turned on when he was fifteen and Melissa Cummings, his big crush, had let him touch her breasts for about three seconds.

Who was he kidding? Melissa's breasts had nothing on Nichole Masters's teeth biting down on him. "Nichole," he growled.

She smiled against his mouth. "Hmm?"

It wasn't easy, but he forced himself to back away. "I'm seconds from taking you down to the floor with me, so I'm going to leave."

"Just wanted to make sure you thought about me today."

"Mission accomplished. My body pressed against yours is all I'm going to think about." He told Dakota to come and walked out while he still could.

* * *

Jack decided to make Dakota happy and take her for a ride before he dropped her off at home. After that, he'd go to the grocery store and get something to make Nichole for dinner. Maybe by the time he got there, he'd think of what to make.

When he and Dakota went for their rides, he would explore different roads. He was driving down a country lane he'd never been on. "Pretty out here, huh?"

Dakota glanced at him, then stuck her head back out the window, her silly grin in place. He passed a sign before the words on it registered. At the next driveway he came to, he turned around. "Asheville Service Dogs," he read aloud to Dakota when he stopped in front of the sign. "Never knew this was here."

A dog raced across the yard and dropped a ball at a man's feet. The man noticed Jack's truck idling at the end of his driveway and waved. Jack lifted his fingers from the steering wheel, returning the wave. He had time to kill, and curious, he drove to the house.

"You're going to have to stay in the truck," he told Dakota. She sighed her resignation, then stuck her head back out the window.

As Jack approached the man, he noted a row of kennels behind the house. "Howdy," he said, holding out his hand. "Jack Daniels."

"Ron Kitterman." He glanced at Jack's truck. "You got a dog you need training?"

"No, Dakota's already trained. She's a retired military dog. Not that she's happy about that, but she was hurt."

"Looks like you were, too," Ron said, his gaze on Jack's arm.

"Yeah, same IED got us both."

"What can I do for you, Jack Daniels?"

"Nothing really. Dakota and I were out for a ride, and I saw your sign. More curious than anything."

"You interested in a tour?"

"Sure."

"First introduce me to your dog."

He walked with Ron to the passenger window and put his hand on Dakota's head. "Friend." She sniffed the hand Ron held out, then her gaze dropped to the dog sitting at his feet, staring back up at her.

"Belgian Malinois, smart dogs," Ron said.

"They certainly are. I've had three working dogs, two shepherds and this one. All good dogs, but Dakota's the best I've ever had."

"She behave if you let her out?"

"Yeah, but she's fine in the truck." His concern was more for Ron's dog. The setter's ears were back as it warily watched Dakota, not a friendly gesture.

"You retired?" Ron asked.

"No, just on medical leave for a couple of months."

"What are you doing to keep busy until you can go back?"

Jack shrugged. "Besides going to therapy three days a week, not much." And that was starting to get to him. It hadn't at first, because he was hurting too much to even think of doing anything, but now...he was restless.

"Hmm," Ron said.

What did that mean?

Ron pointed to the small house. "That's our office. I have a part-time assistant who keeps up with the paperwork and stuff. Back here are the kennels. We have fifteen dogs we're working with right now. This is my operation, and I have two full-time trainers and three part-timers on the payroll. We also have volunteers who spend whatever time they can here."

That caught Jack's interest. "Doing what?"

"Cleaning kennels, keeping the dogs groomed, playing with them. Things like that."

"Could you use another volunteer?" It would certainly help keep him from climbing the walls, which he was about ready to do.

"Sure, especially someone like you who has the training to work with dogs."

"Who are you training them for?" Jack asked.

"Civilians. We specialize in service dogs, you know, for people who are wheelchair bound or can't do things for themselves."

"So that's different from a therapy dog?" A friend of Jack's who suffered from PTSD had been given a therapy dog. Wade had admitted to Jack that he'd been close to eating his gun when he got the dog, and he credited his dog with saving his life.

Jack got that. He was in a better frame of mind having Dakota with him. She was good company, gave him a reason to get up in the mornings, and calmed him after his nightmares. And she wasn't even a trained therapy dog.

"Why don't you come back tomorrow? Spend some time here seeing what we do and if you think you'd like it?"

Jack glanced at Ron. "I have therapy in the afternoon, but I could come in the morning."

"See you in the morning then, Jack Daniels. We get started at nine."

"I'll be here." He grinned as he walked back to his

truck. An afternoon ride had turned into a volunteer job. The only negative was that he'd be leaving Dakota alone more than he liked. Maybe he could eventually bring her with him.

"You're not going to believe this, my friend," he said when he got in the truck. On the way home, he told Dakota about his new job. When she looked at him, her grin gone, he sighed. "No reason to be jealous. You'll always be my number one girl."

She made a sound that he interpreted as *humph* in dog speak, then gave him the cold shoulder as she stuck her head back out the window.

"Be that way," he said, then turned his thoughts to what to feed Nichole for dinner.

## Chapter Eleven

"He's a hundred percent better since I've started working with him," Nichole said at the end of Rambo's training session. He was even behaving better when she brought him with her to the River Arts District. He still had his puppy moments, but they were fewer and farther between, thankfully.

Jack leaned down and massaged Rambo's shoulders. "I'd be questioning my training skills if he wasn't." He straightened, then glanced at her. "But a hundred percent better still isn't the dog he can be for you. We'll get him there."

She especially liked the *we* part, meaning that Jack would still be around to help her train Rambo. He seemed different tonight. Happier. He was quick to laugh or make a joke, but there'd always been something lingering in his eyes that had made her think his laughter and joking around was a front for the pain he tried to hide. She didn't know if it was physical pain or mental or a combination of both, but it had been there from the first day she'd met him until tonight.

"Something's different about you," she said. At his raised brow, she lifted her hand to his cheek. "You seem happy."

He leaned into her palm. "You make me happy."

"I hope so, but so is something else."

His eyes glittered like a child's at Christmas. "I had a great day." He took her hand. "Come on. I'll pour you a glass of wine and tell you about it while I make you one of my favorite dinners."

"Can I help do anything?" She was sitting at the small table in his kitchen. He handed her a glass of wine, then twisted the cap off a bottle of beer for himself.

"Nope. You just sit there and look pretty while keeping me company. I did all the prep this afternoon. You like Mexican, I hope."

"Who doesn't? Although if we're having Mexican, I think I'd rather have a beer." She pushed her untouched wine aside.

"My kind of woman." He popped the cap off another bottle and brought it to her. "Trade you for a kiss."

"Seems fair."

He set the beer on the table, curled his fingers around her hair and tugged her head back, then covered her mouth with his. As he kissed her, his hand drifted to the curve of her breast, and he lazily drew circles with his thumb. Even with the barrier of her T-shirt, his touch sent shivers flowing through her.

"How important is dinner to you?" she said somewhat breathlessly when he let her up for air.

"Oh, no you don't. I'm romancing you by way of feeding you my best meal. No dirty stuff is happening until after I've impressed you." He brushed his thumb over her nipple, sending more quivers through her, then winked as he stepped away. "And then all bets are off."

"Oh," she whispered. "Can we eat fast then?"

He waggled a finger at her. "Nichole, you need to learn patience. Good things come to those who wait."

"Says who?"

"Hell if I know."

God, she loved that mischievous glint in his eyes. She bet he'd been a handful as a little boy. "You're funny."

"I used to be."

"But not anymore?" Why did he think that when he easily made her laugh?

"Didn't have much to laugh about after getting hurt. Things are starting to amuse me again, though. A part of that is that I'm healing, and I'll be back with my team soon, and a part of that is because of you. You make me happy."

How was she supposed to resist falling for him when he said things like that? When he looked at her as if she was the reason for that sweet smile on his face? Did she even want to try? Not really, but she had to. Once back with his team, he'd forget about her. But he was here now, and she was going to enjoy him while she could.

"I had an interesting day," he said, leaning his back on the counter. "Did you know there's a service dog training facility out on Old Mill Road? That's out past Leicester."

"No, I've never been out that way."

"It's a pretty drive. We'll take a ride there sometime. Anyway, I stumbled on the facility and met the owner."

"That sounds like something you'd really enjoy," she said when he finished telling her about the volunteer opportunity. She loved how his eyes lit up with excitement.

A buzzer chimed, and he shot her a grin over his shoulder as he opened the oven door. "Yeah, it does. And I'm going a little stir crazy with nothing to do except physical therapy three days a week, so it gives me someplace else to go."

A few minutes later he placed a salad and a plate of Mexican lasagna in front of her. She'd never dated a man who'd cooked for her, never been with a man who'd made her feel special. Bit by bit, he was chipping away at her heart. How would he react if he knew that?

He'd been up-front that he would be leaving, and she guessed that it was best if she hid these growing feelings she had for him. If he knew that she was falling for him, he would disappear.

The food was delicious but the serving huge. She pushed her plate away after making her way through half the meal. "I can't eat another bite. That was delicious. What else can you cook?"

"Why? You looking for a personal chef?"

"Wouldn't that be awesome? My dream man is both a chef and hairdresser, and since this is my fantasy, he's amazing in bed."

His grin was positively wicked. "Got two of those covered, but tomorrow I'll enroll in hair styling school."

She tapped her fingers over her chest. "Be still my heart."

He shook his head. "Stilling your heart is not the objective tonight. In fact—"

Pink's song "Trouble" sounded from his phone, and he groaned. "Grammie." He scooted his chair back. "Sorry. If I don't answer, she'll just keep calling until I do."

"So, 'Trouble' is her ringtone?" That was funny. She needed to meet his Grammie.

"Yes, and more fitting than you can imagine." He grabbed his phone from the counter. "What's up,

Grammie?" As he listened, his eyes widened, then they slammed shut. He dropped his phone against his leg, opened his eyes, and looked at her. "Please tell me today is April first. Lie if you have to."

Oh, boy. What had his grandmother done now? "Sure, for you I'll lie. It's April Fool's Day."

"I knew I could count on you." He put his phone back to his ear. "Take it down right now, Grammie... I don't need help finding a girlfriend. I have one."

A few seconds after saying that, he pressed his phone against his leg again. "I didn't mean to say that. Now I have to bring you to Saturday morning pancake breakfast."

Without waiting for her answer, he slammed the phone to his ear again. "She might be busy." He rolled his eyes. "No, I'm not making up a fake girlfriend."

Nichole's amusement grew with each minute he talked to his grandmother. Finally, she couldn't hold back her laughter. His gaze fell on her, and he narrowed his eyes. *Not funny,* he mouthed, but his lips twitched.

"No, I do not need a backup plan in case it doesn't work out. Take it down, or I won't bring Nichole to breakfast... Yes, it's a pretty name, and no, I'm not sending you a picture. Gotta go, Grammie. See you Saturday."

"What did she do?" Nichole asked after he disconnected. Instead of answering, he walked out of the room, returning moments later with a laptop. After sitting in the other chair, he logged onto the computer.

"I never should have taught her how to use a computer," he muttered.

"Uh-oh. That doesn't sound good."

"I didn't think she could top the cock sock, but I was wrong." He turned the screen toward her.

"She put you on a dating site?"

"If only that was all she did. Read my bio."

Hello. I'm Jack
A man with impressive sacs
I have other remarkable parts
And I'm not just talking about my heart
I will treat you like a queen
Even give you my spleen
If you are the girl of my dreams
I will make you steam
As you cry out my name
When we play our bedroom games
I will make you mine
For all time

Jack watched Nichole read the ridiculous poem or whatever it was that his grandmother had posted, no doubt with Dirty Mary's help. Amusement filled her eyes, and she pressed her lips together as she tried not to laugh.

He sighed. "Go ahead and laugh."

"I'm sorry," she said after regaining her composure. "Now I know where you got your sense of humor. Your grandmother's a riot." She scrolled down the page. "And look, you have seventeen responses already."

He slapped the laptop closed. "Grammie can answer them, 'cause I'm not."

"Aren't you even curious? The girl of your dreams might be there."

He stroked a finger over her bottom lip. "The girl of my dreams is sitting right in front of me."

"Oh," she whispered.

"Nichole…" He almost asked her if she'd wait for him when he was on deployment, but neither one of them were ready for that question yet.

"Hmm?"

"I'm going to kiss you," he said instead, swallowing the words hovering on the tip of his tongue.

"Yes, please."

Surprising him, she crawled onto his lap, straddling his legs. He put his hands on her hips, stared into those beautiful golden-brown eyes, and wondered what it was about her that had him thinking of a future with her. And even more remarkable, he was good with it.

He lifted a hand to the back of her neck and brought her mouth to his. Her lips were soft against his, her scent washed over him, and he knew that he was lost to this woman. He deepened the kiss, his tongue invading her mouth, needing to taste her, and damn, she tasted delicious.

She pressed against his chest, and he could feel the rapid beat of her heart, proof that she was as affected as him. He growled his satisfaction. Their breaths mingled until he didn't know where his ended and hers began.

"I want you, Nichole. I need you." He didn't care that he'd just given her power over him by admitting his need for her. She could rip him to shreds, and he'd let her. But maybe that was easy to believe because he knew to the bottom of his heart that she wouldn't.

He stood with her wrapped around him and headed for his bedroom, the dogs hot on his heels. "Stay," he said, kicking the door closed before they could come in.

Rambo whined, but Dakota was silent, and he knew she'd positioned herself in front of the door where she could stand guard. Rambo whined again as he scratched the wood. Dakota gave a sharp bark, one Jack recognized as a reprimand. He smiled when silence followed.

"Wish he minded me the way he does her," Nichole said.

"Don't wanna talk about the dogs right now." He still held her in his arms, her legs wrapped tight around his hips. Just having her pressed against him was playing havoc to his self-control.

"Me either." She touched her lips to his.

He turned, then fell back on the bed with her sprawled on top of him. Jack had never been much on kissing. It was too intimate, too much like saying there were feelings involved. But then, he'd never had Nichole to kiss. He slid his hands under her T-shirt.

"Off," he said, the word coming out as a command.

She pushed up, gave him a sexy smile, and then pulled the shirt over her head, tossing it carelessly aside. Holding his gaze with hers, she reached behind her and unhooked her bra, letting the straps slide down her arms. She raised her brows as she crossed her arms, holding the bra against her breasts.

Little tease. "Drop it," he ordered.

"I'll think about it."

She was playful in the bedroom, and he liked that. "While you're thinking, I'll just do this." He put an arm around her back and flipped them, snatching the bra off as they rolled.

"Where did it go?" she said, peering down at herself.

"Away."

"Sneaky," she said, grinning at him. "They teach you sneak techniques in SEAL school?"

"Baby, I learned how to steal bras as a young whippersnapper." That got him a laugh. "What? You don't believe me?"

"Oh, I do. I'm just visualizing you as a"—she made air quotes—"young whippersnapper going around and stealing bras off clotheslines."

"That's not what I meant, and you know it." Damn, he really liked this girl.

"What else did you learn while whippersnapping?"

"The answer to that is best shown."

"Then show me what you got, sailor."

"Yes, ma'am." He skimmed his fingers up her stomach to her breasts. "So beautiful."

The navy had taught him discipline and control, and it was going to take every ounce of those teachings to not embarrass himself because every sexy inch of her had him teetering on the edge. No woman had ever gotten to him the way this one did, and that had him thinking of possibilities.

Who was this man thinking of a *forever*, a word so foreign to him that he should be breaking out in a cold sweat? Instead, as crazy as it sounded in his head, he was all in.

Was she?

## Chapter Twelve

"You're staring at me," Nichole said. Desire—hot and heavy—had been in his eyes as he'd gazed at her breasts, but something else was in them now, something soft and deeper.

"I'm a guy. Breasts are our kryptonite." His gaze traveled up to her lips. "A woman's mouth falls into that category, too, because of what it can do." As if in agreement, his erection pulsed against her core.

She grinned. "That is such a man thing to say."

He smirked. "We're simple creatures. Truth, I want you so bad, baby, that I'm not even sure of my name right now."

"Names are overrated." She tugged on the hem of his T-shirt. "Off."

"Yes, ma'am." He covered her mouth with his, and impressing her with his stealth skills, had them both undressed before she knew what was happening.

That was because the man knew how to kiss, and when he did, the world ceased to exist, even the loss of her shorts and panties going unnoticed. From her mouth he moved to her neck, nibbled and sucked until he had her moaning, then he licked his way to her breasts.

Settled between her legs, his erection teased her as it

rubbed against her while his talented tongue and fingers played with her breasts. Need was a fire raging inside her, every nerve ending sensitive to his touch. It was too much…it wasn't enough.

"Jack," she murmured.

"Hush, I'm busy here." He slid his hands down her sides to her hips, then trailed a path to her stomach. Then lower. And lower.

He was very busy, and his busy was good. No, simply good didn't come close to what he was doing to her, to the things he was making her feel. It was… "Mind-blowing."

"Yeah?"

She'd said that aloud? When she came undone against his mouth, he gave a grunt that sounded like pure male satisfaction. He climbed back up her body, lowered himself over her, and kissed her as if he wanted to devour her, as if she was the oxygen he needed to keep his heart beating.

As for her own heart, she thought it might pound itself right out of her chest.

"I'm burning up for you, Nichole. If you knew all the things I want to do to you—"

"Like what?"

"Dirty things. Things that are going to make you moan my name, then beg me to make you come. But I'm not going to."

"You're not?"

"Not until you can't take it anymore, and then you're going to scream my name." He sucked her earlobe into his mouth, biting down on it, sending delicious tingles through her.

"You like hearing your name that much?" Was that raspy, breathless voice hers?

"Coming out of your mouth, yes." He lifted onto his elbows, putting most of his weight on his good arm, and stared down at her, his blue eyes dark and hungry. "You might be…no, you are the most beautiful thing I've ever seen in my life."

"For you, I want to be." And she did want to be beautiful to this man in a way she'd never needed to for any other. She scraped her fingernails down his chest, smiling when he closed his eyes on a shudder. "Make love to me, Jack."

"Hell, yeah."

He reached over to the nightstand and grabbed a condom that he'd apparently put there when he'd stripped them of their clothes. The man really was stealthy.

"Do you feel how perfectly we fit together?" he said after slipping into her, then stilling as if he felt their connection as deeply as she.

"Yes," she whispered. Her *I'm not going to fall for this man* walls were crumbling around her as if they'd been erected with no more than sand, easily blown away by a mere breeze. Although there was nothing mere about Jack Daniels.

He was going to break her heart.

"What's a girl to do?" Nichole glanced at Dakota and Rambo, both sitting at her feet. Dakota whined, seeming to grasp Nichole's thoughts. Unable to sleep, she'd slipped out of bed to sit in Jack's living room and consider her options. There were only two, really. Keep seeing Jack until he left her behind to nurse her broken heart, or walk away now, only suffering minor damage.

Hard choice, that. What were the chances that he'd want a long-distance relationship? That by his time to leave he would ask her to wait for him? Slim, maybe? He'd been up-front with her that he wasn't looking for anything permanent. Even after saying he wanted to romance her, he hadn't said a thing that gave her hope he might ask her to wait for him. Maybe he would, maybe he wouldn't when it was time for him to leave, which left it up to her to decide if she should walk out his door right now or crawl back into bed with him.

"Okay, guys, bark once for taking a chance on Jack or twice for I'm crazy for even thinking of doing that."

Dakota barked once. Nichole blinked. No way that dog understood the question. Rambo—apparently taking his cue from Dakota—barked. Once.

"That's easy for you two to say. It's not your heart on the line."

When she'd climaxed, shattering in his arms, for a moment she'd thought they were having an earthquake. It had been that explosive, like nothing she'd ever experienced before. And when Jack had reverently whispered her name in her ear and held her close as his body trembled after his release, she'd felt cherished. That maybe he was letting her into his heart. She'd never been a gambling girl, but perhaps he was worth the risk.

"Burning up!"

At those shouted words, Dakota's ears pointed straight up as she jerked her gaze to the hallway, then she raced away. Nichole followed, stopping at the door to Jack's bedroom and taking in the scene illuminated by the moonlight shining through the window. He thrashed on the bed, his legs tangled in the covers.

Dakota put her front paws on his chest, licked his face, then barked.

Jack sat straight up in bed, his chest heaving. He buried his face in the fur on Dakota's neck with such familiarity that Nichole knew his nightmare wasn't a one-time occurrence. Her heart was breaking like she had believed it would, but not for the reason she'd thought.

This man needed her. But she sensed that he wouldn't want her seeing him like this, so she quietly slipped away, returning to the living room. Had he been dreaming that he was burning up? A nightmare of when he'd been hurt by the bomb?

Unsettled, she roamed around the room, stopping when she came to an end table she hadn't noticed before. The table was next to a well-worn recliner that she guessed was Jack's favorite seat when watching TV. She smiled at seeing the figurine he'd insisted on buying from her. Sitting behind it was a metal sculpture of a dog that she recognized as one of Forest Ellers's. An image of a man in military camouflage kneeling in front of a dog formed in her mind, and she wished she was at her studio.

She brushed her fingers over the girl and dog figurine, then returned to the sofa, tucking her legs under her. Tomorrow she'd search online for a mold of a soldier and dog. If she could find one, she'd make it for Jack.

"Hey, you weren't in bed."

Holy hotness. The man standing a few feet from her blinking sleepy eyes, his hair tousled, and wearing only a pair of dark blue boxer briefs, would have been her deepest fantasy if only she'd known there was a man like him to fantasize about. No reason she couldn't start now, though.

"Did you miss me?" She patted the sofa cushion. With those words, she realized she'd made her decision. She wasn't walking away. If the result of that was a broken heart, so be it.

He settled next to her. "You weren't there," he said, sounding grouchy.

"My bad." She didn't want to tell him that she'd spent the past hour debating the wisdom of continuing to see him. She leaned her head against his shoulder. "Mmm. You're as good as sitting next to a furnace. That'll come in handy in the winter." Not that it would do her any good. He'd probably be on the other side of the world somewhere.

Jack glanced down at her. "My heat is yours, baby. Did I wake you up?" He didn't stay the night when he hooked up, but since this was his house he couldn't leave, another reason he never brought women home. And he hadn't seen Nichole as simply a hookup, even from the beginning. This woman had him breaking all his rules.

"You didn't." She grinned up at him. "I should be dead to the world after our little marathon, but I think you invigorated me instead."

"Yeah? Need some more invigorating?" He picked up her hand and put it palm down on his leg. "And Nichole? There was nothing little about that."

"Couldn't resist pointing that out, could you?"

He snorted. "I'm a man. We're sensitive about size." He glanced around his living room. It looked better in the soft glow of the lamp she had turned on than it did in the light of day. "You said something about a person's home telling you about them. What does mine tell you about me?" He really was curious to hear her answer.

Her gaze traveled around the room. "It's not the typical bachelor pad I would have expected."

"Probably because it was my parents' house."

"I see a mother's hand here. Where are your parents?"

"Dead." When she hissed a breath, he said, "Sorry. Didn't mean to say it like that, but it's still hard to think of them gone. They were hiking, something they loved to do, when a sudden storm came up. Lightning struck before they could get back to the car or find shelter. They both died instantly, so at least they didn't suffer."

If anything, he'd always thought it would be them being notified by the navy that he'd been killed, that they would be the ones to mourn. The only blessing was that they would never have to hurt the way he had when his commander gave him the news.

"Oh, Jack. I can't imagine how hard that must have been to lose both at the same time." She slipped her hand into his and squeezed.

"I'll never stop missing them, but they're together, so there's comfort in that." He brought her hand to his mouth and kissed her fingers. The sun was peeking over the mountains, and he wanted to crawl back into bed with Nichole, spend another hour buried in her sweet body, and then a little more sleep curled around her. But first they needed to talk about Gregory.

"Can we talk about your ex for a minute?" She wrinkled her nose but nodded. "Have you filed a restraining order on him yet?"

She sighed. "No, but I guess I need to do that."

"Yeah, you do. His following us the way he did the other night, the way he's watching you, that's not good."

"I know. I'll do it in the morning, okay?"

"Good. With that business out of the way, I have other things in mind." He waggled his eyebrows like a silly cartoon character.

"Do you now?"

"Oh yeah." He scooped her up and carried her to his bedroom. The dogs followed, and after lowering her to his bed, he pointed at Dakota's bed. "Sleep," he said. Rambo followed Dakota, curling up next to her. With the dogs settled, he turned his attention to Nichole.

It should scare him how much he liked seeing her in his bed, but he couldn't deny the longing to wake up to the sight of her next to him every morning. He eased his body over hers, then nuzzled her neck.

"I can't get enough of you, Nichole," he said. "Why is that?"

Wednesday afternoon, after his physical therapy session, Jack walked into the gun range with a smile on his face. It was his best day in a long time. *And night,* he mentally added. Even his nightmare hadn't put a damper on his mood.

After Nichole had left, he'd gone to Asheville Service Dogs and worked there for five hours. Although he'd been assigned grunt work—cleaning kennels, giving dogs a bath, and mowing the grass—and not paid a penny, he'd loved every minute of it.

Between spending the night wrapped around Nichole and his time at Service Dogs this morning, he was a happy man. Now he was meeting her brother, and he was even looking forward to that. It would give him a chance to get a bead on the kid. Nichole's ex seemed to have some kind of hold on Mark, and Jack intended to find a way to cut the ties between Lane and Mark.

Jack arrived at the range thirty minutes before Mark, giving him time to get set up. Since no one touched his guns, he rented a 9mm handgun suitable for beginners, ear and eye protection, and purchased a box of ammo for Mark to use.

He'd use his Glock 19. Nervous about how his arm would do, he headed to the range to get off a few practice shots before Mark arrived. Fifteen minutes later, he packed his gun away in disgust. Before he'd hurt his arm and shoulder, he would have hit the bullseye every single time. Now he couldn't hit it once. Sure, he'd come close the first few times, but close didn't cut it. He massaged his upper arm, appalled by his performance and his quivering muscles.

*What if the damn arm is never right again?* No! It would heal, and he would get back to his team. He just had to work harder, double up on his physical therapy even if Heather didn't approve. More time at the gun range, too, practicing until he had perfect aim again.

His name was paged, meaning Mark had arrived. Jack picked up his gun case and headed to the front. After the attendant checking Mark in reviewed the rules and procedures, and Mark signed the waiver that he understood and would obey, Jack took him to the range.

"You ever shoot a gun before?" he asked.

"No, but I'm deadly on games. Had lots of time to play them when I was sick."

Jack set the items he'd rented on the shelf. "Okay, first thing, this is a real gun, not a game."

"I know that, man."

"No, I don't think you do." He studied the young man

staring back at him with a smirk on his face. He was a little under six foot and thin. There was intelligence in the eyes so like Nichole's, but he had an attitude problem. Nichole had said her brother had been babied most of his life because of the cancer, and he got that. He'd probably be hard pressed not to do the same if it was his kid, but it was time for Mark to grow up.

"We gonna shoot or what?"

"We're going to or what, and if I think you've paid attention when I go over gun care and safety with you, then we'll shoot. If I don't think you're taking this seriously, then we'll call it a day."

"Fine."

"And lose the attitude." Not giving Mark a chance to answer, Jack picked up the handgun. "This is a nine-millimeter, a good gun for a beginner. The first rule, the golden rule of guns, is to treat every gun as if it's loaded."

"Is it?"

"No, but always assume so. Never, ever point a gun at a person while you're at the range, even if you're positive it's not loaded. That will get you banned for life, and rightly so."

Jack went through his spiel, pleased that Mark's eyes hadn't glazed over by the time he finished. "Any questions?"

"Yeah. What kind of gun do you have?"

"A Glock nineteen."

"That's a bad gun. Can I shoot with it?"

"No one touches my guns but me. You ready to give this a try?"

"Been ready."

"Then put on the earmuffs and safety glasses." Jack put his personal ones on. He loaded the handgun with ammo, then pointed it at the floor as he handed it to Mark. "Let's see what you got."

The kid wasn't bad for a beginner. He shot with his legs braced apart and his eyes steady on the target. Jack let him go through the box of ammo, and toward the end as he adjusted to the gun, he was hitting the bullseye.

"That's it for today," Jack said, pulling off his ear protection when the last bullet hit the target. "You did good." Truthfully, the kid was a natural.

"Aren't you going to shoot?"

"Nope. I reserved the time for you." No way was he going to embarrass himself in front of Nichole's brother, who no doubt thought Jack would dazzle him. Before he'd been hurt, he would have. The reminder of that soured his good mood.

"Can we do this again?"

The hopeful look in Mark's eyes was impossible to say no to.

"Sure. I'll give you my phone number. Call me when you're ready to go again." Jack hadn't asked Nichole how old her brother was, but he guessed early twenties. He seemed younger, or maybe it was just that Jack felt years older than he was. War would do that to a person.

"Wanna go get a beer?"

"Not today." He was not going to make Nichole's kid brother a drinking buddy. But… "You doing anything tomorrow morning?"

Mark's eyes lit up. "We're gonna come here again?"

"Nope. I have something else in mind. You still staying at your sister's?"

"Uh-huh. She said I could stay there for two weeks."

"Great. I'll pick you up at eight-thirty."

"In the morning?"

Jack swallowed a chuckle at Mark's alarmed expression. "Yep. Wear old clothes." No reason the kid couldn't make himself useful instead of hanging around, being useless. If nothing else, it might help keep him away from Lane and out of trouble.

"So, what are we doing?"

"It's a surprise." Although he doubted Mark would think cleaning up dog shit would be a particularly good surprise. It was going to be fun.

## Chapter Thirteen

"I hit the bullseye a couple of times at the end," Mark said as he sat at the kitchen island eating a bowl of ice cream. "Next time we go, I'll hit it every time."

Nichole added a lemon slice to her glass of iced tea, then leaned back against the counter. She wasn't sure how she felt about that. He'd been bouncing around like a kid on a sugar high ever since coming home, and she loved that he was excited about something. It was the guns she wasn't crazy about. She hadn't said anything to Jack because she hoped spending time with him would be good for Mark. She just wished they were doing something together besides her brother learning how to shoot.

"And I'm going with him in the morning."

"To the gun range again?" Once was one thing, but on a regular basis? That didn't please her.

"No. He won't tell me where we're going. Said it was a surprise. What do you think we're gonna do?"

"I can't imagine." But she was sure going to call Jack later and find out. Mark's phone buzzed, and since it was face up on the counter, she could see the screen. *Lane!* Damn it, why couldn't he leave Mark alone?

"Yo," Mark said. He listened for a moment. "Nah.

I'm gonna pass. I have to be somewhere early in the morning, so I'm hitting the sack soon."

*Thank you, Jack.* It was the first time she'd heard her brother turn Lane down.

Mark glanced at her. "Ah, she's in the shower right now."

She frowned. Whatever she might be doing was none of Lane's business.

"Yeah, later, dude." He set his phone down. "He wanted to talk to you."

"I have nothing to say to him."

"Figured that." He pushed his empty bowl aside. "So, he really did hurt you?"

"I would never lie about something like that. I know you're an adult and can choose your own friends, but he's bad news, Mark."

"He's always been cool with me."

With that said, he walked away. She sighed when she heard the guest room door close. Lane was using Mark as a means to get to her, but her brother refused to see that. Her ex-boyfriend could care less about anyone but himself. Unfortunately, Mark was going to have to figure that out for himself. If she tried to tell him, he would only dig his heels in.

She grabbed Rambo's leash, clipped it to his collar, picked up her phone, then walked outside. "Go potty." While he sniffed the bushes, she called Jack.

"It's magic," he said in greeting.

"Pardon?"

"I was sitting here thinking about you and you called. That's magic of the best kind."

She smiled. "Yeah?" He was such a charmer, and she didn't think he even tried to be. It was just natural to him. And she liked that he was thinking about her.

"Mmm-hmm. It would be even better magic if I wished you here and poof, there you were on my lap."

"If you could make that happen, I'd be super impressed."

"Sadly, my lap is still empty. Sure wish you were here, Nichole."

So did she, but she'd spent all of last night with him, and she didn't want him to get tired of having her around. "Um, I wanted to thank you for spending time with Mark this afternoon. That's all he's talked about since coming home."

"Okay, change of subject here. I preferred talking about you straddling my lap, but hey, I can go with the flow. You're smiling."

"How do you know that?" She totally was.

"I just do. So, Mark. I enjoyed spending time with him more than I thought I would. He's a good kid—"

"He's twenty-two."

"Maybe in age, but not in maturity."

She couldn't argue with that.

"It's time for him to grow up, though."

Her thought exactly. "I know, but how do I make that happen?"

"You don't, other than forcing him to stand on his own two feet. It's up to him to decide what being a man means."

"You're right. It's just hard to stand back and watch him drift through life. I really do appreciate your spending time with him. I have to admit that I'm not crazy about his learning to shoot a gun."

"You should have told me. I wouldn't have taken him there."

"No, it's okay. That's just me. I'm not a fan of guns.

He said y'all are going somewhere tomorrow but you wouldn't tell him where."

Jack's chuckle rumbled through the phone. "He probably won't like it. I'm taking him with me to the service dogs place. He'll be cleaning kennels and whatever else they need us to do."

"Well, that should be interesting."

"No doubt."

"Anyway, thanks."

"Welcome. Now can we get back to how I was sitting here thinking about you?"

"Okay. So exactly how *were* you sitting?"

He laughed. "Funny girl. When can I see you again?"

At the sound of the low rumble of a motorcycle approaching, she pulled Rambo's leash, bringing him back to her. "Gotta go. Call me tomorrow, okay?"

"Nichole?"

She disconnected, then ran to the door. Seconds after she stepped inside, the motorcycle passed without stopping. It could have been someone else, but bikes were rare on her street. When there was a motorcycle anywhere near her house, it was almost always Lane riding it.

After she'd ended things with him, he hadn't gone away quietly, had called until she'd blocked his number—which had made him furious—and he had unexpectedly shown up numerous times. Then suddenly he'd disappeared for about six months. She'd felt nothing but relief that he'd given up. Now that he was coming around again, it made her wonder about those months he'd gone quiet.

This morning she'd gone to the courthouse to file the restraining order. Apparently, it wouldn't go into effect until Lane was served with papers and there was a hearing. The last thing she wanted to do was face him in front of a judge, but maybe that would get it through his head that it was over between them.

A girl could hope.

Jack turned onto the gravel lane leading up to the dog kennels. He glanced at Mark. The kid was looking around with a confused expression on his face.

"What's this place?"

"They train service dogs for civilians." He figured Mark was going to be disappointed that it wasn't a paintball place or something along those lines. "We're volunteering our time this morning."

"Doing what?"

He didn't sound excited, but Jack had expected that. "Whatever needs to be done."

"You got me up to do this?"

"Yep. It's gonna be fun."

"If you say so."

An hour later, after they'd hosed down all the kennel floors, Jack leaned against one of the fences and watched Mark bathe a Labrador puppy that was hellbent on licking his face off. The kid laughed as he tried to rinse off the puppy. Mark was as soaked as the dog, and although he'd whined about cleaning up dog shit, it was obvious he was enjoying himself.

"Stop it, Murphy," Mark said, laughing as he pushed the puppy's face away.

Jack swallowed his smile. While the kid—and that was how he thought of Mark even though he was legally considered an adult—was distracted and would answer without thinking, Jack said, "What kind of job would make you the happiest?"

"Creating video games."

"Do you know how?" He didn't know anything about that, but he did know someone who did.

"You mean like coding?" Mark grabbed a towel, then wrapped it around Murphy before picking him up.

"Yeah. Have you created any?"

"A bunch, but most of them aren't too good. Just basic stuff. The last one is pretty good." He shrugged. "I think so, anyway."

Jack rarely played video games these days. The popular ones—kill your opponent or aliens or whatever— held no appeal to a man used to war and the real deal. "Have you shown it to anyone or tried to do anything with it?"

"No. Don't really know who I could show it to."

"I do."

"For real?"

*Gotcha,* Jack thought when the kid's eyes lit up, hope shining in them. "Yep. I'll make a deal with you. You come here, volunteer your time with me in the mornings, and I'll give my friend a call."

Clint Alba wasn't exactly a friend, but the brother of Jack's teammate, Noah. Clint designed video games for a living, and from what Noah said, had made a name for himself in the industry. Jack had met Clint twice and he seemed like a nice guy. Hopefully nice enough to be agreeable to taking a look at Mark's game.

"Sure. Got nothing better to do in the mornings. Does it have to be so early, though?"

"'Fraid so." Maybe the early mornings would keep him from staying out late with assholes like Lane Gregory.

"That sucks, but okay. When are you going to call him?"

"This afternoon. Might take me a day or two to catch up with him." First, he'd have to get in touch with Noah and get Clint's phone number. Hopefully his team wasn't out on an op and unreachable.

A dusty white truck pulled to a stop in front of the kennels, and Ron Kitterman got out. "Jack, good to see you back." His gaze fell on Mark. "And who's this?"

"Mark Masters, another volunteer. Mark, this is Ron Kitterman, the owner of this place."

"Always good to have another pair of hands. You got any experience with dogs?"

"No, sir."

Jack cringed. He should have cleared it with Ron before bringing Mark out here. He hoped the man wouldn't send Mark packing.

"Like I said, we can always use the extra help, but don't try to teach the dogs anything. They have specialized training, and even teaching one to sit messes things up."

"I won't," Mark said. "And thank you, Mr. Kitterman."

If nothing else, the kid had manners.

Ron glanced at Jack's truck. "Where's that dog of yours, Jack?"

"Home. Would you have a problem with me bringing her here?"

"No. Just keep her away from the other dogs."

"Not a problem."

"Well, I got some calls to make," Ron said. "You boys are doing a good job."

Mark watched him walk away. "He seems nice. What do they train these dogs for?"

"To assist people with disabilities, stuff like picking up things a person might have dropped and opening doors. They're different from therapy dogs that are trained to give emotional support."

"I never thought about those being two different things. Pretty cool that dogs can do stuff like that, though."

"Yeah, it is." And calming a man down after a nightmare was high on Jack's list of pretty cool.

After dropping Mark off at Nichole's, Jack went home, showered, dressed, and then loaded Dakota in his truck. He stopped at a deli and bought two ham and cheese on sourdough sandwiches, two bags of chips, and two bottles of water. But the clincher—at least he hoped— were the two dark chocolate cupcakes with raspberry frosting. Leaving there, he headed for the River Arts District.

The thing was, he couldn't get Nichole out of his head. He wanted her under him, over him, wrapped around him, but the most surprising, he wanted her next to him. That last not having a thing to do with sex. He wanted her in his life.

Since leaving on his last deployment, up to the first night he'd spent with Nichole, he'd been sex deprived. That had been a record for him, but he'd let the woman who'd taken one look at his arm and freaked out freak him out.

Why he'd even decided to track down his middle-of-the-night caller was a mystery, one he had no interest in solving. He wasn't a man to question a gift, and so far, Nichole was turning out to be the best gift he'd ever received.

Today he'd offer her decadent cupcakes. Maybe someday he'd offer her his heart.

*Maybe.*

# Chapter Fourteen

Nichole sold her last fairy with the silver glitter on her blue tulle dress. She'd only made five of them, not sure how they'd sell. Adding the glitter had been a moment of inspiration when she'd gone to her studio the morning after spending her first night with Jack. Happier than she'd been in a long time, she'd felt like she'd been sprinkled with fairy dust. As a lark, she'd made the first fairy and had liked it so much that she'd made four more.

She'd also sold a set of mugs, several expensive bowls, and had another commission for dinnerware. It was turning out to be a good day, and she still had the afternoon to go. Adding to her great mood, Rambo was actually behaving. His training sessions, both with Jack and the ones with just her, were paying off.

It was lunchtime on Thursday, and Nichole's gaze strayed to the aisle. Jack had surprised her yesterday by showing up with lunch. Would he do the same today? She'd spent the night at his house again, but he hadn't said anything about seeing her later when she'd left.

Instead of the man she hoped to see was one she had zero desire to talk to, and he was headed straight for her.

"Swear to God, Rambo, if you so much as wag your

tail at Trevor the Rat Bastard, you'll never get another treat so long as you live." Rambo wagged his tail. "Stop it," she growled.

"Nichole, you look really nice today."

She grabbed her dust rag, then turned her back on him and started cleaning her pottery.

"Come on. I just want to talk to you, okay?"

Desperation tinged his voice, and it could only mean that the theft of her commission wasn't going so well for him. Too bad, so sad.

"Nichole! Turn around, damn it." He came around the table, toward her.

Rambo growled. Well then, her dog was learning how to do his job. Extra treats for him tonight.

"Fine, keep your back to me, but you can still listen. My last offer was a damn good one, but I'll sweeten the pot. I'll give you—"

"La, la, la, la, la, la," she sang as she put her hands over her ears. Nothing like reverting to being a twelve-year-old.

"I don't think she wants to talk to you, Trevor."

Hearing another voice, Nichole glanced over to see Forest Ellers, the metals artist, arms crossed over his chest as he coldly stared at Trevor.

"None of your business," Trevor said.

Forest shifted his gaze to her. "Do you want to talk to him?"

"No. Not today. Not tomorrow. Not ever."

"You okay then with me making this my business?"

"You betcha." She picked up the end of Rambo's leash. "I'm going to take him for a short walk. Back in a few minutes." Maybe Trevor would leave if she wasn't here.

When she returned five minutes later, as she'd hoped, Trevor was gone. She stopped at Forest's table. "Thank you. He's refusing to take no for an answer."

"I'm guessing he wants you to help him meet the deadline on the commission he stole from you?"

"Where'd you hear that?" The only person she'd told about Trevor's treachery was Jack, and she knew he hadn't said anything.

He laughed. "You know nothing is a secret around here." He glanced across the aisle at Andrea, the stained-glass artist who had the booth next to hers. "You told Andrea when you got the commission, then she overheard you and Trevor the last time he was here begging you to save his ass."

"Oh. Well, thanks for getting rid of him."

"It was my pleasure. No one really liked him in the first place, then pulling this stunt showed his true colors. He'll get the cold shoulder from now on in the artist community."

If she wasn't so furious with Trevor, she might feel sorry for him. Getting blackballed by his fellow artists meant he wouldn't get any support for his art shows or referrals to anyone looking for commissioned pottery. But he'd brought it down on himself, so not her problem.

Back at her booth, Rambo headed for his water bowl. It didn't look like Jack was going to show up bearing lunch, so she decided to get a salad from the little café located in the warehouse. Now would be a good time to go since there weren't any customers nearby.

"Let's take another walk," she said to Rambo. He was learning what the word *walk* meant, and his ears perked up. She'd only taken a few steps when she saw Lane headed toward her.

"Crap!" What was this? Asshole Man Day? Unfortunately, her restraining order hadn't taken effect yet or she'd be on her phone, calling the police.

"Hey, Nichole." Lane walked around the table, stopping a few feet from her.

She lifted her gaze to the ceiling. "Universe, what did I ever do to piss you off today?"

"Huh?" Lane said.

"Go away, Lane. Like far, far away." Rambo put himself in front of her and growled. She wasn't sure why the friendliest puppy in the world had suddenly decided to play guard dog, but he was definitely getting extra treats tonight.

"I miss you, Nic."

"No, you don't. You just want what you can't have." She sighed. "We're over, and there's no going back. I just want you to leave me alone." There was the cold glint in his eyes that she was used to seeing lately. Lane didn't like to be told no, always wanted his toys and everyone else's, too. Even ones he could care less about.

"Go out with me tonight. By the time I take you home, if you don't ever want to see me again, I'll disappear."

Lane was also a liar. She'd caught him lying many times during their time together, and sometimes it was about things that didn't matter. He had no intention of disappearing before he got what he wanted.

She had a feeling that Jack was a part of Lane's reason for his insistence that he wanted her back. The minute he became aware that another man was sniffing around in what he considered "his territory," he was back to protect what was his.

"No, I'm not going out with you."

His eyes went from cold to mean, and this was the Lane that scared her.

There was a mall cop always on duty in the warehouse, and she scanned the aisle, looking for him. She didn't see him, but she did see Jack, and her heart sputtered, both from relief and…well, just the sight of the beautiful man coming her way. He carried the same hard-plastic cooler as he had yesterday when he'd brought her lunch.

The easygoing man she'd kissed goodbye this morning was gone, though. In his place was a warrior moving with purpose, raw power radiating from him so strongly it was almost visible. Not a sound warned of his approach, not even footsteps. *Stealth mode,* she thought. He stopped a few feet behind Lane, who was still stupidly unaware that he was in the crosshairs of a deadly predator.

"It would probably be a good idea to leave," she said to Lane, feeling like she should at least warn him.

"Not until you agree to go out with me. I'll pick you up at seven."

"You should take the lady's advice and go," Jack said in a voice that dripped menace.

Lane spun to face Jack. "You!"

Jack didn't respond, only speared Lane with an ice-cold hard stare. Like a junkyard dog spoiling for a fight, Lane charged, his fists swinging, aiming for Jack's face.

"Idiot," she murmured. Her incredibly stupid ex didn't have a clue who he was messing with. She expected Jack to do some kind of impressive ninja warrior moves. What he actually did was swing the cooler at Lane's head, who stilled as if stunned, and then crumpled. Jack caught Lane's shirt, slowly lowering him, preventing him from hitting the concrete floor face-first.

Once Lane was flat on the floor, Jack lifted his gaze to her and cocked a brow.

"My hero," she said.

A crowd had gathered around them, and the mall's security cop pushed through. "What's going on here?"

"They were fighting," someone said.

The cop glanced from Lane, out cold, then to Jack, and then pulled out what looked like a taser. "On your knees, hands behind your head."

Jack dropped to his knees, set the cooler next to him, and linked his fingers behind his neck.

Nichole pointed at Lane. "He started it, Mel. Jack was only protecting himself."

"What she said." Forest Ellers stepped up to them. "It was self-defense. The man went for him, and all Jack did was bonk him on the head with the cooler."

Nichole choked on a giggle.

Mel glared at her. "You think this is funny, missy?"

She sort of did, but she decided it was best not to admit it. Of all the security people, Mel Secur was the one she liked the least. It was not a secret that he wanted to be a "real" cop, and he'd applied for the job numerous times but always failed the physical test. She also wasn't sure he'd pass whatever mental test the Asheville Police Department required. Mel liked power, was judgmental, and she was pretty sure he lacked a heart.

He walked behind Jack, whipping out handcuffs. "Don't move if you know what's good for you, douchebag. Put your arms behind you."

Nichole rolled her eyes.

Jack barely refrained from rolling his eyes. Just his

luck that a rent-a-cop with a make-my-day-attitude was on duty. Two people had already said that Lane Gregory had come at him. This situation didn't require attitude and handcuffs.

Secured by cold metal around his wrists, Jack looked up at Nichole. "Your lunch is in the cooler."

"Aw, you're so sweet," she said.

"Only for you." Damn, he loved that smile of hers.

"You have the right to remain silent," Rent-A-Cop said.

"Fuck happened?" Gregory said, then groaned.

Nichole leaned down. "You got bonked. Deservedly so."

"Let us through!"

Jack glanced over to see EMTs pushing through the growing crowd. Half of the people surrounding them had their phones up, recording the ridiculous proceedings. If his commander saw him now—handcuffed and on his knees—Jack would have a lot of explaining to do. He didn't doubt that he'd be all over Facebook in minutes. Praise Jesus that his commander thought Facebook was the devil incarnate and never ventured on to the site.

The two EMTs kneeled on each side of Gregory, slapped a neck brace on him, loaded him on a board, then whisked him away. Jack took inventory of the places he was starting to notice. His knees didn't like the concrete floor, the handcuffs on his wrists were too tight, cutting off blood flow to his fingers, and his shoulder was throbbing. He was getting too old for this shit.

Nichole put her hand on his shoulder. "I'm sorry."

He frowned. "For what?"

"For dragging you into my mess."

"Babe, you can drag me anywhere you want to."

She smiled at him. He smiled back at her. His heart

did that funny bounce thing that he blamed totally on her. He hadn't wanted to find the girl of his dreams before his time in the military was over, but as his Grammie would say, "Life bites you in the butt when you least expect it." He wasn't exactly sure what that meant, but it seemed to fit. He sure hadn't expected Nichole, or for her to ramrod her way through all his relationship rules. But she had, and he wasn't sorry.

"No touching the prisoner," Rent-A-Cop said.

Now he was a prisoner?

"What do we have here?"

The smirk on his new friend's face told Jack that he wouldn't live this down, not even after offering to buy Heather's husband a lifetime of beers. But at least it was a friendly face. "Deke, my man, fancy meeting you here. How's Heather?"

"As beautiful as ever. What trouble have you gotten yourself into?"

"Dunno. You'll have to ask him." He pointedly glared at Rent-A-Cop. A thought occurred to him. He'd only planned to drop off lunch for Nichole before heading to his doctor's appointment, the one Heather had made for him without asking first. An appointment he wouldn't make now.

"Whatcha got here, Mel?" Deke said.

"A ten-forty-four, Officer Matthews."

Deke shot Jack an amused glance. "A riot, huh?"

"Ah, no, I mean a ten-forty."

"Hmm, a fight in progress. Looks like you got it all handled. I'll just be on my way then."

"Hey," Jack said. Was Deke really going to leave him here on his knees with a squirrelly pretend cop pointing a taser at him?

"Aren't you going to arrest him?" Rent-A-Cop said.

Deke glanced at Jack with entirely too much amusement in his eyes, then shifted his gaze to the security guard. "Sure, why not?" He leaned down and put his hand under Jack's elbow. "Up with you, troublemaker."

"But he didn't start it," Nichole said as Jack struggled to his feet.

"Good seeing you again, Nichole. I'll let him have one phone call." Deke grinned at her and winked.

"Ah," she said, grinning back at him. "Don't forget to frisk him," she called as Deke led him away.

Jack glanced back at her. "Enjoy your lunch."

"Thanks, and don't worry. I'll come bail you out of the slammer."

"Y'all are having way too much fun with this," Jack muttered.

Deke snorted. "Highlight of my day. Can't wait to tell Heather."

"Asshole." He'd gathered from the exchange between Deke and Nichole that he wasn't actually going to be hauled off to jail. But his shoulder was hurting like the dickens with his arms bound behind him.

"I've been called worse." They stepped out of the building. "Wanna tell me what that was all about?"

Jack turned his back to Deke. "First get these off me." When he was freed, he flexed his fingers, and then rubbed his upper arm.

"You okay?"

"Damn shoulder."

"Hope you didn't do more damage. He had those handcuffs too tight."

"No shit. So I stopped by to bring Nichole lunch before I headed to my doctor's appointment, which I'm going to

miss now. Your wife isn't going to be happy about that."
He told Deke what had happened between him and Gregory. "I don't like the dude, but I hope he's okay."

"Let's find out." After making a phone call, Deke said, "My partner is checking with the hospital now and will get back to me. Nichole needs to get a restraining order on her ex."

"She's filed for one. I guess she has to wait for a hearing now."

"Good. The court hearing happens pretty fast after a restraining order is filed." Deke's phone buzzed. "Matthews here." He listened, then, "Thanks. I'll be back at the station shortly."

"Well?" Jack asked.

"He's fine, just raising a stink, demanding you be arrested for assault. You need to watch your back with this guy, Jack."

"I know, and I will. I'm more worried about Nichole." A man who wouldn't take no for an answer couldn't be trusted, and he didn't think she was taking the situation as seriously as she should.

"Might be a good idea not to go back in there today if you don't want Mel tasering you." Deke laughed like that was funny. It was not. "See you and Nichole Saturday."

"Yeah, man. Looking forward to it."

Now what was he supposed to do with his afternoon? He'd missed his doctor's appointment, which was okay with him, but Heather wasn't going to be pleased about that. He couldn't go back inside and hang out with Nichole because he had no desire to get tasered. He thought about it, and then texted Nichole.

How about I take Rambo for the afternoon?

Why?

Some training.

Sure.

Great. Can you bring him out front?

Be right there.

"Sorry," he said when she walked out. "Figured it probably wasn't a good idea to show my face inside."

"Mel tends to get carried away." She handed him Rambo's leash. "When Lane went for you, I thought you'd go all ninja warrior. Instead you bonked him with a cooler, and it ended before it started."

"There were all kinds of ways I could have reacted, but I would have hurt him more than just knocking him out for a few minutes."

She put her hand on his arm. "Lane doesn't forget slights. He's going to want revenge."

"Probably." He put his hand over hers. "I can take care of myself, Nichole. It's you I'm worried about. What time are you leaving today?"

"Around six."

"Okay. I'll be back before then."

"You're a good man, Jack." She lifted up on her toes and kissed him. "Not to mention sexy as all get-out."

"I'm a lucky man," he murmured after she walked back inside.

# *Chapter Fifteen*

At Jack's insistence, Nichole was back at his house. "I should be in my studio making pottery."

He made a pouty face. "Poor Jack. Ranks second to mud."

"It would sound better if you said clay." She and Jack were sitting on his back deck, she nursing a glass of wine and he a beer. They'd grilled hamburgers for dinner, and after eating, they'd played with the dogs until both were worn out. The two were now sprawled out side by side. Rambo was out cold, but Dakota's eyes were ever alert.

"Easier to feel sorry for myself when I'm compared to mud."

That little boy smile of his charmed her every single time he used it on her. He was such a paradox. If she didn't know it—hadn't seen him in warrior mode—she would never be able to guess he was a SEAL. He was just so easygoing and cheerful.

His phone buzzed, and he pulled it out of his pocket. "Been waiting for this call." He put the phone to his ear. "Jack Daniels here."

As she listened to him, she realized he was talking about her brother and games. What was that about?

"He's created a few of them," Jack said. "Says the last one is the best. He showed it to me this morning. It looks pretty good to me, but what do I know about video games? Thought maybe you'd be willing to take a look at it."

Her brother had created video games?

"Awesome. Thanks, man. I'll give him your number, and you two can talk."

"Who was that?" she asked after he disconnected.

"Clint Alba, the brother of one of my teammates. He's apparently a big name in the video games industry."

"I don't understand. Mark has a game?" How did she not know that?

"He never told you?"

"Ah, no. I mean, I know he loves to play those things. When he was sick, they helped keep his mind occupied on something besides hospitals and stuff. But I didn't have a clue he knew how to code or had created his own games." She was sure going to ask him why he'd kept that a secret.

She set down her wine, and then crawled onto Jack's lap, straddling his legs. "And you're going to help connect him to someone with influence in the industry?"

"Yes, but it might not go anywhere. I meant it when I told Clint that I was impressed with the game, but video games aren't my thing, so I really don't know if Mark has something good."

"You're an awesome man, Jack Daniels." Not only was he taking Mark with him to the service dog place in the mornings, but now this. She cupped his cheeks. "I think you need to be rewarded."

"Yeah?"

"Oh, yeah." She lowered her mouth to his. Dear God, she loved kissing this man. When he slid his hands along her sides, then to the curves of her breasts, she slapped them away. "No, I'm in charge tonight. I need to show you my appreciation for being so awesome."

His grin was wicked as he dropped his hands down to his sides. "Appreciate away then."

"Oh, I plan to." She had never taken over before when with a man. She'd never cared to. Sex was great, especially with a skilled lover, and she'd always been perfectly fine with the man calling the shots.

But…and it was a big one, one she'd never wanted or needed before. But she wanted to own this man who so easily laughed yet could morph into a warrior at the blink of an eye. He turned her on like no man before him. She wanted him begging for mercy because of her. His backyard was private, and it was getting dark, adding to their concealment.

"Take off your shirt," she said, tugging on the hem.

"Yes, ma'am." He wrapped his hands around hers, and together they got him bare-chested to her great satisfaction. Mama Mia and all the other exclamations her woman-sisters had ever shouted at seeing a picture-perfect male chest, stomach, and abs.

When he sneakily tried to slip fingers under her shirt—aiming for her breasts, she was sure—she slapped his hands away again. "For a man trained to obey orders, you're doing a piss-poor job of it."

He laughed. "You make it impossible to keep my hands to myself."

"Try harder," she said as she kissed a path from his mouth to his chest to his left nipple, the first one she came to. She swirled her tongue around it.

"Harder is happening without my even trying." He rocked against her to prove his point. "See?"

Did she ever. "Forget see. I feel you." She continued her trek down his body, and when she reached the waistband of his jeans, she said, "Can you get these off with me still wrapped around you like your favorite blanket?"

He actually growled. "Babe, I'm yours to command." He stood, and holding her against him with his good arm, he toed off his shoes, and shucked his jeans and underwear in less than a minute.

"You're a very talented man when it comes to clothing removal."

"Ah, but I have you as a reward at the finish line."

She wrapped her arms around his neck, sucked his earlobe into her mouth, then nipped the lobe.

"Hell, Nichole," he said, dropping heavily onto his chair. "Killing me here."

"Don't worry. I know CPR." She settled over his lap again, and when he put his hands on her hips, she grabbed them and pressed them down on the chair arms. "No touching."

"You're a mean woman."

"Oh, I think I can change your mind on that." She pressed her mouth to his, his soft lips fitting to hers like puzzle pieces meant to be connected. When she stroked her tongue along the seam of his mouth, he opened. Chest to breasts, she could feel the hard thumps of his heart. She was doing that to him—making his heart race—and that knowledge spread warmth through her body.

Their tongues tangled, and she could taste the flavor of the malt beer—rich and tangy—he'd been drinking.

Kissing Jack was potent, and pleasure streaked through her body. His scent surrounded her, his heat seeped into her skin, and her nerve endings suddenly felt electrified. Her body hummed as if a thousand bees buzzed under her skin.

"Nichole," he murmured against her lips.

The need she heard in his voice fueled the flames already heating her blood. "I know," she whispered. Her gaze traveled over his chest and stomach. As a SEAL, he had to stay in shape, and he was doing a fine job of it.

"I'm holding on by a thread here, baby. You keep looking at me like that, and these hands you won't let touch you are going to disobey."

"Then I'll have to punish you."

His eyes flamed with desire. "Promise?"

"Hush." She put her mouth on his chest, hiding her smile. A man had never looked at her like that, as if she were the hottest thing to ever straddle his lap. It did wonders to a girl's confidence.

She danced her fingers over his very perfect abs while swirling her tongue around his nipple. He jerked upward, pressing his erection against her belly, sending an aching need into the deepest part of her. She thought she would never tire of this man, and as much as she craved to feel him inside her, filling her, she wanted to give him a gift.

"You don't have to do that," he said when she dropped her knees to the wooden deck and curled her fingers around his shaft.

"I said to hush," she said again.

He gave a strangled laugh. "Hushing now."

Again smiling to herself with the knowledge that she was torturing him in a really good way, she licked her way from the bottom of his erection to the tip. He hissed, the sound coming from deep in his throat. *I'm doing this amazing thing to him,* she thought. It was not something she'd particularly enjoyed before him, but he could easily become her favorite snack. He tasted salty, like the sea, like something she could never get enough of.

From the corner of her eyes, she saw his hands grip the arms of the chair. He was close, and she lifted her gaze to his face. He was watching her, watching her tongue lapping on him. It was the hottest, the sexiest thing she'd ever seen. She firmed her lips, tightening them on him.

He put his hands on her head and tried to push her away. "I'm going to come."

She swatted those annoying hands away. She wanted to know how he tasted when she was the one who'd brought him to this state. Lifting her head, she said, "Come in my mouth." Then she wrapped her lips around him again.

"Baby," he growled as he put a hand back on her head.

*I know,* she thought, swallowing his essence, visualizing that part of him settling in all the parts of her—her mind, her heart, her soul. It was true. She did know. They had something special. Did he feel it, too?

As the last of his tremors faded, Jack pulled Nichole up until she was eye level with him. "That was…" The words filing through his head—amazing, incredible, awesome—seemed inadequate. "Incredible," he finally settled on. "You didn't have to do that but thank you."

"I know I didn't. I wanted to."

He kissed her and tasting himself on her mouth was

sexy as hell. He wanted her plastered to him skin to skin, but she still had clothes on. That needed fixing. He put his hands on her waist and lifted her to her feet. "You have too many damn clothes on."

A sexy smile curved her lips. Holding his gaze, she pulled her T-shirt over her head, tossing it on top of his, revealing a lacy white bra. "Leave it," he said when she put her hands behind her back to unhook it.

Next were her shorts. His eyes tracked her movements as she slid them over her hips and down her legs, revealing white bikini panties that matched the bra. "Beautiful." He should have had oxygen standing by.

"Leave those on, too." He held out his hand. "Come here."

She put her hand in his, and he pulled her to him. When she was straddling him again, he moved her hands to the chair arms. "Same rules for you, sweetheart. It's my turn to play." He chuckled at her scowl. "Like my Grammie says, 'You get what you sow.' Now, where should I start?"

He dipped a finger inside the edge of her bra. "I think here with this sexy piece of lace."

Goose bumps rose on her skin in the wake of his fingers as he trailed them over the curve of her breast. Dropping his hand to her waist, he leaned forward and clenched the bit of lace edging the top of her bra between his teeth. He tugged it down, exposing her nipple.

"My prize," he murmured, then swirled his tongue around the little bud, and then he sucked it into his mouth. Her breathy sigh was music to his ears, a love song that he could listen to over and over and over.

He reached behind her and unhooked the bra. The straps slid down her arms, and with her eyes focused on his, she removed it, tossed it aside, and then put her hands back on the arms of the chair.

"Carry on," she said, lifting one hand in a royal wave, as if she were the queen commanding her subject.

"Yes, ma'am." They grinned at each other, and in the playfulness between them and the silly grins, his heart did that twitchy thing again. Instead of being afraid of it like he had when it first started happening, he welcomed it. Surprised himself with how much he wanted more with her.

He trailed his fingertips down the valley of her breasts, over her stomach, then lower. "I need to taste you." He slid a finger inside her, into her wet heat. "Here."

"Yes, please," she said, making him smile.

"Not an easy thing to do here." He stood with her wrapped around him. "Bed." Leaving their clothes scattered on the deck, he carried her inside. Both dogs followed them in, and once again, he closed the bedroom door, keeping them out.

He lowered her until she was sitting on the edge of the bed, and then pulled a pillow behind her. "Lie back and spread those sexy legs for me."

When she hesitated, he sat next to her, slid his hand around the back of her neck, and lowered his mouth to hers. He'd seen the shyness in her eyes and the pink blush in her cheeks, had understood. He was a man. He had no qualms about walking around naked. Pink wouldn't color his cheeks if she told him to spread his legs for her. He would eagerly comply.

Women were different, though. They were shy about their bodies and their sexuality. At least that had been his experience. He'd never understand why that was. Women and their bodies were beautiful things to behold.

He peppered kisses over her skin as he worked his way down her body, her tense muscles relaxing under his touch. Reaching his goal, he slid off the bed to his knees. His gaze hungrily roamed over her.

"So beautiful."

He put his hands on her thighs and set his mouth on her, his tongue relentlessly stroking that secret spot until she was panting and begging for more. She bucked against his mouth, shattering as she cried out his name. Desire crashed through him with the force of an out of control train barreling down the tracks sans brakes.

"Need you, baby. Now." He pushed up, and after grabbing a condom from the nightstand, he rolled it on, and then stretched out next to her.

She tilted her head toward him, and he lost himself in the eyes that turned soft as she looked at him. He didn't know what made her different from the next woman, but he honestly didn't care the reason. It was just what it was.

"Hi," she said with a dreamy smile on her face.

"Hi," he answered, smiling back as he trailed his knuckles over the soft skin of her cheek.

There was something deeply intimate in this silent moment between them, a shared connection, one that he'd never felt before. And he knew. This was a girl that he could fall in love with, who he could cherish until his dying day.

"Nichole," he reverently whispered. A minute ago, he'd been so lust-filled and on the edge that he'd been ready to slam into her, taking her hard and fast. Something had changed in that shared moment, in their exchange of smiles. Now he needed to worship her, show her without words what was in his heart.

He cradled her neck, pulling her mouth to his, brushing his lips over hers. He draped his leg over her thigh, put his hand on her hip, and pulled her close to him, skin to skin, until there was no space between them.

Her body melted into his, and he slowly entered her. When they were face to face, chest to breast, heartbeat to heartbeat, he sighed from the contentment and pure pleasure of finding a home in her. She answered his sigh with one of her own, and happiness filled him from the knowledge that she too was feeling this thing between them.

"Nichole," he said again as he truly made love to a woman for the first time in his life.

Time seemed to float away, so lost was he in her body, in the scent and touch of her. Her gentle hands explored every inch of him, as if she were learning him. She didn't shy away from his scars, and the caress of her fingers over his damaged skin brought a sting to his eyes. He closed them, afraid she would see his tears and not understand. He wasn't sure he understood why he felt like crying.

Maybe because before now he hadn't believed he could ever be this happy.

As much as he wanted to make love to her like this all night, he was nearing the edge, his release building to the point of no return. It seemed imperative that they share this moment.

"Come with me, baby," he whispered into her ear. He slid his hand between them, his finger finding her sweet spot.

A shudder traveled through her, one he felt each

place their skin touched. "That's it." He let go, falling alongside her. Their harsh breaths mingled as they both tried to get air back into their lungs.

"What just happened?" she said when she was breathing again.

He lifted onto his good arm and stared down at her. "Everything." He kissed her—claiming her—all the gentleness he'd felt earlier gone.

"Everything," he said again.

## Chapter Sixteen

*Everything.* Several days had passed since the night Jack had said it, and that one word still echoed in Nichole's mind over and over. It held so much meaning, but what if she had put more significance into it than was there?

Although he'd not said anything more to give her a hint of his feelings, it seemed as if things between them had changed. There was a new intensity in the air when they were together, and sometimes she'd catch him watching her. She had the impression there was something on his mind, but so far he was keeping his thoughts to himself. The curiosity as to what was going on in his head was so strong that she'd practically bitten her tongue more than once to keep from asking him.

Maybe today he would clue her in. It was Saturday morning, and she was going to join Jack and his grandmother for their Saturday pancake breakfast. She was looking forward to meeting the woman who made cock socks for her grandson. That was one of the funniest things ever, and she wondered if his Grammie and Dirty Mary would have something today that would embarrass him. She hoped so, although she doubted they could top the cock sock.

The doorbell rang, and Rambo's chin hit the floor

as he scrambled to get his feet under him to go find out who'd come to see him. Since she'd learned her lesson, she peeked through the eyehole to make sure it was Jack.

"Hey, you," she said after opening the door.

She'd only left him a few hours ago, after spending most of Friday night with him. She had taken him to her favorite Mexican restaurant, and then they'd gone back to his house, ripped their clothes off, and had given rutting bunny rabbits a run for their money. He'd wanted her to spend the night, but she hadn't wanted to show up to meet his Grammie looking like she'd not slept a minute because she'd royally gotten it on all night with the woman's grandson.

"You're looking mighty pretty this morning, Miss Masters." He grinned wickedly as he pulled his sunglasses down and peered at her over the rims, letting his gaze travel over her.

"Such a charmer, Mr. Daniels." Was there a man sweeter—and sexier—than this one? If so, she'd never met him.

"Just speaking the truth, ma'am."

She eyed him up and down. "You're not so bad yourself." Standing in front of her was sex on two legs, and already knowing the things he could do to her, she wanted nothing more than to grab his hand and tug him along with her to her bed.

He took a step closer, then leaned down until his mouth was inches from hers. "If I wasn't afraid my Grammie would kill me for missing our pancake breakfast, I'd have you in bed in sixty seconds flat," he said as if reading her mind.

Then he wrapped his hand around her neck and

kissed her. Kissing Jack Daniels was her new favorite thing, and when his tongue invaded her mouth, she moaned. Too soon, he pulled away.

"Let's go before I decide Grammie killing me is worth getting us both naked and sweaty."

"Grammie, this is Nichole Masters. Nichole, my Grammie, Elizabeth Daniels."

"It's a pleasure to meet you, Mrs. Daniels." Nichole held out her hand to the woman who, with her white hair, wire glasses framing kindhearted blue eyes, and pearls around her neck, could be the poster child for what grandmothers should look like.

"Call me Lizzy, my dear." Instead of shaking hands, she pulled Nichole into a hug. "Don't wait too long to marry him. I need great-grandbabies before I die."

"Ah…" Nichole glanced helplessly over her shoulder at Jack. He looked back at her with amusement shining in the eyes he'd clearly inherited from his grandmother.

"Grammie, let go of the poor girl, and stop scaring her away with talk of babies."

The older man standing behind Jack's grandmother snorted. "Good luck with that, son. She's not going to stop until you give her one."

"Three would be nice, dear," Lizzy said.

Nichole gulped. She wasn't even sure what her and Jack's relationship was, but an image of a little boy up to no good with Jack's eyes and boyish grin popped into her mind. *Oh, thanks for that, Grammie.*

Jack put his hand on the other man's shoulder. "Nichole, this is Harold Robinson."

"My beau," Lizzy said, her eyes lighting up as she beamed at Harold.

"Mr. Robinson, nice to meet you."

He shook the hand she held out. "The pleasure is all mine, dear."

"We got you a present," Lizzy said, picking up a small gift bag from the table next to her.

Jack groaned. "I was hoping you'd skip that little tradition knowing I was bringing Nichole today."

"Oh, it's not for you, Jackie. This one's to welcome Nichole to the family."

"Aren't you sweet?" She should have brought something for his grandmother. Flowers would have been nice. "Can I open it now?"

Jack stared at the bag, suspicion in his eyes. "I wouldn't if I were you."

"Hush." Lizzy tapped him on the arm. "You'll scare the poor girl."

He glanced at her. "Be afraid, Nichole. Be very afraid."

How horrible could a present from a grandmother be? Of course, this was the woman who'd knitted him a cock sock and had signed him up on a dating site, so maybe she should be afraid. She warily peeked inside, and not seeing anything resembling a family jewels warmer or worse, she reached in and took out a rose-colored organza bag. In it were two small brown bottles.

"One is clary sage oil," Lizzy said. "It's good for enhancing the female libido."

Nichole blinked. Next to her, Jack made a snorting-choking sound.

"The other is rose oil, which increases a woman's sex drive."

"Seems redundant," Jack quipped.

His grandmother poked him in the ribs. "You can never have too much of a good thing."

"Ah…" Nichole was at a loss for words. Jack was right; little old ladies were not to be trusted.

"Tried to warn you," Jack muttered. "Grammie, I don't think—"

"There's more." Lizzy took the bag from her. She pulled out a small three-legged silver pot. "This, my dear, is a fertility ritual candle. It… Well, here, read it for yourself." She handed Nichole a cream-colored card.

Jack was entirely too amused, as was Lizzy's boyfriend. The two men appeared to be barely holding in their laughter. As she silently read the card, she bit down on her cheek to keep from laughing. The last thing she wanted to do was hurt his grandmother's feelings.

*All items used in the creation of this candle were cleansed with white sage. All of the crystals were also cleansed in moon water and the candle was born during the full moon. This candle is perfect for performing your fertility spell casting.*

"Well?" Jack said. She handed him the card, and after reading it, he snorted. "Really, Grammie. Moon water?"

"There's one more thing," Lizzy said, ignoring him. She removed another organza bag, a lavender one this time. She handed Nichole a bag of polished rocks. "These are moonstones. They aid pregnancy and childbirth."

"Well…um, thanks."

"Have you given any thought to names for my great-grandbabies? If not, I have some ideas."

"Ah…"

"McHottie! You're here."

At Jack's groan, Nichole glanced at the woman barreling toward him. She was rail-thin, had bright orangy-red hair, cherry-red lips, and blue eyeshadow. She wore leopard-print leggings, glittery silver sandals, and a black silk blouse with the top buttons undone. Large silver hoops dangled from her ears, and each of her fingers sported a ring. Her lined face attested to her eighty-something years.

This had to be Dirty Mary. Nichole grinned. The artist in her loved every inch of the colorful, free-spirited woman. Nichole stepped next to Jack.

"McHottie, hmm?" she murmured.

"Don't you dare start calling me that."

"Hot damn," the woman Nichole assumed was Dirty Mary said, planting herself in front of Jack. "My fantasy in the flesh." She reached for Jack's arm and squeezed his biceps, then shot Nichole a mischievous grin. "Is he this *hard*"—she fluttered her eyelashes—"all over, sugar?"

"What do you think?" Jack made a choking noise, and Nichole couldn't help it, she laughed.

"Mary, stop pawing my grandson." Lizzy pulled Mary's groping hand away. "Did you bring it?"

"Got it right here, all warmed up for him." She stuck her hand inside her shirt, then pulled out a small dark blue bottle.

Jack's eyes widened and he stepped back when she tried to hand it to him. "What is that?"

"Goldenrod oil. Guaranteed to boost the male libido." Mary held the bottle up to the light. "How does it work?" Her gaze fell to the zipper of his jeans. "Do you rub it on your—"

"Stop!" Jack put his hands over his ears.

It was all just too hilarious, and unable to hold back any longer, Nichole burst into laughter. The two ladies were a hoot, and that they could cause a strapping SEAL's face to turn fire-engine red was an added bonus.

"Not funny," Jack grumbled.

Oh, but it was.

After ordering something to drink while they waited for Deke and Heather to arrive, Jack shifted to face Nichole. They were seated at a table at one of Asheville's sidewalk restaurants. A full moon hung low in the cloudless sky, not far from them a street musician softly strummed his guitar as his raspy voice sang a ballad, and next to him was a beautiful girl, making for a perfect summer night.

"Grammie called this afternoon. Made me promise to bring you back next Saturday. Apparently, you're her new favorite person."

Somehow they'd all ended up going out to breakfast this morning—him, Nichole, Grammie, Harold, and Mary. There had been much laughter at his expense, which he'd pretended to grump about but hadn't at all minded.

The way Nichole had quickly bonded with his grandmother and Mary had only solidified his conviction that he wanted Nichole past the expiration date he'd originally set in his mind. He didn't want her to merely be a pleasant memory when he returned to his team. He wanted more...much more.

"I love your grandmother. Both her and Mary are a riot."

"If you say so." His grin betrayed the grumpy attitude he was going for.

"Deny it all you want, but I saw you trying not to laugh all through breakfast."

He shrugged, unable to deny it.

"When Mary asked our waiter for his phone number, telling him she was a cougar on the prowl for fresh meat, I almost spit out my coffee." She grinned at him. "And you. Your coffee went down the wrong pipe. I thought for a minute that you were going to choke to death."

He'd thought so, too. "It was a close call." Breakfast had been Dirty Mary Unplugged. Even their waiter— who'd miraculously managed to sidestep Mary's questing fingers—had ended up laughing so hard that he'd been distracted, refilling Harold's coffee cup until it overflowed.

"That's a beautiful song," she said, her gaze on the street musician.

"It is," he answered, his gaze on her. He wasn't sure what he did to deserve her but felt like the luckiest son of a bitch right now.

Their waiter returned with Nichole's glass of wine and his locally brewed beer. That was one of the things he loved about his town, all the microbreweries putting out some damn good beers.

After the waiter left, he lifted his mug. "To my gorgeous girlfriend."

"Oh, and who's that?"

"Dirty Mary, who else?" He smiled, loving that low, throaty sound when she laughed. "Silly girl. I mean you."

He'd hesitated to use the word, not sure if she was

ready for the label, but he was. And wasn't that a trip? A damn good one, though. If she was on the same wavelength as he, that was.

"How many girlfriends have you had?" she asked.

"Only one that was serious before you, the one I told you about. What about you?"

"Well, you know about Lane." She swirled her finger around the rim of her wineglass, and he suspected that being linked to Gregory embarrassed her.

He took her hand, linking their fingers. "Yeah, we don't have to talk about him. Any other boyfriends?"

A soft smile curved her lips. "A few, but the only really serious one was my first boyfriend, Tate."

As she told him about her motorcycle-riding bad boy from high school who'd stolen her heart and then had died riding his bike, Jack tried not to be jealous of a dead boy.

"I've given it a lot of thought, and I think I saw Lane as a way to recreate a time in my life when I was really happy. At first, he reminded me of Tate." She shrugged. "Until he showed his real colors."

"That makes sense. You never had closure with Tate, never got to see what could be with him."

"Well, I was sure wrong about Lane." Golden-brown eyes peered up at him. "After him, I decided I didn't like being girlfriend material."

His heart plummeted to his stomach.

"But for you, I'd like to give it another try."

His heart righted itself.

"Great. That's great." *That the best you can do, slick?* In his defense, he was still struggling to recover from the freefall when he'd thought she was going to refuse the girlfriend label.

He lowered his head until his lips were a breath from hers. "Really great," he murmured, then claimed her mouth in a kiss that extinguished the world around them, and the only thing that mattered was her.

"Get a room," said a voice he recognized.

Jack chuckled against Nichole's lips. "Tell him to go away." He reluctantly let go of her, sat back in his chair, and eyed Deke before turning a smile on Heather. "You pick this bum up on the street? I thought you were more discerning than that."

She laughed as she sat in the chair Deke pulled out for her. "He started following me, and when I couldn't ditch him, I decided to feed the poor bastard."

"Hey," Deke said, sitting next to her. "I'm the best thing that ever happened to this woman."

"True, that." Heather softly smiled at her husband. "Hi, Nichole," she said, waving.

Nichole fluttered her fingers. "Hi, you two. Nice to see you both again."

"Still wondering why you're hanging with this scoundrel." Deke lifted his chin toward Jack. "No accounting for taste, I guess."

She chuckled. "Yeah, apparently not."

When he got his own soft smile from his girlfriend, contentment settled in Jack's soul. She put her hand on his leg, and he put his over hers. It was an intimate act, something couples did, and his insides melted into a soppy mess. But it was a mess he was good with, something that was still taking him by surprise.

When the waiter arrived to take Deke and Heather's drink order, she asked for an iced tea and Deke ordered a beer. After he left to get their drinks, Heather looked wistfully at Nichole's wine.

"That's one thing I'm definitely going to miss," she said.

Nichole's eyes widened, and then she grinned. "Congratulations!"

"For what?" Jack asked.

Deke rolled his eyes. "Dude, are you really that dense?"

"Apparently." Then it hit him. "You're pregnant?"

"We are," Deke said with a shit-eating grin on his face.

And who could blame him? Suddenly Jack wanted it all, too. The wife who looked at him as if he hung the moon, one he loved to pieces, the babies…all of it. He'd even erect a white picket fence around his house if that was what it took to make the dream a reality. And he wanted it with the beautiful, sweet woman sitting alongside him.

Dinner was excellent, and the company fun. Jack really liked Deke and Heather and hoped they would continue to deepen their friendship. He could tell Nichole liked them, too, and they her. The girls had even exchanged phone numbers so they could make plans to meet for lunch one day.

When they returned to his place tonight, he would ask her if she would wait for him when it was time to return to his team. He felt fairly confident that she would give him a yes, but there was a sliver of doubt there. Maybe waiting around for a man who might never make it home wasn't her thing.

## Chapter Seventeen

"I had a great time," Nichole said as she followed Jack into his house. "Deke and Heather are a blast."

"Yep."

One word answers were all that she'd gotten from him since leaving the restaurant. He seemed preoccupied…or had she said something wrong? She hated thinking that. It was shades of being with Lane and wondering what she'd done this time. She'd promised herself she would never let a man intimidate her again, but she was feeling like that now.

"Jack, if I did or said something wrong, how about you just spit it out instead of giving me the cold shoulder?"

He stopped so suddenly that she plowed into his back. He turned to face her. "Why would you think that?"

"Because you're not talking to me. That's exactly how Lane acted when I did something to piss him off."

A muscle ticked in his jaw. "I'm not Lane. I'll never be him, so don't compare us. Honestly, I'm insulted that you would think me anything like him." He swiped a hand through his hair as he let out a sigh. "I'm sorry if I made you feel like I was upset with you. I'm not. Far from it, in fact. There's something I want to talk about, and I'm just nervous, is all." He sheepishly shrugged. "I was preoccupied on the way home with practicing what I'd say to you. How I'd say it."

Lane had never apologized, and that right there was proof that he wasn't Lane. "Okay, and I'm sorry I jumped to conclusions. Lane conditioned me to expect the worst, a habit I'm trying to break." She put her hand on his arm. "And I know you're not Lane, not even close." But now he had her nervous. Was he having second thoughts about wanting her as his girlfriend?

He took her hand. "It's a beautiful night. Let's sit on the deck for this talk." He reached down and scratched Dakota's head. She'd been patiently sitting at his feet—waiting to be noticed—since they'd walked in and come to a stop. Someday Rambo would behave that well. Hopefully.

"Okay, but I need to call Mark and make sure he let Rambo out."

"While you do that, I'll make us something to drink. What would you like?"

"Water's fine." She'd had enough wine for the night. Any more and her mind would be too fuzzy to listen to whatever he had to say.

After talking to Mark and being assured that he had let her dog out, she joined Jack on his back deck.

"We'll share," he said when she glanced at the one glass of water on the table next to him.

Sharing was a good sign, right? When she went to sit in the chair on the other side of the small table, he shook his head as he held out his hand to her.

"Over here, girlfriend."

Okay. He wasn't breaking up with her. The tension

that had been building dissipated. She put her hand in his, and he pulled her down so that she was sitting with her back to his chest. He wrapped his arms around her.

"So," he said, then nothing.

She waited, trying to guess what he wanted to say, but nothing came to her. "So?" she prompted.

"Yeah, so." He rested his chin on her shoulder, then nuzzled her neck.

If he kept that up, she was going to forget he had something to say that she wanted to hear. She leaned back, moving her face until they were almost lips to lips.

"Jack, I'm dying here. It's like you're purposely torturing me with whatever it is you're having trouble saying."

"I don't mean to torture you," he murmured into her ear, his breath warm on her skin.

"In about sixty more seconds I'm going to attack and drag the words out of your mouth." She felt his lips curve on her neck. "And stop smiling."

"You're sexy when you get feisty."

"Jaaaack!" She bumped her head against his chest.

"We're officially boyfriend and girlfriend, right?"

"Yeah, and?"

"Where do you see our relationship going?"

She knew the answer. They had an expiration date— the day he left to return to his team. He'd been clear on that. It wasn't what she wanted, but she would respect his rules. Knowing she was falling for him, she was trying to protect her heart, holding that fragile organ back as much as she could.

"You're thinking real hard there, Nichole."

"I'm not sure what you want to hear." Was this his

attempt to make certain that even though he'd given them a label she didn't get the wrong idea?

He nuzzled her neck. "How about if I go first?"

"Okay." She braced herself for the reiteration of his rule. No matter how much it hurt, she wouldn't cry. At least not in front of him.

"I really only have one question. Will you wait for me?"

She blinked. Had she heard him right? She leaned to the side so she could see his face. "You mean when you're on deployment?"

"Yes. Will you be here when I get back? Write to me? Skype with me when I can manage it?" He glanced away, then focused back on her. "Be faithful?"

For a moment she bristled that he would imply she wouldn't be true to him, but then she remembered that his one girlfriend had cheated on him while he'd been overseas serving his country. She'd probably be worried about the same thing if something like that had happened to her.

She slid her hand into his, lacing their fingers, then brought their hands to her chest, over her heart. "I have never and would never cheat on a man I was involved with. If the day ever came when I didn't think our relationship was working, I'd talk to you about it. If you happened to be on deployment when that happened, I would still be true to you, and when you came back, we would talk. But, Jack, I don't see myself ever wanting anyone but you."

His mouth crashed down on hers.

Jack believed her, which was a miracle in itself considering how many years he'd been skeptical of a relationship working with a woman as long as he was in the military. It was her, though, the reason he trusted this thing between them was real. She was beautiful inside and out, honest, sweet, and kind. And, oh yeah, sexy as hell.

"I will be faithful. That is my promise to you," she said when they came up for air. "But I expect the same from you."

"Baby, you're the only woman I want in my bed, the only one my heart has room for."

She squeezed his hand. "Those are two of my favorite places to be."

"Good." He stood, bringing her up with him. "Let's dance."

"Now?"

"Why not?" Dancing was something he loved to do, and not just because he was good at it.

As a boy, he'd hated when his mother roped him into the dance lessons the times she was a boy short. He'd much rather have been working on cars with his dad or hanging out with his friends. As a grown man, he appreciated those lessons and his skill on the dance floor. He'd learned early that women loved a man who had the moves.

He brought up his phone's playlist, choosing the one with songs perfect for dancing the tango, then he pulled Nichole close to him. "Remember what I said about the tango?"

"That you'd teach me?"

"That, too, but I also told you that it's making love with your clothes on. Personally, I think it's the most sensual dance there is. The steps can get complicated, but we're going to keep it simple for now."

"That's good since I'm not such a great dancer."

"You will be when I finish with you." He winked, and her smile went straight to his heart and his lower regions. Hell, holding her in his arms and not taking her right down to the deck and having his way with her was going to be a test of his wills.

"The first thing you have to remember is that the tango is something you feel, not something you do. We're just going to sway here for a few minutes while you close your eyes and feel the music." He put his mouth next to her ear. "Let the music flow through you, Nichole."

She was stiff at first, but as they swayed, her muscles relaxed, along with her breaths. "You're feeling it," he said after a while when her body finally sensually swayed as she moved with him.

"It's… I don't know how to explain it."

"You don't have to. I get it." And he did. Most people didn't try to feel the music when they danced, but when they did, their body would respond to the beat, move with it, embrace it. It was a beautifully sensual thing.

"Now we'll start with the embrace. That's where our hands go. We'll be a mirror image of each other." He took her left hand in his right one, holding them both out to the side. "For now, put your other hand on my shoulder." He slid his right hand down her side, resting it on her lower back.

"Is it weird that I'm kind of turned on right now?" she said.

"If it is, then we're both weird."

Truth, kind of turned on was the understatement of the year. She was a natural, which pleased him. It also had him sporting an erection that threatened to rip its way right past the zipper of his pants. He couldn't remember ever wanting a woman this much. He gritted his teeth, determined to teach her a little more of the dance steps before he showed her exactly what she did to him.

"The most important thing to remember is to trust your partner. Let your body feel my weight, to feel where I'm going, to feel me because I'll always take you with me."

She stilled, causing him to stumble. "Are we still talking about the tango or us?"

"Both," he said, then scooped her up in his arms, ignoring the screaming protest from his damaged shoulder. Her tango lessons could wait for another day. He was done. This woman was either going to be his salvation or his hell. He hoped for the first but was willing to risk the latter.

She had the power to break him, to be the reason he never again trusted another woman. But he would trust her while praying that he would never let her down. As he carried her to his bedroom, he shut out the whispering voice saying that was a distinct possibility.

## Chapter Eighteen

Jack's doctor's appointment was today, and Nichole waited for his promised call. Things had been going great since they had committed to each other. Almost too great.

They were spending their nights together, Rambo was a new and improved dog under Jack's tutelage, Mark was evolving into someone she actually liked—again because of Jack—and, no kidding, she could actually tango. Not at Jack's level of expertise, but she wasn't embarrassed to dance it with him in public, which they'd done twice now.

He hadn't lied when he'd said it was making love with their clothes on. The second time he'd taken her dancing, when the music had ended, she'd dragged him to the ladies' room, pushed him up against the door so no one else could enter, and then had her way with him.

"Damn, baby, that was hot," he'd rasped afterward. "I might have to tango with you every night if this is what it does to you."

"It's you that does this to me," she'd said.

There were so many facets of Jack, which made him endlessly fascinating. There was the SEAL who was a protector as she'd learned firsthand each time Lane made an appearance. And living inside his ripped body, under all those hard muscles, was a soft heart. One that had tracked down his wounded dog, bringing Dakota home to heal. He was a man who gave hours of his time away volunteering at the service dog place.

For a highly trained warrior, he was a surprisingly patient man, whether he was teaching her to dance or dealing with her rambunctious puppy. What she loved the most about him, though, was the way his eyes turned soft when he looked at her. She was falling hard for him, but that didn't worry her anymore. Not since he'd admitted to feeling the same and wanting to continue their relationship through his deployments.

It would be hard, knowing he was in danger and worrying that he'd return safely to her. But he was a man worth every single sleepless night she knew she'd have, wondering if he was safe.

She glanced at the clock. His doctor's appointment was three hours ago. He should have called her by now. Apprehension curled its slithery fingers around her. Something was wrong. Jack always kept his promises.

"Where is he, Rambo?" Her dog looked up from his place next to the edge of her table where he'd been quietly watching people passing by. *Quietly* was the key word and something she appreciated. She called Jack, getting his voice mail.

"Hey, it's me. I was just thinking of you. Give me a call when you get a chance."

Unfortunately, she was stuck here until at least five, or she'd go to him. When her phone vibrated, thinking it was Jack, she swiped the screen, belatedly realizing it was Turner Hutchins's name showing. What did he want?

"Nichole speaking." She was still furious with him and didn't want to talk to him, but she was too curious to hang up on the man who'd given Rat Bastard Trevor the commission he had promised her.

"This is Turner Hutchins. How are you, Nichole?"

So now she was supposed to play nice after what he'd done? "Is there a reason you're calling me?"

"There is. I haven't been able to get ahold of Trevor. Since he said you're teaming up with him on my dishes, I thought I'd get an update from you."

Damn Trevor! "I am not and will not be helping Trevor with your dishes, Mr. Hutchins. I would, however, appreciate getting my samples back."

A few seconds of silence, and then, "Trevor has those."

Just as she thought. "I see. Then we have nothing else to say. Good day."

Let him stew on that. Obviously, Trevor was avoiding Hutchins, which meant that Trevor wasn't going to deliver what he'd promised, at least not on time. Turner Hutchins hadn't blinked when he'd given Trevor the commission she'd been promised, so she didn't feel any sympathy.

It was a hard lesson learned, but she had more important things to think about, namely, where the devil was Jack, and why hadn't he called? There was probably a reasonable explanation—the doctor was running really late, maybe Jack met up with Deke for a beer, or...well, she couldn't think of another reason why he wouldn't have called.

Those were explanations, but she didn't believe they were true. One thing she'd learned about Jack was that if he said he was going to do something, he did it. Even if he was meeting up with Deke or anyone really, he would have called her. Something was wrong. She just knew it.

The building's manager wasn't going to be happy if he came by and saw her booth's night-gate closed, but she didn't care. She couldn't ignore the feeling that Jack needed her.

After she locked up for the night, she loaded Rambo into the car. She'd drop him off at home before heading for Jack's house. When she walked inside, Mark grabbed her and danced her in a circle.

"What was that for?" she asked when he let go.

A big smile lit his face. "I just got off the phone with Jack's gamer friend. He likes my game, and he has some suggestions for improving it."

"That's great, Mark." There were so many things to thank Jack for. She just needed to find him so she could thank him properly—lots of kisses would be a good start.

"Have you talked to Jack this afternoon?"

Mark shook his head. "No. I called him as soon as I got off the phone with Clint...that's his friend. Got Jack's voice mail, so I left him a message. I was kind of hoping he might want to meet up for a beer. You know, a little celebration." He shrugged. "I know it's not a done deal, but it's cool that someone in the business is actually going to give me feedback on my game."

"That really is awesome. I'm headed over to Jack's now. If he doesn't have plans, we can all three go celebrate."

"Great. I'm gonna grab a shower. Call me after you talk to him."

"I will."

"Nic," he said when she reached the door.

She glanced back at him. "Yeah?"

"Thanks. I know I've been a pain in the ass, but I'm working on being a better me."

*So much to thank Jack for.* "And I'm really proud of you." She walked back and hugged him. There had been a time when she and her parents had thought he wouldn't live long enough to see him grow into a young man. She'd been so exasperated and annoyed with him for the last year or two that she'd forgotten to be thankful she still had her brother. "I love you," she whispered.

He slipped his arms around her. "Love you back."

Leaving him to shower and dress, she headed to Jack's house. He wasn't home. Could a doctor's appointment last this long? Possibly if there was a problem. Her worry for him intensified.

She peeked in the front window. "Hey, girl," she said at seeing Dakota staring back at her. If he didn't have his dog with him, then he must still be at the doctor's. Deciding she wasn't leaving until she saw him, she settled on his porch swing, took out her phone and brought up her Kindle app. Thirty minutes later she realized she was spending more time watching the road than reading, so she set her phone down next to her.

"Where are you, Jack?"

Jack was stinking drunk. Where locationwise he'd arrived at this condition he wasn't exactly sure. He looked around him, narrowing his eyes in an attempt to see through his blurry vision. He'd stopped here sometime after leaving the VA hospital, the doctor's words a fucking echo in his fucking head.

Dr. Patel had peered over the rim of his glasses and said the words that had knocked Jack on his ass. "The muscles in your shoulder and arm are permanently damaged. You will never be back to one-hundred percent."

*Permanently damaged. Permanently damaged. Permanently damaged.*

He would never return to his team, no matter how much they needed him to. He leaned his elbows on the bar and dug his fingers into his scalp, wishing he could scrub those words out of his mind.

Where the hell was he, anyway? He remembered driving around for an hour—or maybe days—while ignoring the ringtone he'd assigned to Nichole. Each time the Temptations' "My Girl" had sounded, he'd picked up his phone, fully intending to answer. He'd promised her he'd call her after his doctor's appointment, and he was a man who kept his promises. Well, he used to be that man before the doctor had said the fucking words that had Jack now sitting in a... He blearily peered around again. As best he could tell he was in a biker bar.

Hooyah!

Each time Nichole had called, he'd wanted to talk to her. Needed to. But he hadn't been able to because then he'd have to admit what a failure he was to his team... to her. The military was all he knew, and now he had no future, nothing to offer her. She deserved a man who had a future, a place in this world. That wasn't him. Not anymore.

He slammed his empty beer bottle down on the bar. "Again!"

The bartender warily approached him. "Maybe you've had enough?"

Jack growled. "I say when I've had enough."

A miniscule voice he was determined to ignore tried telling him that he didn't act like this. But he was entitled to act like an ass. Not every day a doctor got to ruin your life. The doctor's report would probably land on his commander's desk bright and early tomorrow morning.

Goodbye fucking Jack. You're no use to your team anymore. A farewell *hooyah* to you, boyo.

"Saw your truck outside, thought I'd have a word with you."

Jack grinned at hearing the voice of Nichole's ex. He swiveled on the barstool—barely managing not to fall off—and met the gaze of the man he'd very much like to put a hurt on for all the times the prick had hurt Nichole.

"Got nothing to say," he said, glad that he'd managed not to slur his words. He wouldn't start something, but if the asshole wanted to mix it up, Jack's black mood made him ready for a fight. Before his doctor's appointment, he would have worried about doing more damage to his arm. Now, he gave zero fucks.

"Then you just sit there and listen, 'cause I got something to say. Stay away from Nichole."

"Go to hell." Done with this conversation, Jack turned back to his still empty bottle.

"I'm talking to you," Gregory said, pushing Jack's shoulder, the damaged one.

"Touch me one more time, asshole, and you'll need to see a doctor about your broken fingers."

"You two start something in here, and I'll call the cops. Take it outside if you're gonna fight." The bartender snatched away Jack's empty beer bottle.

Jack watched the bottle disappear into the trash. "Rather have another beer."

When on duty, he'd do whatever he had to in the service of his country and to protect his teammates. Off-duty, different story. He wasn't a fighter. He didn't have anything to prove and walked away if trouble started brewing. All he wanted to do right now was sit on this barstool and drown his misery in alcohol.

"Pussy." Gregory sneered. "Afraid I'll—"

"I've been afraid of things you can't begin to imagine. You, not so much." Jack slapped his hand on the counter as he stood. "A word of advice, though. You really ought to walk away while you still can."

He should probably clue the douchebag in that he was messing with a SEAL, one highly trained in the art of combat, including how to kill a man with his bare hands.

Gregory snorted. "Quaking in my boots, pal. I'll be waiting outside." He took a step away, then paused. "You can leave with your pretty-boy face still intact. All you gotta do is get the fuck out of Nichole's life."

The miniscule obligation he'd felt to tell Gregory who he was took a hike. Jack was a firm believer in karma. Why else on a day he had zero fucks to give had he ended up in a biker bar that Gregory apparently frequented? He followed the man out.

"Look," Jack said, stopping a few feet in front of Gregory. "This is bullshit. Nichole doesn't want you in her life, and that has nothing to do with me. Respect her wishes, and we don't have a problem. No need for fists."

When Gregory came at him, Jack sighed. "So be it," he muttered.

Using the man's forward momentum against him, Jack leaned back, and when Gregory was close, Jack grabbed his wrist. He used his strength to twist it enough to hurt as he swept his leg behind Gregory's ankle and tripped him. Gregory hit the pavement face-down, and Jack crouched, pressing his knee into the man's upper back.

"Had enough?"

"Go to hell."

He twisted the wrist harder. "I forgot to mention that I'm a SEAL, so oops on that. What that means is I know all kinds of ways to put a serious hurt on you without breaking a sweat. Witness the fact that you're eating dirt right now, and I'm not even breathing hard."

Maybe if Gregory knew he was messing with a SEAL, he'd be smart enough to go away and leave Nichole alone. When Gregory tried to buck him off, Jack rolled his eyes. The dude was an idiot.

"Here's how this is gonna go. I'm going to let go of you. If you come at me again, I really will hurt you. If you bother Nichole again, I promise that I'll make you sorry. So be smart and forget you ever knew her."

He glanced up to see the bartender standing a few feet away, his arms crossed as he watched them. Jack stood and stepped back. "He's not smart, this one," he said to the bartender.

"You've had your fun, now I want both of you gone."

Jack dipped his chin. "Works for me."

The bartender disappeared back inside, and Jack was halfway to his truck when he heard footsteps pounding on the asphalt. Spinning, he wasn't surprised to see Gregory heading for him. Well, he'd warned the asshole. As soon as the man's knee was in striking distance, Jack kicked, the heel of his boot landing hard on Gregory's kneecap. Gregory screamed as he crumpled to the ground.

Jack leaned over him. "Believe it or not, I'm still taking it easy on you. But my patience is wearing thin. This is your last warning."

* * *

Jack jerked awake at the sound of loud motorcycle pipes. Where the hell was he?

He scanned the area around him, his gaze passing over the biker bar and then jerking back to it. He was trained to process intel, and what he processed had him frowning. He'd been in that bar only…he glanced at his watch. Two hours ago?

Damn it. He had the feeling he needed to remember. There was the doctor snatching Jack's world out from under him, and then he'd stopped at the first bar he'd come to. Right, he'd been happily drinking until Nichole's ex had shown up.

*Nichole.*

He fumbled for his phone in the pocket of his jeans. As he blinked to clear the haze out of his eyes, his gaze fell on his bloody knuckles. He frowned at them, then looked up, zeroing in on the bar's parking lot. Nothing to be seen there, and he let out a sigh of relief. He hadn't left a dead body in his wake.

At least he hadn't been stupid enough to try to drive home. He remembered thinking that he would call an Uber, but then he must have fallen asleep. Since he still had no business driving, he made the call, arriving home thirty minutes later.

Seeing Nichole's car in his driveway and her sitting on his porch swing, he almost told the Uber driver to keep going. She was the last person he wanted to see right now. His mood was too black, and he didn't want to talk about his afternoon…none of it. Not his doctor's appointment, not the shoulder that would keep him from returning to his team, not his fight with her ex, and especially not the parts he couldn't remember.

## Chapter Nineteen

Nichole frowned at the unfamiliar car pulling up behind hers. When Jack stepped out from the back, she realized it was an Uber, and that was puzzling. Maybe his truck had broken down.

"Hey," she said when he was on the porch. He swayed, and she frowned as she studied his face. He stared back at her with bloodshot and unfocused eyes. He was drunk!

"Jack?"

He turned away, fumbled with his keys, finally managing to unlock his door, then disappeared inside. What was she supposed to do? Leave? Follow him inside? The only thing she knew he had planned for the day was his doctor's appointment. What had happened between then and now?

Dakota walked out the door he'd left open, came to her, and if Nichole wasn't mistaken, the dog wore a worried expression. She knew her master, and if there was something wrong with Jack, Dakota would pick up on that. Maybe it was her imagination, but Dakota seemed to want her to do something.

"What's going on, girl?"

Dakota whined, then walked to the door. She glanced

back at Nichole. The dog wanted her to come inside. Had Jack purposely left the door open so she'd come in? The way he'd looked at her, though, made her wary. He clearly hadn't been happy to see her on his porch. Dakota whined again.

"I wish you could talk so you could tell me what's going on."

She took a deep breath, then followed Dakota. The dog led her through the living room and to the French doors leading to Jack's back deck. He was sprawled in a chair, a beer in his hand with three unopened bottles on the table next to him. His gaze was on the mountains, but his eyes were so unfocused that she doubted he saw them.

"Jack?" She slipped onto the chair on the other side of the table. "Can I have one?" she asked, picking up one of the bottles. She hadn't known him a long time, but she'd been with him enough to know being drunk wasn't his normal.

"You need to go home," he said without looking at her.

"Please, tell me what happened." She touched his arm and felt like crying when he flinched. Her gaze fell on his hands, on the bloody knuckles. "Jack?" she gasped. "You're bleeding."

He held up his hands, frowned, and without a word, twisted the cap off a second beer, guzzling half of it. Dakota, sitting at his feet and staring at him with worried eyes, whined. Deciding she wasn't leaving until she found out why he was pouring beer down his throat like a man living in hell and beer was the only weapon against the fire threatening to consume him, she tried to twist the cap off the bottle she'd picked up.

When she was unsuccessful, he sighed, snatched the

bottle from her, opened it, and then set it next to her on the table with enough force to cause beer to geyser out the top.

If she didn't know that he was a gentle soul, a sweet man with a kind heart, his anger would have scared her, would have sent her fleeing. But no matter his rage, she trusted him. Knew he wouldn't hurt her.

"What happened at your doctor's appointment?" It had to be something related to that.

He finished off the remaining beer in his bottle, staggered to his feet, stumbled over Dakota, and caught the railing to keep from faceplanting to the deck. "Damn dog," he muttered.

At the door he paused, his chin dropping to his chest. "My shoulder's permanently damaged. Won't be returning to my team."

"Oh, Jack, I'm sorry."

She knew what returning to his team had meant to him, and what a devastating blow it was that it wasn't going to happen. She would never admit it to him, however, but tremendous relief flowed through her that he wouldn't be putting himself in danger again.

"Sorry doesn't get me back to my brothers." He finally looked at her, the warmth for her that used to be in his eyes gone. "That's all that mattered to me. You know the way out."

Nichole glanced down at her chest, almost expecting to see a knife stabbed through her heart. She startled when he went inside, the door slamming behind him. The tears pooling in her eyes stung, and she tried to swallow past the lump in her throat.

*That's all that mattered to me.*

How could six words hurt so much?

* * *

"You were supposed to call me after you got to Jack's," Mark said when she got home. "Are we still going out to celebrate?"

She'd completely forgotten about that. What she wanted to do was crawl into her bed and pull the covers over her head, but there was so much excitement in his eyes. She couldn't bring herself to disappoint him, so she buried her hurt and forced herself to smile.

"Jack's not feeling well, but yes, you and I are going to celebrate your amazing future as a game creator. Give me time to take a quick shower and change."

"Yeah, okay."

At seeing the disappointment on his face, she wanted to march back to Jack's and give him a piece of her mind. Not that it would matter to him. She treated Mark to dinner and then claimed a headache when he wanted to go to a downtown nightclub.

Later that night, alone in her room, she called Rachel.

"Hey, girl. What's up?" Rachel said.

"Just missing you. Why can't you get hired for a movie filming around here?"

"That would be awesome, but that's not why you're calling. What's wrong?"

Nichole sighed. "How can you read me so well from three thousand miles away?"

"I got magic, remember?"

"You do, and it's spooky."

"So spit it out. What's got you sounding like you lost your best friend?"

"Remember the guy I told you about?"

"The SEAL?"

"Yeah, him. Things were really going great. He even

asked me to wait for him while he was on deployment."
Nichole swallowed past the lump in her throat. What if
he no longer wanted that?

"That's great, but?"

"But he found out his shoulder's permanently damaged from the bomb—"

"What does that have to do with the two of you? It
doesn't mean you can't still be together, right?"

"You'd think so, but he came home drunk after his
doctor's appointment, and he was pretty mean."

"I'll come there and make him sorry if he hurt you.
You got out of an abusive relationship. You sure don't
need another man like that."

"No. Jack would never physically harm me. He just
hurt my feelings. If something like that was going on
with me, I'd turn to him for comfort and support. He
doesn't want me anywhere near him."

"It's a man thing. When something goes wrong,
they're like a hurt dog that just wants to crawl in a
hole, lick its wounds, and growl at anyone who dares
to come near. It's the equivalent of a girl pity party, but
without the ice cream and wine. Don't take it personal."

But she did. "So, every time something doesn't go
his way, he'll shut me out? That doesn't work for me."
She was falling hard for him, but if that was going to
be how it was with them, she'd rather end it now before
he owned every piece of her heart. Besides, she didn't
matter to him.

"Then don't see him anymore. It's as simple as that."

It hurt to think of never seeing Jack again, and she
squeezed her eyes shut against the burn.

"Not what you want, huh?" Rachel said when she
didn't respond.

"No, but it's the smart thing to do." When she'd left Jack's house, she'd told herself that once he got past his disappointment, he'd realize he didn't mean what he'd said. But his shutting her out had festered, growing from just being hurt to questioning their relationship if that was the way he dealt with problems.

"Listen, you really like this guy, so give yourself some time to think. Is walking away from him what you really want to do?"

"I don't know." She hated feeling torn. Her brain said walk away, but her heart didn't want to listen.

"Let me play Dr. Phil for a minute."

"Can I stop you?"

Rachel laughed. "Nope. Lane messed with your head, and now you're afraid to trust your judgment. You also came out of that mess determined to be on equal footing with any man you had a relationship with."

"I'd say I'm finally making smart decisions." So why did it hurt so much?

"Are you really?"

"I don't know, Rach. I just don't know."

Jack groaned when he opened his eyes to the sun shining in his living room window. And what the hell was that pounding? His head? He blinked several times, then frowned. Apparently, he'd crashed on his sofa, even still had his boots on. When he stretched his neck, a pain shot up his skull.

The reason for getting a drunk on hadn't gone away but getting plastered didn't solve any problems. He was a SEAL, and SEALs sucked it up. That didn't change even when he soon wouldn't be one. As for his future...

he didn't have an answer to that question except that one thing hadn't changed. He still wanted Nichole in his life.

An image of her walking away last night—hurt on her face and in her eyes because of how he'd treated her—filled his mind. He didn't remember anything he'd said to her, but he did know he needed to apologize. All she'd wanted to do was comfort him, be there for him. Being drunk and angry was no excuse for how he'd rejected her. He pushed up, then dropped his throbbing head into his hands. He was an ass.

When he picked up Mark, he'd see Nichole and, well…grovel. He should pick up some flowers on his way over. And chocolate because he had a feeling he owed her a big apology. He wished he could remember exactly what to apologize for.

He glanced at his watch. "Shit!" He should have been at her house an hour ago to get Mark. First, he needed to call Ron and let him know they were running late. He hated disappointing the dogs as much as he did Ron. Seemed like he was letting everyone down. He sniffed under his arm. A shower was definitely in order. He smelled like sweat and beer. And why were his knuckles bloody?

What was that damn pounding?

"Police. Open the door."

"The hell?"

Before he reached the door, it was kicked in and four uniformed cops fanned out in front of him, two with guns drawn. Jack stuck his hands in the air. What the devil was going on?

Dakota growled, and the cop closest to her aimed his gun at her.

"Friends," he quickly said. "Down." She lowered

her belly to the floor, but she wasn't quite believing the strangers in the room were friends. Her eyes were alert on the men, and her ears were pinned back.

Jack leveled his gaze on the officer pointing his gun at her. "She's a highly trained military dog, owned by the government." Well, she used to be, but they didn't need to know that she was no longer their property. "She won't attack unless I tell her to."

"She does and government dog or not, I'll shoot her."

Jack gritted his teeth, biting back an angry retort.

"On your knees, feet spread, hands on your head," one of the officers barked while the two without their guns out took positions on each side of him.

Jack complied without hesitation. "What's this about?"

Instead of answering, one of the cops next to him snapped a handcuff around his wrist. "Hands behind your back," he said.

This was getting to be a habit he didn't like. Once he was cuffed, he was ordered to stand. When he was on his feet he was frisked. The position they had his arms in was hurting his shoulder, but he pressed his lips together and kept quiet. He had no idea what was going on and could only conclude that they had the wrong house. If that was what it was, it would be cleared up soon enough.

An older man wearing plainclothes walked in, and Jack noted the detective's badge clipped to his belt. He stepped in front of the officers and eyed Jack. "Check the house," he said.

Three of the four cops disappeared while one stayed with the detective. "Guns," one yelled from the direction of his bedroom.

"I'm a Navy SEAL. Of course I have guns." He was ignored.

His weapons were piled on the dining room table, and Jack was losing his patience. If they were going to threaten his dog and manhandle his guns, he wanted to know why.

He glanced at his broken door. "Can someone please tell me what's going on?"

"You're under arrest for assault and battery on Lane Gregory."

"Whoa there. The dude came at me. All I did was defend myself."

The detective's gaze roamed over him. "Strange that he's in a coma after getting in a fight with you."

"No way. All I did was take him to the ground and twist his arm when he tried to attack me. There was even a witness, the bartender. Ask him. He'll tell you the same."

"We talked to him. He said that's all he saw you do, but he also said he went back inside while you still had Mr. Gregory down."

"I did not put Gregory in a coma." Jack wondered who in the universe he'd pissed off. First learning that his shoulder was permanently damaged, and he wouldn't be returning to his team, getting in a fight with Nichole's ex—where he did not do anything to put the man in a coma—and then running Nichole off with hurt in her eyes.

*What about the part you don't remember and the blood on your knuckles?* There was no way, though, that he would put a man in a coma. He just wouldn't have. Wouldn't have needed to take it that far.

"He was found behind the building a few hours after

your fight with him. No one else was seen near him. Took us a while to identify you, then we found your truck in the bar's parking lot. Why did you leave it behind?"

Because he was an idiot and had gotten too drunk to drive. "I want a lawyer." And that was all he was going to say from this point on.

The detective walked around him. "When you get him to the station, get pictures of his hands," he said to the officer.


So this was what an interrogation room looked like. Handcuffed to a bar bolted down to the tabletop, Jack glanced around, his gaze sweeping past the wall painted barracks gray and landing on the large mirror. He wondered who was watching him from the other side.

They'd brought him into this room over an hour ago. The chair was hard, his butt was numb, his throat as dry as the godforsaken Afghanistan desert, and his brain on the verge of exploding.

How had he gone from waking up yesterday morning with his future set and the girl of his dreams in his life to sitting in a police interrogation room charged with putting a man in a coma, his future gone, and probably the girl.

The door opened and Deke walked in. He took a seat across from Jack. "I have to say you're the last person I expected to see handcuffed to this table."

"I didn't do it, Deke. Yeah, we got in a fight, but when I left, the man had nothing more to complain about than a sore wrist and knee." That was his story, and he was sticking to it despite the black hole in his memory. There was just no way he would have hurt a man that badly, even an asshole like Gregory. He had to believe that, because if he had, he was a disgusting human being and deserved whatever they threw at him.

"I believe you." He glanced at the camera mounted on the wall. "But the detective on the case doesn't."

"What happens now?" Jack eyed the camera. He doubted his friend was winning any points by talking to him.

"You stop talking and wait for a lawyer. You got one you want to call?"

"Not off the top of my head." It wasn't like it had occurred to him to have a criminal defense attorney standing by.

"I doubt you qualify for a public defender. I have someone I can recommend if you want. She's one of the best."

"Yeah. Thanks."

Deke slid a business card across the table. "Her cell number is on there. You probably won't go up before a judge until tomorrow, so that means a night in jail."

"Damn, that means Dakota will be locked up in the house. That's my dog."

"Want me to take care of her?"

"Yeah, man. I'll owe you."

"You don't owe me shit, Jack. How do I get to her?"

"There's a key box next to my back door." He glanced at the camera, then the two-way mirror before sliding his free hand across the table and tracing four numbers with his index finger.

"Got it," Deke said.

"They broke my front door, so you might not need a key. They let me put Dakota in my bedroom. She'll be wary of you, but she won't bite or attack unless commanded to by me. Tell her you're a friend, and she'll let you put her leash on her. It's on a hook in my mudroom."

"I'll head over as soon as I leave here. Does Nichole know what's going on?"

"No."

"Want me to call her?"

Jack thought about it, then shook his head. "She doesn't need my shit dumped on her."

"You don't think that should be her decision?"

"No." After the way he'd treated her, and then hadn't been able to apologize, the last thing he wanted was for her to have to deal with his mess.

"Okay, have it your way." He stood. "Don't let anyone make you their bitch tonight."

"Funny. And thanks for putting that image in my head."

"You're welcome." He smirked, then walked out, leaving Jack alone again.

Jack stared at the card in his hand, then lifted his gaze to the window. "I want my phone call."

# *Chapter Twenty*

"Jack didn't show up this morning and he hasn't called," Mark said when Nichole walked into the kitchen, heading for the coffeepot.

He was probably too hungover. "Have you called him?"

"Yeah, but he's not answering. I left a message but haven't heard back." He frowned. "We're supposed to be at the dog place. It's not like him to blow that off."

She sighed as she poured a cup of much needed coffee. Sleep had been elusive as her mind had bounced all night from never seeing Jack again because it was the best thing for her to that would mean…well, never seeing him again. When she'd tried to imagine her life without him in it, she'd buried her face in her pillow and cried.

She should be standing by him, helping him get through this, but…his team mattered more than she did. That was the kicker, what she couldn't get past. She understood why he'd gone straight from the doctor to getting drunk, although she would have preferred for him to come to her. Getting drunk didn't solve anything. But apparently, she wasn't important enough for him to come to when his life took a turn he hadn't foreseen or wanted. That was why she was doubting they had a future.

Rachel was right. Lane had messed with her mind, but she'd also come away from her time with him resolved to only be in a healthy relationship with a man. She'd thought she'd found that with Jack. Now she wasn't sure.

She didn't know what to do.

"Will you call him?" Mark said.

"No." She needed to be honest with him because Jack could hurt her brother as much as he was hurting her. Maybe not as much, but too close for her liking.

Mark frowned at her. "Why not?"

"Sit." She took her coffee to the kitchen table and sat across from him.

Jack had performed a miracle with her brother, and she didn't want to damage their relationship, or the strides forward on Mark's part. But she couldn't pretend things were still great between her and Jack.

"What's going on?" Mark said. "He's not sick, is he?"

"Not in the way I implied last night, but I do think he has some serious issues he needs to deal with. He found out yesterday that his shoulder's permanently damaged. That means—"

"He won't be able to be a SEAL?"

"I don't think so." She stared into her coffee, knowing what that meant to Jack, her heart breaking for him. She lifted her gaze to her brother. "He's not taking it well."

"No shit."

"Language, Mark."

Her brother snorted. "I'm not twelve anymore, Nic.

You don't get to reprimand me." He stood and took her coffee cup away. "Let's go. He needs us."

"You go to him. I don't know if he's the best thing for me."

"You're wrong, but I'll let you figure that out."

That was easy for him to say. He hadn't seen how Jack had treated her, hadn't heard what Jack had said. When she was alone, she grabbed her earbuds, clipped the leash on Rambo, and took a long walk, hoping the exercise and fresh air would calm the battle going on between her brain and aching heart.

When Rambo flopped down on the grass, his tongue hanging out the side of his mouth, she glanced around, realizing she'd walked much farther than she'd planned. "Come on, you lazy thing. I'm not carrying you home."

Mark was pacing in her driveway when she returned.

"Did you talk to Jack?"

"He wasn't there. I guess he went to the dog place without me."

Or he was nursing a hangover, maybe still too drunk to answer the door.

"But that's not important right now." He bounced on the balls of his feet. "Lane's in the hospital. A friend called, said he's in a coma."

"Did he wreck his bike?" That wouldn't be surprising considering the way he drove it sometimes.

"No, someone beat him up last night. I'm going to the hospital."

So Lane's temper had finally caught up with him. "I'll take you." Mark was too agitated to drive himself.

"You don't have to. I know you hate him."

She shook her head. "He's not my favorite person

in the world, but I don't wish him harm. Let me put Rambo in his kennel and we'll go."

They weren't family, so they weren't allowed to see Lane or get any information on his condition.

"How about I make you some French toast?" she said to Mark when they returned home. Growing up it had been his favorite meal, one of the few things he had an appetite for when he was going through chemo.

"Sure, that would be great."

"Hey, Mark?" He'd been quiet ever since leaving the hospital. She guessed he was keeping his worry for his friend to himself because he knew how she felt about Lane.

"Yeah?"

"I know Lane's your friend, and it's okay to be worried about him. You don't have to hide that from me."

He glanced down at the floor, then sighed. "I'm feeling guilty. I've been blowing him off ever since meeting Jack."

She kept how much that pleased her to herself. No matter what was going on between Jack and her, she would pick Jack to be her brother's friend over Lane any day.

His gaze lifted to hers. "The thing is, I haven't been liking Lane so much lately."

About time. She also kept that thought to herself as she grabbed the carton of eggs from the refrigerator and the bread from the pantry. "There's no reason for feeling guilty for not admiring a man who thinks it's okay to hit a woman."

"Jack would never do that," he said.

"No, he wouldn't." The doorbell rang. "Get that,

would you?" She hoped it wasn't Jack finally showing up. She had no idea what to say to him since her brain and her heart were still waging war.

"Nichole, this is Detective Matthews. He says he needs to talk to you."

Weird. Why was Deke here to see her? She turned off the burner, then smiled as she faced Jack's friend. "Deke? This is a surprise."

He didn't smile back.

Mark glanced from her to Deke. "You know him?"

"I do. He's a friend of Jack's."

"Cool," Mark said. "Have you talked to him today? He was supposed to pick me up this morning. We're volunteering at a service dog place."

"I have. He's…ah, he's busy with something right now. Nichole, can we talk in private for a minute?"

At seeing the serious look in Deke's eyes and the odd way he'd answered Mark's question, she knew it had something to do with Jack. "We can talk outside."

Mark frowned and stepped closer to her. "Why can't you talk in here? Is she in trouble or something?"

"No," Deke said. "I just need a few minutes of her time."

She put her hand on Mark's arm. "It's okay." It was the first time that he'd tried to be protective of her. Maybe he was finally growing up, and no matter what happened between her and Jack, she knew he'd played a part in her brother's new attitude. She'd always be grateful to him for that.

"It's about Jack, isn't it?" she said as soon as she and Deke stepped onto her porch.

"Yeah. He's in trouble, Nichole. He's in jail, accused of beating up your ex-boyfriend."

"What? You're saying he's the one who did that to Lane?" She gave a hard shake of her head. "No way."

"He says he didn't do it."

"Of course he didn't. Jack is one of the kindest souls I've ever known. Who's accusing him of such a ridiculous thing?"

He leaned back against the railing. "No one. He actually did get in a fight with Gregory yesterday afternoon, but Jack claims all he did was twist Gregory's arm and take him down to the ground. There was a witness who backs up Jack's story that your ex started the fight, and he did see Jack take Gregory down, but the witness walked back inside before the fight was over. A few hours later, Gregory was found unconscious behind the bar."

"I just can't believe Jack would hurt him that bad. I don't believe it."

"I don't either. The reason I'm here telling you is that there's history between you, Jack, and your ex, and I'm going to have to tell the detective on the case that. I wanted to warn you that he'll want to talk to you."

"I'll tell him the same thing. Jack didn't do it."

"Unfortunately, the detective's made up his mind that Jack did, especially since this isn't the first time there was an altercation between Jack and Gregory, which he's aware of. When he finds out there's history between the three of you, it will only confirm what he believes."

"Then we have to find out who did do it."

"Hopefully Gregory will wake up and tell us that."

"Can I see Jack?" She didn't doubt him, but she wanted to look into his eyes when he told her he hadn't put Lane in a coma.

He sighed. "I talked to him this morning. I'm sorry, Nichole, but he doesn't want to see you right now."

Because she didn't matter to him.

The bunk's sheet felt like sandpaper, and Jack was pretty sure it hadn't been washed since the last inmate used it. The first thing he was going to do when he got home was take a long, hot shower.

On the bed above him, his cellmate was flying high, talking about God knew what. Nothing he said made sense. In between his gibberish monologues he sang sad country songs. The dude actually had a good voice, so Jack preferred the singing.

"Imma a federal cadaver dog, ya know."

Jack couldn't help chuckling. The man came out with the most outlandish things, and this one was something he'd claimed to be numerous times. Jack guessed him to be in his fifties, but because of his drug-ravaged face, he could as easily be years younger than he looked.

"Shut the fuck up," someone from another cell yelled when the man started singing again.

His cellmate started crying. Jack groaned and pulled the pillow over his head. He'd tried pot when he was in high school, hadn't liked how spaced out it had made him feel, and had decided drugs weren't for him. If he was ever tempted, though, he'd remind himself of his cellmate, and that would cure him of any desire to mess with that shit.

Since there was no hope of sleeping with a roommate who jumped from babbling about who knew what to singing to crying at the speed of an incoming missile, Jack let his thoughts drift to Nichole.

He missed her.

* * *

"Daniels!"

Jack jerked up, thinking he was back with his team and his commanding officer was bellowing his name. Had he slept through roll call? Then the words to George Jones's "He Stopped Loving Her Today" sounded from above him, reminding him that he was in a jail cell and not with his team. He rubbed his eyes, surprised he'd apparently drifted off after all.

"Sir?" Jack said, his automatic response to anyone in authority.

"Follow me."

He was led to the same room he'd been in yesterday before they'd booked him. An attractive woman sharply dressed in a gray business suit sat at the table. He was handcuffed again to the metal bar bolted to the table.

"I'm Vickey Boyd, your attorney. Have a seat." She eyed the police officer. "You may leave us now."

"Thank you for coming," Jack said when they were alone.

"Deke called in a favor, otherwise I'd have referred you to one of the other attorneys in our firm since I'm not taking new clients at the moment."

"Well, thank you both then."

"You go up before the judge in an hour, so let's get to it. I've read the police report. Now I want to hear it from you. Start with why you were at the bar getting drunk in the middle of the afternoon. I gather from Deke that's not your usual behavior."

Jack felt his face flush. The lady was no-nonsense, and he liked that, but it was embarrassing that he'd put Deke in the position of having to make excuses for him. He'd gone from never even having a speeding ticket to being arrested, accused of putting a man in a coma, and all because he'd decided the answer to his problem could be found in the bottom of a beer bottle...make that bottles, plural.

Everything that had made him happy when he'd woken up the day of his doctor's appointment was gone. He couldn't be a SEAL with a shoulder that kept him from shooting straight. That hurt, but what hurt the most was the damage he'd done to his relationship with Nichole. What did he have to offer her now? Answer, nothing.

"No, I don't hang in bars, and I don't get drunk. As a rule." He sat back, wishing he didn't have to bare his soul to this woman he didn't know. But he did, so he told her everything, from the news he'd gotten from his doctor and why that had been upsetting to the point of deciding to get a drunk on through when he'd been arrested.

As he related the events leading up to him sitting handcuffed in a police department interrogation room, one thought kept running through his head. Failure wasn't an option for a SEAL, yet he was failing at every turn. As much as he wished his teammates were here to support him, he was glad they weren't. He didn't think he could handle the disappointment he'd see in their eyes.

The only thing he didn't tell her was about blacking out. He'd given it a lot of thought, and as drunk as he was, he was sure there was no way he would have forgotten dragging a body to the back of the building. He remembered putting Gregory to the ground, and he remembered stumbling toward his truck after that. There was also a fuzzy memory of falling down, but he couldn't swear to it. If he had put his hands out to catch his fall, that could explain his bloody knuckles.

"And that's it until the cops broke my door in yesterday."

"Unfortunately, there aren't cameras outside the bar to back up your story," she said when he finished. "There are cameras inside, so that's how they were able to track you down."

"The only thing I hurt on that man was his wrist and maybe his knees." He had to believe that.

"That doesn't matter—"

"It does to me."

"But not to me. Guilty or not, it's my job to protect your interests and make sure the law works as it should." The hint of a smile appeared on her face. "It is a plus when the client is innocent, which I believe you are."

"Thanks. That's important to me. What happens now?"

"We get you out on bail." She gave him a dollar figure. "That's my best guess estimate on what your bail will be. It helps that you don't have a record and Deke said you own a home here. Can you cover it? If not—"

"Not a problem." He glanced down at the orange jumpsuit. "Any chance of getting my clothes back before I go to court?"

"Sorry, no. You'll be taken in with the other prisoners going up before the judge today. I'll do all the talking, so don't piss me off and open your mouth."

Caught by surprise by her saying *piss*, he laughed. "Yes, ma'am."

"The only time I want you to talk is when you're asked what plea you're entering. That's where you'll say not guilty. Anything other than that comes out of your mouth, you can go find yourself a new lawyer."

"Got it." Jack had been trained to the gills on following orders, and Deke was right. This lady was sharp. He wasn't about to do anything but obey her, especially if it meant he'd be at home in a few hours where he could take a hot shower.

"I'll want a list of character witnesses. Family, girlfriend, teammates who might be available to testify."

"What else do you need from me?" he asked, avoiding telling her his only family was Grammie, and no way would he put her through a trial. His teammates would gladly testify on his behalf if they weren't over seven thousand miles away. As for a girlfriend…he just didn't know. He wasn't sure who he was anymore, and what woman would want a man possibly headed to prison?

"That's it for now. Be in my office in the morning at nine, and I'll fill you in on what to expect as we go forward. Do not under any circumstance talk to the police without me present, and that includes Deke. He'll be obligated to inform the detective on the case anything you say to him."

He felt as if he was being isolated, and for a man used to having his team at his six, he was…lost.

## Chapter Twenty-One

"It seems there's bad blood between your old boyfriend and your new one."

Nichole kept her gaze steady on the man who'd introduced himself as Detective Margolis. "You're wasting your time trying to pin this on Jack. He would never hurt someone like that."

Two days had passed since she'd learned Jack had been arrested, and he still hadn't called or tried to see her. No matter how much that hurt, how much of a jerk that made him, this detective was never going to convince her that Jack had almost killed Lane.

She glanced around the room, then down at the bar bolted to the table that she assumed was meant for handcuffs. Had Jack been in this room, his wrists cuffed to the bar so he couldn't pull a fast one and escape? Probably, and that made her sad. When the detective had called her, requesting she come to the police station for an interview, she'd gladly agreed. It was her chance to help Jack.

"We have a witness to the fight, Nichole. It wasn't their first altercation. I have a statement from your mall security that your boyfriend knocked out Mr. Gregory, sending him to the hospital."

She bristled at the way he said *boyfriend*, as if he had a bad taste in his mouth. And damn Mel. "I'm telling you again. Jack. Did. Not. Do. This. As for the incident at the artisan's mall, Lane attacked Jack, and Jack was only defending himself. Instead of trying to find evidence where there isn't any, you should be looking for the person who really is guilty. Believe me, the people Lane hangs out with are not the cream of society."

Everything she said was true, but she couldn't get the vision of Jack's bloody knuckles out of her head. Was it possible he had done what he was accused of? He'd been pretty drunk when he'd arrived home. What if… No, he didn't do it, and she resented the detective for making her doubt Jack.

After a few more questions from the detective attempting to get her to say something negative about Jack, she stood. "I'm done here. I can't and won't help you convict an innocent man who is serving his country, who was injured in the line of duty, and who is a hero." She needed to talk to Jack, ask him straight out if Lane was in a coma because of him, look him in the eyes when he answered.

"I'm not finished, Nichole."

"Well, I am." She took one last look at the black metal bar, her heart hurting at the thought of Jack being handcuffed to it.

After getting the call from the detective, she'd phoned Deke, wanting to know what to expect. She could tell he was uncomfortable answering her questions, and she understood she was putting him in the middle. Even so, he'd walked her through what would happen, and she appreciated that. The best thing he'd told her was that unless she was charged with something, she was free to walk out whenever she wanted.

She wanted, so she did.

When she arrived home, Mark wasn't there. She called his cell. "Where are you?"

"At the dog place."

Even though Jack had ghosted him, Mark was still volunteering his time there each morning. Her little brother really was growing up. A month ago, he wouldn't have cared about being responsible.

"Have you heard from Jack?" he said. "He's still not calling me back. I'm getting really worried."

"We need to talk. When will you be home?" Not wanting to see his disappointment in his new hero, she hadn't told Mark about the accusation against Jack and that he'd been arrested. She couldn't put it off any longer, though. It was better that he heard it from her, and not someone else.

"I'm finishing up, so I'll be there soon. What's going on?"

"We'll talk when you get here." She disconnected before he could ask more questions, then took Rambo out. It was such a pleasure to walk him now compared to how he'd been before Jack's training. Everyone was new and improved since Jack had entered her life. Whatever happened between them going forward, he had shown her what it was like to be in a healthy relationship. She would never again settle for less.

That was good, but she didn't want anyone else. She wanted Jack, but when a man told you what mattered to him and you weren't on that list…well, she had her pride. He'd been drunk when he'd slung those words at her. When someone was plastered, they had no filter.

The things they said were their truths. How was she supposed to get past that?

"Would you be happy living in a convent, Rambo?"

That wouldn't work. She liked sex too much to do without for the rest of her life. She couldn't imagine never again feeling a man's body wrapped around hers while he whispered dirty words into her ear, of seeing his male-satisfied smile when she shattered in his arms.

The problem was that Jack had ruined her. She didn't want to be with some other man. Even if she cried herself to sleep again tonight, she couldn't stand by and watch a good man's life ruined. She would do everything in her power to right the wrong being done to him.

*But what if he really is guilty?* an annoying voice said in her head.

That voice could take a hike. If Jack was capable of doing something like that, then she would never again trust her judgment in men. She really would check herself into a nunnery as long as she could bring Rambo and her trusty vibrator along with her.

Rambo excitedly barked a greeting to Mark when he saw her brother standing on the porch, waiting for them. She unclipped his leash. "Go see your favorite guy." Actually, Mark was his second favorite, Jack his first, but whatever.

She jogged up the porch steps. "Hungry? Want to order a pizza?" Her brother was always hungry, and she didn't want to have a serious conversation with him while he wasn't paying attention because his mind was on food.

"You're weirding me out, Nic. You tell me to come home because we need to talk, and then you want to know if I want a pizza. What's going on?"

"A lot." She glanced at Rambo. "Let's get him inside and fed, then we'll talk."

After filling Rambo's bowl, she went into the living room. She sat on the sofa, curling her legs under her. Mark settled on the opposite side.

"Talk," he said.

"It's about Jack." With the exception of what Jack had said to her—that was between the two of them—and his bloody knuckles, she told her brother everything that had happened from Jack's doctor appointment until now.

"No way. Jack wouldn't hurt someone enough to put them in a coma. He just wouldn't. Even if he lost his cool and did do something like that, he's too smart to just dump Lane behind the building."

She hadn't thought of that, and he was right. Come to think of it, she couldn't believe Jack would disappear from Asheville Service Dogs without explanation. "Has he explained to anyone at your dog place why he's not showing up?"

"Not to anyone I've talked to, but the owner's out of town for a few days. Jack probably talked to him."

Both she and Mark had called Jack, gone by his house at various times—Mark more than her—and it was as if he'd disappeared from the face of the earth after being released from jail.

Jack walked back into his house after being away for two days. Following him in, Dakota made a noise that sounded like a sigh of contentment at being home again. "Home sweet home, huh, girl?"

He'd made a quick trip to Virginia to see his home base commander, preferring to explain in person the shitstorm he was in the middle of. Captain Pendley wasn't happy about the charges against Jack, but said he believed in Jack's innocence, which was a relief. When Jack updated him on the condition of his shoulder, he'd encouraged Jack to consider other opportunities besides opting out of the navy. Jack appreciated the captain's optimism that the mess he was in would be straightened out, so he'd agreed to think about it. Problem was, he couldn't see himself at a desk job, about all he was fit for.

Before he left, he'd called both his attorney and Deke so they'd know where he was. He hadn't heard from either of them since then, so he could only assume that nothing had changed, that he was still going to be prosecuted. A quick call to Vickey Boyd confirmed his assumption.

"Damn it to hell," he muttered after hanging up.

He stared at the phone, longing to call the one person he wanted to talk to the most. No, he wouldn't, couldn't do it. If he couldn't prove his innocence, he would go to prison. It was one thing to ask Nichole to wait for him when he went on deployment. He would not ask or expect her to wait around for a man who would have the title of ex-convict when he got out. She was the best thing that had ever happened to him, and he couldn't bear her someday thinking he was the worst thing that had ever happened to her.

She was better off without him, and although he regretted the way he'd treated her, he hoped she hated him now enough not to be sad. He was sad enough for the both of them.

The other person he needed to talk to was Ron Kitterman. He'd had a brief conversation with Ron before going to see his commander. Hoping that by the time he got back home the cops would have realized they had the wrong man, he'd only told Ron that he had to return to base for a few days. Since his innocence was still in question, it was time to level with the man. He unpacked his duffel, then headed for Asheville Service Dogs.

Ron wasn't there, but one of the volunteers said he was expected back any minute. Since he owed Ron an explanation and apology, he decided to wait. What else did he have to do?

A few minutes later, a car pulled up and a young woman got out. A small boy exited from the back seat. She looked around, and seeing him, headed his way.

"Do you work here?" she asked.

Jack wasn't sure how to answer. Did he still work here? He guessed that would depend on how Ron felt after Jack talked to him. "Yes, ma'am." It was the only thing he knew to say without dumping all his shit on her.

"My daddy needs a helping dog," the boy said.

"Then you've come to the right place." A helping dog… Jack liked that. He guessed the boy to be around eight. "I'm Jack. The man you need to talk—"

"Daddy was in the war. He has PS… PT… What does he have, Mama? I can never remember."

"He has PTSD, honey." She turned sad eyes to Jack. "He's out of the army now, but he's not the same." She glanced at her son. "We're worried about him."

"Is he disabled from an injury?" he asked.

She shook her head.

"I'm sorry, ma'am, but it sounds like you need a different kind of dog from what we train here."

"So he can't have a dog?" she said.

She looked like she was about to cry, and Jack couldn't bring himself to send her away. Her husband was a brother-in-arms, and he couldn't turn his back on a brother in need. He squatted in front of the boy. "What's your name, buddy?"

"Nigel. But Mama and Daddy call me Junior. My daddy was Nigel first."

"Well, Junior, if I help your daddy get a dog, your dad will have to go through training with it. Since the dog will be living in your house, you'll have to learn about a therapy dog right along with your dad. Are you good with that?"

"Yes, sir. I want him to be happy again."

The problems Jack faced paled against this boy's longing to have his happy father back. "Then let's see what we can do to make that happen." He stood. "Mrs...."

"Jacoby. Brenda Jacoby. You can really help us?"

He really could, but not if he was in prison. What could he promise this woman and her son and be able to follow through on before he disappeared without an explanation? He could at least find them a good dog match and get them started while finding someone to finish the dog's training.

"As I said, the dogs here are trained specifically for people who are disabled." He eyed the car that was at least ten years old. "It's possible the owner will consider training a dog for what your husband needs. He'll return shortly, and you can speak with him. Have you considered the cost of a trained dog?"

"Maybe a thousand dollars? I was hoping I could make payments."

"Mrs. Jacoby, you'd be looking at a minimum of ten thousand, probably more."

Her eyes widened. "Dollars?"

"Yes, ma'am."

Junior tugged on her arm. "Mama, you can have the money in my piggy bank."

The boy was breaking his heart.

Tears pooled in her eyes. "That's so sweet, honey, but I'm afraid we still won't have enough."

"I can help you, though. If you want me to."

"How can you? Are you going to write me a check?"

He heard the sarcasm in her voice, but it was the defeat in her eyes that gutted him. "I wish I could, but what I can do is help you find a good dog, and then work with the dog and your husband." At least until he went to prison, but he'd make sure someone continued the training.

"Why would you do that?"

"I'm a Navy SEAL on medical leave. I'm also my team's dog handler." He wasn't a certified service dog trainer, but he'd talk to Ron, see if he'd certify the dog once he was trained.

"I still don't understand why you'd help us."

"Because, even though I've never met your husband, he's my brother. I have the time and the knowledge. Besides, I'm bored, so you'd really be doing me a favor." Added benefit, it would help keep his mind off missing Nichole.

"Can we go get a dog right now, sir? I'm going to name it Trucker 'cause my daddy loves trucks."

Jack smiled at the boy. "That's a fine name, but it's up to your mother." He met her gaze, let her see the truth of his offer in his eyes.

"I'll pay you what I can," she finally said.

"No, ma'am. We'll find a suitable rescue dog, and you'll have a small fee to adopt it. You'll also need some supplies, but it won't be all that much. I do have to ask, is your husband agreeable to this?"

She put her hand on her son's head. "Go wait for me in the car."

"So we can go get a dog?"

"We'll see." After he left them, she said, "He's not exactly agreeable, but then he's not agreeable about anything these days. In desperation, I told him that I would leave and take our son with me if he refused to do this. I don't mean it, but I don't know what else to do. I only told him that to push him into doing this. I really am desperate."

There were the tears again. "Then let me help you and your family."

"Okay." She glanced at the scars on his arm, then put her hand on them. "Thank you."

Uncomfortable with her gratitude and her soft touch on his mangled arm, he had to force himself not to step away. "Like I said, you're doing me a favor." His first thought had been to take them with him to pick out a dog, but that really wouldn't work.

"There is something you and your boy need to understand. I know he's eager to go right now, get a dog, and take it home. It can't happen that way."

"Why not?"

"Because he'll likely fall in love with a dog that's unsuitable for what your husband needs. Also, the dog needs to come home with me first."

"But he'll be so disappointed."

"A service dog isn't a pet, and that's what your son

will want to make him. The dog needs to come home with me for a while so I can work with it."

"But—"

"Tell you what. After I've worked with the dog for a week, I'll bring him by so you and your family can meet it. But I'm going to be firm on this. Typically, a service dog goes through several years of training. That means your husband's dog will be more of a companion, but it will be trained."

She seemed to think about that for a few moments, then said, "I don't know."

"Would it make you feel better if I promised to keep the dog myself if it doesn't work out?"

"Actually, it would."

They exchanged contact information, and since Ron still wasn't back, Jack headed to a no-kill shelter to look for a dog while ignoring his phone's beeping, telling him he had messages.

He was on a mission.

## Chapter Twenty-Two

Nichole smiled at seeing Deke walking toward her. "This is a nice surprise."

"Thought you'd want to know that Gregory's awake and talking," he said.

"That's great news. He said Jack didn't do it, right?"

"Unfortunately, no." He glanced around, his alert gaze landing on the people strolling past her booth. "I shouldn't even be here talking to you, but I can't stand by and watch my friend get railroaded," he quietly said. "I tagged along with Detective Margolis when we got the call from the hospital that Lane Gregory was awake."

"He's saying Jack did that to him?" She'd thought Jack couldn't break her heart any more than he already had. She was wrong. Never again would she trust her judgment in men.

"Yes, but only after Margolis told him that Jack has been arrested for the assault."

"That doesn't seem right. Shouldn't he have been asked first who did it before Jack's name was brought up?" Her belief in Jack returned.

"Yes, and Margolis and I had words about it after we left the hospital. He told me to butt out of his investigation. Unfortunately, he's made up his mind that Jack's guilty, and now with Gregory accusing him, he considers the case closed."

"Honestly, I'm not surprised Lane would jump on Jack being punished, whether he's guilty or not. Isn't there something you can do?"

"I can go to my captain, and I will if it comes down to it, but he won't appreciate me putting my nose in another detective's case any more than Margolis does. Not to mention, I have to work with Margolis after this is over, and he's the kind of man who'll cause me as much trouble as he can."

"What can we do?" Whether Jack wanted her involved or not, she couldn't stand by and let Lane ruin his life. She might not matter to him, but he mattered to her. Besides, it was because of her that Jack was in this mess. Lane wouldn't have fixated on Jack if not for her, if he hadn't gotten it in his head that the only reason she wouldn't come back to him was because of Jack.

"My hands are tied. At least for now. Your brother is friends with Gregory, so I thought maybe he could get your ex to tell him who really beat him up."

The last thing she wanted was for Mark to get anywhere near her ex, but she might not have a choice if it meant getting the truth out of Lane. "Let me think about it."

"I understand." He stuffed his hands in his pockets and stared down at the floor for a moment before lifting his gaze to hers. "I hate asking this, but I'd appreciate it if you kept our talk between us. Even from Jack. He won't like you having anything to do with your ex."

"I have no desire to cause trouble for you at work or to have Jack upset with you. But I hope you meant it when you said if it becomes necessary, you'll talk to your captain."

"I will."

After Deke left, she glanced at her watch, and since it was almost five, decided to close up early. As she drove home with Rambo, she tried to decide what to do. As much as she didn't want Mark involved, he was a grown man who'd changed for the better because of Jack's influence. Maybe it was his decision to make.

"Honestly, I wasn't sure who you'd believe, Lane or Jack," she said after arriving home and telling Mark what Deke had said. "I mean, you've been friends with Lane longer than with Jack, so—"

"Lane wouldn't hesitate to lie if it served his purpose. What are we going to do to help Jack?"

"There's only one thing I can think of, and that's get Lane to tell us who really did beat him up." What she really meant was Mark would have to do it, but he'd have to come to that conclusion himself. Although his loyalty seemed to be transferring to Jack, he'd hero-worshipped Lane until recently. She wouldn't ask him to choose between them.

"I don't want you anywhere near him, Nic, so I'll do it."

Nichole stood outside Lane's hospital room door that evening. Even though Mark had his phone recorder activated, and she could listen to the conversation later, she strained to hear.

"You need to keep your sister away from that asshole," Lane said. "He's dangerous. Look what he did to me."

"Yeah, I know. I told her not to trust him, but she's hardheaded and bossy," her brother replied, causing her to scowl. "What I don't get is how one dude got the better of you. Come on, man. You're badder'n that. I've seen you take on big-assed dudes and them lookin' a hell of a lot worse than you in the end."

Nichole held her breath as the silence stretched out. That was clever of Mark to challenge Lane like that, but he wasn't going to take the bait.

"The day one dude gets the best of me is the day ya might as well bury me in the ground. Ain't gonna happen."

And there it was! Nichole slapped a hand over her chest, pressing against her racing heart. *Please, Lane, tell him it wasn't Jack,* she prayed.

"Whatcha mean? The cops are saying it was just Jack Daniels that made your face look like it was bashed in by a baseball bat. It sure ain't pretty, bro."

Her brother's language skills were deteriorating by the minute. Even though she hated hearing him sound like an ignorant dolt, she understood that he was matching Lane, who really was a dumb bonehead.

"You gonna rat me out to your sister?"

"Nah, man. I ain't no snitch. 'Sides, she's so fed up with me that she don't believe a word I say anymore."

Her brother had missed his calling. He belonged on stage.

"You repeat what I'm gonna tell you, and I'll come find you," Lane said.

Nichole shivered, knowing Lane meant it. She shouldn't have let Mark walk in that room.

"Read you loud and clear, bro. So, what really did happen?"

"I got in a little trouble with some badass dudes. They were looking for me. My bad luck, they found me right after Daniels left. I can take on two and come out on top, but three? Not a fucking chance."

"Damn, that's some bad luck."

Her brother had done it! He'd gotten the proof they needed that Jack hadn't done it. She pumped a victory fist in the air. She felt guilty for the little bit of doubt that had crept into her mind over the past few days, but Jack was partly to blame for that. If he'd seen her, talked to her, told her he was innocent, those snippets of doubt would have never popped up.

*Now get out of the room, Mark.*

As soon as they got home, she called Jack, wanting to tell him about the recording, but got his voice mail again. He could ignore her phone calls, but he couldn't ignore her if she was at his door first thing in the morning.

I'm on the way over.

Jack read the text message from Nichole, then deleted it. He now had a record, and he was probably going to prison. His attorney had called to tell him that Gregory was awake and talking, claiming that Jack had been the one to beat him up. Had he? He didn't want to believe he could lose it so badly that he'd put a man in a coma and not remember. Damn that black hole in his memory.

She was on the way to his house, and there wasn't anyone in the world he wanted to see more—including his SEAL brothers, whom he loved to the depths of his heart—but if he saw her, he'd lose his resolve to do the right thing. He owed her an apology, a big one, but he'd do it in a letter. Or maybe he shouldn't. It would be better for her to let her hate him.

He loaded Dakota in his truck and left. Nichole

needed to realize he wasn't good enough for her, not anymore. "Cry Me a River," he heard his buddy Double D sing in his ear. Jack snorted. DD was forever quoting song titles that managed to fit any situation. Even though Noah Alba—Double D because he always carried a pair of dice once belonging to his father in his pocket—was on the other side of the world, he'd somehow managed to ghost himself into Jack's stateside life.

Damn, he missed his teammates. He missed Nichole even more.

He'd visited a no-kill shelter yesterday afternoon but hadn't found a suitable dog for the Jacobys yet. Since this was going to be a fast-tracked training, the dog needed to be young but past the rambunctious puppy stage.

He found the perfect candidate at the second shelter of the morning.

The dog was a golden retriever–German shepherd mix with intelligent brown eyes and a calm temperament that the shelter had named Larry. The shelter's vet estimated his age close to three years old.

After filling out the paperwork and paying the adoption fee, Jack clipped the leash he'd brought to the dog's collar and walked him outside. He squatted in front of Larry. "Here's the deal, pal. Your new name is Trucker, and you're going to have a special job in life. Time is of the essence, and your intelligent eyes tell me you're a quick learner. That's important considering…well, I'm not going to get into all that right now."

Trucker's gaze stayed on him, his ears perked up. It was a good sign. "Let's just say that I've got a mess on my hands, but that's got nothing to do with you other than we're gonna have to work fast." He stood. "Come on, Trucker, there's someone you need to meet."

As he'd guessed, Trucker right away recognized Dakota as alpha and lowered his head in submission. That was going to make things easier since he planned to use Dakota in the dog's training. After introducing them, he got both dogs loaded into the truck, Dakota in the front passenger seat and Trucker in the back.

The first thing he did when he got home was give Trucker a bath. After drying him off, he let the dog explore the house. While Trucker was investigating the different rooms, Dakota sat at the entrance to the hallway, her ears up, listening.

"We have an important job," he told her. She glanced at him. "Yeah, we have to get him trained for one of our brothers in need. You up for it, girl?"

If it hadn't been for his dog, he wasn't sure what his mental state would be. When he'd first arrived home, she'd helped him stay calm, had been there to get him through his nightmares, had given him a reason to get up in the mornings. He'd taken care of her, and she'd returned the favor tenfold. Now they would pay it forward, giving another brother a tool to help him get better.

Dakota disappeared down the hallway, returning a minute later with Trucker following her. She led him to her bed, and when he curled up on it, she walked to Jack, settling down at his feet. It grew quiet, too quiet. He slapped a hand over his bouncing leg. A run, that was what he needed.

After changing into shorts and running shoes, he headed out, leaving Dakota to keep watch on Trucker. He'd hoped to outrun his thoughts, the future he no longer had, the worry that he was going to prison, and most of all, the ache of missing Nichole. It wasn't happening, so he ran faster.

## Chapter Twenty-Three

Jack hadn't been home, and he still wasn't answering his phone or responding to her texts. Nichole was dying to tell him that Lane had admitted to Mark that he was lying when claiming that Jack had beat him up, but she didn't have a clue where to find him.

After arriving at the River Arts District and getting her booth opened, she called Deke, told him about the recording and how she and Mark had obtained it.

"It's doubtful his attorney will be able to get it allowed in court as evidence, but she needs to hear it," Deke said. "If nothing else, Detective Margolis won't be able to ignore Gregory's confession."

"Thank God." The detective had already wasted almost a week trying to nail Jack for something he didn't do. "We copied it to a thumb drive, so Mark can drop it off to her."

He gave her the attorney's contact information, then said, "It's great that you got it, Nichole, but you and your brother stay away from Lane Gregory from now on. He's bad news."

"I know, and we will." She was embarrassed that she'd ever had a relationship with a man like Lane. "The good news is that my restraining order against him has been processed." The hearing had been yesterday, and when Lane hadn't shown up to protest it, the judge had granted the order. Nichole hadn't bothered to mention that he wasn't there because he was in the hospital.

"That is good news. Now the cops can act if he comes anywhere near you."

"And believe me, I will call them if I see his face."

He chuckled. "You better. Talk to you later."

"Okay. And, Deke, thanks for everything."

"I've only done what I felt was right."

She hoped Jack realized what a great friend he had in Deke. Next she called the attorney's office, expecting to have to leave a message. Instead, Ms. Boyd was available to talk. Nichole introduced herself, then told her about the recording.

"Can you get that to me today?" Ms. Boyd said.

"My brother can drop it off to you. Will it help?"

"At the very least, it will get the detective on the case off Jack's back and looking for the real guilty person."

"That's great. My brother will drop off the thumb drive shortly."

After talking to Mark, she called Jack's number again. When she got his voice mail, she didn't leave a message. She'd already left three, and he was making it clear that she didn't matter to him, that those words hadn't just been drunk talk. And for the first time since he'd slung those hateful words to her, she really believed him.

"Darn it, Jack." Also, for the first time, she acknowledged what her heart had been trying to tell her. She was in love with the man, not just falling for him.

Lane had fascinated her, much like her first high school biker bad boy had. Where a high school bad boy had been pretty much harmless, a grown-up one like Lane wasn't. As it turned out, Lane hadn't been even close to fun. He hadn't been a bad boy with a soft heart and an enthusiasm for life like the first boy she'd loved. It had taken her entirely too long to realize that, so stupid her. She'd finally found a good boy to love, and where had that gotten her? Heartbreak, that was what. Maybe she wasn't meant to be in love.

That was a sad thought that hurt deep in her heart. She squeezed her eyes shut against the stinging tears. This wasn't the place to have a meltdown.

"These fairies are adorable," a woman said.

Nichole blinked away the tears. "Thank you." She forced a smile she didn't feel. The woman was holding one of her glittery fairies that Nichole had made on a night when she was bursting with happiness. Would she ever feel that way again?

The customer tilted her head, her gaze on Nichole's watery eyes. "Are you okay?"

"Yeah. My allergies are killing me today." She just had to get through the day, and then she could go home and have that much needed meltdown.

The rest of the day seemed to last forever, but it was finally time to close up. She debated going by Jack's house one last time, then decided it was up to him to make a move...or not.

When she got home, she ignored Mark trying to talk to her, ignored her dog for the first time since she'd gotten him, went into her room, closed the door behind her, kicked her shoes off, got in bed, pulled the covers over her head, and quit trying to pretend her heart wasn't broken.

Mark knocked on the door. "Nic, are you okay?"

No, she wasn't. She cleared her throat. "I'm fine. Just tired."

"Have you talked to Jack?"

"No. Have you?"

"I've tried, but he's still not calling me back. I think we should go to his house."

"Have at it."

"Don't you want to come with me?"

"I'm really tired, Mark."

"Oh, okay. Want me to make you something to eat?"

"No thanks." All she wanted was to hide under the covers and for the world to go away. Rambo whined as he scratched on the door.

"Can I let him in?"

She sighed. "Yeah, and then go away."

Rambo bounded in as soon as Mark opened the door. He jumped on the bed and tried to lick her face off. She buried her nose in his fur. At least her dog loved her. The meltdown she'd been holding at bay all day broke free and her tears were hot on her cheeks.

Gutted. That was what she was. Jack might as well have carved her heart out with a rusty knife.

She couldn't sleep. Every time she closed her eyes, Nichole saw Jack's smile. She heard his silly jokes, saw his lopsided grin when he knew he'd amused her. She felt his hands glide over her skin as he stared down at her with heat in his blue eyes, and in the deep hours of the night, alone in her bed and heartsick, she grieved for what would never be.

When light from the sunrise filtered around the edges of her window shades, she put on her ratty pottery clothes, and after taking Rambo out, she headed for her studio. She was running low on her glitter fairies, so she decided it was a good time to make some more.

Or not.

"Damn it," she muttered when she messed up another one. Coming in here had been a mistake. All she could think about was the night she and Jack had recreated the scene from *Ghost*. The only thing she'd accomplished the past two hours was being even more miserable.

Her eyes burned from the ocean of tears she'd shed, and her throat was raw. Angry at Jack and even angrier with herself for falling in love with him, she grabbed the fairy she'd messed up and threw it just as her brother walked in. It hit his chest, then shattered when it fell to the concrete floor.

"Whoa!" He picked up the largest piece. "Didn't like this one, huh?"

"How'd you guess?"

"Seemed pretty obvious. Jack's here. He wants to talk to you."

"Jack?" Her heart bounced madly in her chest.

"Yeah. I didn't tell him about the recording. Thought maybe you'd want to."

"I'll be there in a few minutes." Fortunately, she could get to her bedroom without passing through the living room. In the bathroom, she cringed when she looked in the mirror. The few minutes turned into twenty—the time it took to get the tangles out of her hair, put on a little makeup to try to conceal her puffy eyes, and a quick change into her favorite sundress. If this was going to be the last time she saw Jack, then she wanted him to see what he was going to be missing.

She took a deep breath as she walked down the hall-way. Jack stood at the window, looking out, and she wanted to go to him, wished he would wrap his arms around her and promise that they would be all right. Even though it felt like an ice pick had pierced her heart, she kept her distance.

"Hello, Nichole," he said before he turned to face her. "I should have talked to you before now."

"Yes, you should have. At least returned my calls. I know you've had an awful week, but I have to say it's not fun being ghosted." Mark wasn't in sight, so she guessed he'd taken Rambo for a walk, which she appreciated. "I—"

He held up a hand. "I really am sorry about that, but you're better off without me."

Men were idiots. "Don't you think that should be my decision? Unless you just don't want to be with me anymore."

"I'm sorry, but..." He stared down at the floor, then lifted his gaze to hers. "I don't have a job or won't soon. Not that it'll matter since I'll be in prison. The thought of you having to visit your boyfriend in prison..." A visible shudder ran through him. "I just can't do that to you. You deserve better."

"Stop saying that. Besides, you're not—"

"Okay, but it's true."

The ache inside her turned to anger. "You know what? You're right. I deserve a man who sees me as a partner, someone to stand by his side through the good times and the bad. I need to *matter* to him. So just take yourself off and go feel sorry for yourself." She turned away from him. "You know the way out," she said, throwing his own words back at him.

His shoulders slumped, and he nodded, then left. She should have told him he wasn't going to prison, that Lane had confessed that it wasn't Jack who'd hurt him. She'd let her anger get the best of her.

She walked to the window and peered out. As his truck backed out of her driveway, leaving her house for the last time, taking her heart with him, she buried her face in her hands and whispered his name.

"Jack."

Walking out the door of Nichole's house, knowing he'd never see her again, was the hardest thing Jack had ever done. Facing the charges against him, missing his team... Those things were nothing compared to losing Nichole.

He wasn't sure he'd ever be able to forget the hurt in her eyes. He was an ass. He was right, though, and she'd figure out soon enough that she was better off without him. And if the reverse didn't apply to him, so be it. That was what love was, wasn't it? Doing what was best for the other person, even if it meant sacrificing your own happiness?

His first impulse was to get drunk enough to deaden the pain in his chest, but the last time he'd done that, he'd ended up in jail, so it probably wasn't a good idea.

Since heading to a bar was out, he turned his truck for home. He had a mission to complete before his trial started, and that was getting Trucker ready for his new job. He spent the morning working with the dog. Fortunately, Trucker was not only intelligent but eager to please, both him and Dakota.

An idea was brewing, though, something that would enable him to make a contribution to the men and women he would always consider his brothers and sisters, the military heroes who were having trouble adjusting to civilian life, whether from loss of limbs or suffering PTSD. It was a known fact that therapy dogs had an extraordinary ability to ease stress and anxiety, even to the extent of helping to reduce suicides in military personnel.

He was good at training dogs, and it was something he loved. He'd tried to think of other jobs he could pursue, but nothing appealed to him. He was a trained warrior and a dog handler. It was all he knew. Sitting in an office, whether in the public sector or a desk job in the military, would be torture at its worst. He could get a job in construction or the like, but that wouldn't make him happy to get up in the mornings.

The more he thought about it, the more it interested him, to the point that he started researching therapy dog training as soon as he finished his session with Trucker. Although he knew how to train dogs for war, therapy training was different. Tomorrow morning he'd go talk to Ron, see if Ron would agree to train and certify him after he got out of jail or prison, or at least recommend someone who would.

By lunchtime he'd decided on a name and mission statement. His excitement growing, he logged on to his computer and drafted a logo.

*Operation K-9 Brothers*

*Rescue dogs making life better for veterans in need.
Veterans giving rescue dogs a new beginning.*

He'd need to find a graphic designer to improve on it, but he liked it. Fortunately, overhead wouldn't be out of his reach to start. He'd enlisted in the navy the day after getting his associate degree. It had only taken two years to decide college wasn't for him. Other than minor expenses during his twelve-year stint in the military, he'd been able to bank a good chunk of his pay.

Eventually, if he succeeded and was able to grow Operation K-9 Brothers, he'd need to look for sponsorships and donations, but that was down the road. To start, he needed to find a dog or two with the potential to become therapy companions and locate a place to train them. In the beginning, if he had to, he could use his yard, but the grassy area was small and not ideal.

After throwing together a quick sandwich, he ate it standing at the counter, eager to get back to his computer and investigate what dogs were available for adoption in local shelters. He identified several possibilities, but a personal visit would be in order before making a final decision. He was getting ahead of himself, though. Until he got certified, he couldn't move forward. Unfortunately, patience wasn't one of his virtues.

Tomorrow he'd talk to Ron about certification, and then he'd check out some dogs at the…

This was all pointless if he was headed for prison. He was getting excited over something that was probably never going to happen. Tossing his pen down, he paced the confines of his living room. How was he supposed to survive being locked up? He wasn't sure he could.

Dakota whined, drawing his attention. "No, I'm not okay," he told her. What was going to happen to his dog? He needed to make arrangements for her, not be dreaming about a future he'd never have. Who could he ask to take her? Just thinking about giving her away like she was a piece of furniture he no longer wanted made him want to put his fist through the wall. She wouldn't understand his abandoning her.

Because he'd made a stupid decision to get drunk, ending up at the wrong place at the wrong time, he was losing everything. Nichole, his dog, his team, his freedom. Not only that, but the nightmares that had eased off since he and Nichole had been spending their nights together had returned with a vengeance, starting again with his arrest.

How had his life gone to hell so damn fast?

Running was his answer lately to when the panic threatened to drown him, so he headed for the door. His phone buzzed. Taking it from his pocket, he saw his attorney's name on the screen.

"Ms. Boyd, I'm hoping you're not calling with more bad news, although that seems to be the way things are going these days."

"Then you'll be happy with this phone call. I've been in court all day, or I would have gotten in touch sooner. Can you be in my office first thing in the morning?"

"Is that all you're going to tell me?"

"Yes. I'm sorry if I'm being mysterious, but you need to hear what I have for yourself."

Hear? What did that mean? "Yeah, okay, I'll be there."

Jack stared blankly at his phone's screen after disconnecting. She'd said he'd be happy…the only things that would make him happy were if Nichole was in his life, he didn't have to give his dog away, and he wasn't going to prison. As for never being able to return to his team, he'd made peace with that. It was what it was, and a SEAL sucked it up, and then put one foot in front of the other and moved forward.

Was whatever his attorney planned to tell him something that would show him a door out of his personal hell? Too afraid to hope, he went for his run.

"Wow," Jack said, after listening to the recording of Gregory admitting to who'd actually put him in the hospital. He lifted his gaze to his attorney. "Does that mean the charges against me have been dropped?"

She smiled. "Not yet, but they will be. I'll make sure of that."

He closed his eyes and blew out a huge breath. "Okay. Okay then." He hadn't dared to hope that was her good news, and the profound relief made him feel... giddy. Yeah, that was a good word for the happiness bubbling inside him.

Except... "That was Mark Masters's voice. Did you put him up to that?" He didn't at all like the idea of Mark being anywhere near the man, even if it was to prove Jack's innocence.

"No, I wasn't aware of this until after the fact, when Mark brought me the thumb drive."

In that case, Jack saw Nichole's hand in this. As much as he wanted his innocence proven, it wasn't at the cost of putting Nichole or Mark in danger of Gregory's retribution when he found out what they'd done.

There was only one thing to do about that, and that was to protect them from whatever revenge the man cooked up. That meant inserting himself back in their lives, meaning he had a lot of groveling to do.

"Where do we go from here?" he asked.

"I've made a copy of the recording, and it's being delivered to Detective Margolis as we speak. He can't ignore Mr. Gregory's confession, and I believe the charges against you will be dropped in the next day or two."

"Great and thank you."

Ms. Boyd smiled. "I didn't do much. It's Mark Masters who you really need to thank."

Oh, he would, and then right after, he'd have a few words for Nichole's brother for putting himself on Gregory's bad side.

He'd woken up this morning believing life as he knew it was over, and then as fast as all the shit had been dumped on him, it was disappearing just as quickly. What a day! After leaving his attorney's office, he headed to Nichole's, and assuming she would be at the River Arts District, he hoped to catch Mark alone. He had not only let Nichole down, but Mark as well, and he needed to make things right with both.

As for his future, he now had possibilities, ones he couldn't wait to make happen. The one fear left was that Nichole wouldn't forgive him. After the way he'd treated her, he couldn't blame her if she didn't, but he let himself hope that she eventually would. Sitting in that jail cell, thinking he'd lost her, he'd accepted that he loved her. He'd known before then that he was falling for her, but he'd raced past falling without even realizing it.

At Nichole's house, Jack rang the doorbell. Mark's car was in the driveway, so he hoped that meant her brother was home. He was.

"Hey, can we talk?" he said when Mark opened the door.

"A little late for that, don't you think?" Mark said before disappearing back inside the house.

He'd left the door open, though, so Jack took that to mean he could come in. He followed Mark to the kitchen, where the kid resumed eating his half-finished lunch while ignoring Jack.

If he were Nichole's brother, he'd probably do worse than ignore the man who'd hurt her, so he didn't take offense. He stuffed his hands in his pockets as he leaned back against the kitchen counter.

"I messed up," he said. An understatement, that. "First, I need to apologize to you." Mark kept on eating, ignoring him. Since he deserved the silent treatment and more, he continued on. "I'm sorry, Mark. I have no excuse for treating you or Nichole the way I did."

Mark finally looked at him. "I don't care about me. You hurt her. She tried to hide it, but she cried."

Guilt settled heavy in his chest. "I was an asshole, and I'm sorry for that." There wasn't anything else he could say to undo the way he'd acted.

"It's not me you need to be apologizing to. Look, I get that it sucks you won't be able to keep on being a SEAL…" Mark frowned. "That's what it was all about, right?"

"Yeah. I didn't take the news well, and it was stupid to think getting drunk was the answer. Believe me, I will apologize to Nichole twenty-nine ways to Sunday, but I also wanted to set things right with you."

"I don't know if she'll forgive you."

"That's a possibility, but I'm hoping that she will." Hoping with every beat of his heart.

"Do you love her?"

"Yes." Although he would have preferred to tell Nichole that first, he wasn't going to deny it.

"Okay, we're cool, you and me." Mark narrowed his eyes. "This time. You do anything like that again, especially to my sister, and all bets are off."

"Got it." Jack hid his smile. The man-child was growing up. "There is one other thing I have to say, and that has to do with Lane Gregory. I appreciate what you did, getting that recording, believe me. But you shouldn't have because as soon as Gregory finds out what you did, he's going to come after you."

Jack didn't miss the fear that flashed in Mark's eyes, and he was glad that the kid was smart enough to recognize that Gregory was bad business.

"I know, and I've been thinking about that." He met Jack's gaze straight on. "It was the right thing to do, so I won't say it was a mistake. Probably the best thing is for me to head back to my parents in Florida, but I won't leave Nichole to deal with him alone."

"She won't be because she'll have me, and trust me, I'm fully capable of protecting her. It would be a whole lot easier to do that if I didn't have to worry about protecting you, too."

"What if she doesn't want you around anymore? How will you protect her then?"

"Let's hope that I can get back in her good graces, but if not, I'll shadow her until I'm sure Gregory's not a threat anymore. She'll never know I'm there." She was safe as long as Gregory was still in the hospital, but when he got out, to protect her, Jack would camp out in her yard if he had to.

"You can't watch her twenty-four seven. Besides, that sounds a little stalker creepy."

"Yeah, I can, and making sure she stays safe trumps stalker creepy, don't you think?"

"I guess."

"There's no guessing about it, Mark." He decided to change the subject before Mark had second thoughts about heading back to Florida. "Have you talked to Clint Alba yet?"

Mark's eyes lit up. "Yes! He likes my game, and he had some great suggestions to make it even better. He said we'd talk more after I get it back to him."

"That's great." Finding a direction in life would do wonders for Mark.

"Yeah, and I can work on my game in Florida as well as here. I just hope my dad doesn't expect me to go back to that construction job."

"You're how old?"

"Twenty-two."

"Which makes you old enough to make your own decisions. I think it will make a difference if you have a good talk with him. Tell him what you want to do with your life, and the steps you've taken to make it happen."

Mark seemed to think that over, then nodded. "You're right. I've never told my parents I wanted to create games because I just thought they'd think that was stupid."

"I doubt that will be their reaction, but if it is, so what? It's your life, Mark, not theirs, eh?"

"Yeah, it's my life." He stood, picked up his plate, and took it to the sink. "I'm going to pack up my stuff."

"You leaving today?"

"No, I want to hang around, spend some time with Nichole tonight. I'll head out in the morning." He gave Jack a big grin. "Thanks, man, for everything. I hope you can fix things between you and Nichole. I'd like to have you around."

Jack hoped—okay, prayed—he'd still be around, too. He lifted his hand, and they bumped fists. "I hope so, too, and you're not so bad to have around either." It was somewhat surprising how much he liked the kid compared to when he'd first showed up at Nichole's. He'd like to think he had played a part in Mark finding his place in life. At least then he'd feel like he'd done something right where Nichole and her brother were concerned.

Since Mark was staying over until tomorrow, Jack would wait to try to talk to Nichole. The two of them would be safe for now since Gregory was still in the hospital, so Jack decided to do the one thing that would get his mind off Nichole for a while. He went Operation K-9 Brothers dog possibilities shopping.

## Chapter Twenty-Four

"Jack came by today," Mark said.

"Oh?" Nichole's stupid heart needed to stop doing that bouncy thing at hearing his name.

"Yeah, he wanted to apologize for being an asshole. He wants to apologize to you, too."

Well, he owed her that much, but it wouldn't make any difference because *she didn't matter*. Although he didn't specifically say *she* didn't matter, he might as well have. She wasn't sure there was anything he could say that could put those words to rest in her mind.

"Whatever." She shrugged as if what Jack wanted meant nothing to her. She wished it didn't, but there was still that bouncy heart thing going on, and worse, she hurt. Hurt like she never had before.

Her pain was even showing up in her pottery. Last night, she'd created what she thought of as sad fairy girls. She'd taken two of them to work with her today, and they'd both sold within an hour of opening. That was fine since those miserable fairies were all she felt like making.

"I think you should hear him out."

"Why's that?" She'd let Jack say his piece, but unless he had magic words that could sweep her mind clean of the ones that had ripped her heart out, he would be wasting his time.

"Because men are stupid?"

She couldn't argue with that. "Was that a question?"

"Yeah. No." He laughed when she raised a brow. "It's true. We really can get dumb when our manhood is questioned."

"I never doubted his manhood." Not ever.

"No, but finding out he'll never be fit to be a SEAL again was a hard pill to swallow."

"I get that. The thing is, he as much as told me that all that mattered to him was returning to his team. There wasn't one hint that I mattered to him. I would have been there for him if he'd let me, but he rejected every one of my attempts. If the situation had been reversed, I would have loved to have his support when I was at my lowest."

"That's because you think like a woman."

"Okay, hit me up. How does a man think?" They were sitting on the sofa, and Rambo had his butt perched on the floor between them, his gaze swiveling between them like he was watching a tennis match. Since he was a male, he probably thought she was overreacting, too.

"Embarrassed. Inadequate. A failure. Want me to go on?"

"So what? It makes you guys feel better to be a jerk?"

"Not really, but sometimes we can't help ourselves. Think about it. He was a SEAL for a long time, and he fully expected to still be one for who knows how long. Then he gets the worst news possible, and he didn't know how to process that. But I think he has now. Just hear him out, okay?"

"I'll think about it."

Rachel had said men needed to crawl off and lick their wounds, which fit with what Mark was saying, that Jack was probably embarrassed and feeling like a failure. She got that, but it didn't excuse the way he'd treated her.

She supposed she should consider the fact that he was drunk, but did that make it better or worse? Better because it really wasn't Jack talking, or worse because his words were unfiltered, thus how he actually felt?

They'd been seeing each other long enough for her to know Jack wasn't a heavy drinker. A beer or two seemed to be his limit, and not once until that night had she seen him drunk. His getting wasted was an anomaly, otherwise she'd have walked away before now.

She missed him to the depths of her soul, and then some more. Her mind, wanting to protect her from further hurt, said to be smart, that she didn't need a man in her life who hadn't wanted her by his side, supporting him, when he felt like his life was falling apart. Her heart, though…

"I'm going back to Florida tomorrow," Mark said.

She jerked her face toward him. "What? Why?"

"Jack's worried about what Lane will do when he finds out I recorded our conversation. We both think it's best if I'm not here."

So wrapped up in her misery, she hadn't even thought of what Lane might do when he learned about the recording. She knew better than anyone what Lane was capable of, and she should have put Mark's safety over her heartbreak. Yet Jack had considered Lane's possible reaction and had somehow convinced her brother to return to Florida.

Just another thing to thank him for, and maybe all those things outweighed the one time he'd messed up.

So she'd listen to what he had to say, and then she'd let her mind and her heart battle it out.

Until then, it was her last night with her brother. "Let's make popcorn and watch a movie."

He looked at her with a challenge in his eyes. "Better yet, let's make popcorn and play my game."

"Give me thirty minutes to practice it, and then your ass is grass."

He laughed. "Game on."

Nichole managed not to cry when sending Mark back to their parents. In the short time he'd been here, a different brother was leaving than the one who'd arrived with an attitude. Thanks to Jack, her brother had a bright future ahead of him.

Mark was walking on clouds, and she was thrilled for him. She was also relieved that he was leaving. As far as she knew, Lane didn't know where their parents lived. Her brother's game had been a blast to play, and with a big-name gamer interested, Mark had a purpose that his life had been missing.

After his car turned the corner, disappearing from sight, she headed for her pottery studio. Since she had a lot of catching up to do, it was good that she had the next three days off from her booth.

She had the dinnerware commissions to finish, more sad fairies to make, and she was running low on her glitter fairies and mugs. The day flew by, and when she stood, stretching her aching back, she glanced at her watch, surprised to see it was after five. Other than a few breaks to walk Rambo, she'd been hard at it and was pleased with her progress.

After Mark left, she'd debated between going back

to bed and just staying there for the rest of her life or losing herself so thoroughly in the one thing she could count on to make her happy so that she wouldn't think of Jack. She chose the second option. She was tired of crying, and that was what she'd do if she spent her day in bed, missing him.

"It's wine time," she told Rambo.

He jumped up from his bed, bringing his chew toy with him, his tail wagging with excitement. Both her boys were new and improved from a few weeks ago even. Mark was a joy to be around now, and Rambo's progress was remarkable.

Now, it was only she who wasn't new and improved. Whatever. Someday Jack would be a distant memory. Maybe.

After washing the clay from her hands and arms, she headed into the house. The doorbell rang as she took her first sip of wine. Rambo barked as he raced for the door. As far as she knew, Lane was still in the hospital, but she wasn't taking any chances. She pushed Rambo aside with her leg, then put her eye to the peephole.

"Jack," she whispered.

Of course she had on her ratty pottery clothes, clay under her fingernails, no makeup, and her hair in a messy bun. Well, that was what he got for not calling. She opened the door, wishing that her stupid heart wasn't happy to see him.

"Can I come in?" he asked when she just stared at him.

Without answering but leaving the door open, she headed back for her wine. Deciding she hadn't poured enough for the coming conversation, she filled up the glass. She glanced at Jack, and the uncertainty and vulnerability she saw on his face and in his eyes softened her anger with him, but it wasn't gone completely.

"Beer?" she said.

"I'm taking a few days off on beer."

She bit back a snarky retort. Too bad he hadn't done that a few days ago instead of ending up at a biker bar. "Okay. Let's sit on the patio."

The view from her deck wasn't close to as nice as his, but inside her little house, his presence was so overwhelming that he stole all her air. She could smell his unique—and okay, mouthwatering—masculine scent, even feel his body heat. Never mind that he'd stomped on her heart, said organ was apparently a glutton for punishment, ready to throw itself at him all over again.

Even her mind was wavering. If they had a chance, she needed him to convince her that she mattered to him, but it had to happen where she could still think, and that wasn't standing in her kitchen where his essence surrounded her. Before she walked right into his arms without a word of explanation and an apology from him, she went out her back door. He could follow her or not. His choice.

Jack had never been so unsure of himself or so nervous. If he didn't find the right words, he was going to lose her…if he hadn't already. She hadn't smiled at him the way she used to, before he got stupid and acted like a jerk.

He took a deep breath, then followed her out. Because he was trained to prepare for missions—and this was one of the most important missions he'd ever undertaken—he'd rehearsed what he was going to say. But as he took a seat in the chair next to Nichole's, he didn't remember a word of it. Some operator he was.

Maybe she'd say something, giving him time to get his brain back on track. She didn't, just sipped her wine and stared at the house behind hers, apparently unaware that he was close to climbing out of his skin. He leaned forward, resting his elbows on his knees.

"I fucked up, Nichole, and I'm sorry." That wasn't what he had planned to say. Well, it was, but he'd intended to be more articulate than that.

"I know."

And? Was he forgiven? Kicked out of her life? She remained quiet, and since she hadn't told him to leave, he let himself feel a little hope. He got it, though. A simple *I'm sorry* wasn't going to cut it. She needed him to bleed, and for her, he would.

"When I..." He swallowed past the rock lodged in his throat. It wasn't going to be easy, baring his soul. Although he didn't remember exactly what he'd said to her, he'd hurt her. Because of that, he'd cut open a vein and bleed. He stared at the floor. "Being a SEAL has defined me since the day I made it through BUD/S school." He glanced at her. "That's like SEAL boot camp, and it's damn hard to make it through. Only about twenty to thirty percent of a given class graduates."

"I guess that makes you special," she said, darting a glance at him.

"No, just determined. Anyway, my one and only goal was to heal so I could get back to my team. When I was still in the hospital, the doctors were hinting that there was a possibility I'd never get full use of my arm back. I refused to listen. Not returning to my team wasn't an option.

"I walked into the doctor's office last week as a SEAL. When I walked out, that was no longer true because my arm's permanently damaged. I couldn't deal with that, and that's when I got stupid. The answer to your problems is never in the bottom of a beer bottle. I knew that, but I did it anyway. Mostly I just wanted to forget I'd never be with my team again."

"Because that's all that mattered to you."

Those words sounded vaguely familiar, but he didn't know why, although the way she said them put him on alert. "For a while I thought that was true, and then I met you. You changed everything." He flinched when she snorted. "You don't believe me?"

"After you said that the only thing that mattered to you was getting back to your team? You said that when you were drunk, when you weren't filtering your thoughts, so no, I don't believe you."

"I said that?"

"Yeah, and then you told me to leave."

He was never getting drunk again. Not in this lifetime or the next. At least he remembered why he'd tried to run her off. "I'm sorry, Nichole. If I could take it all back, I would. The thing is, at the time I believed I had nothing to offer you. You deserved more than a man with no future. That's what the drunk me thought. The man sitting here right now is calling that man a drunk-ass fool."

"What is it with men and their stupid egos?" She finally faced him. "So you decided to make the decision for me as to what I deserved?"

"I would have come to my senses when I sobered up, but then I was arrested with the good possibility that I'd be going to prison. You definitely deserved more than a man who was going to be locked up for who knew how long."

"For something you didn't do. There was never a doubt in my mind that you were innocent of that." She stood, went to the deck railing, and stared into her backyard.

He wanted to go to her, but he sensed she had more to say, so he waited.

A few minutes passed, and then she turned. "Here's the thing. I love you, but it's not enough. I want a man in my life who stands by my side, who supports me in good times and bad. In return, I need to be that for him, and you shut me out when you needed me the most. You hurt me, Jack. Who's to say you won't do that again if things don't go your way?"

She loved him, but... His heart didn't know whether to rejoice or cry because of the words that followed her admission. He'd had this idea in his head that the first time they said they loved each other, it would be over a candlelight dinner, or sitting out on his deck under a starry night, or maybe when they were making love. Yeah, he liked that last one.

"I wish I'd said this days ago." He stood, going to her. "When we met, I thought we'd have some fun until it was time for me to return to my team. Then you inched your way into my heart when I wasn't looking, and I started thinking that maybe we could sustain a relationship through my deployments. That you'd wait for me."

"I would have," she whispered.

But not now? He was in the fight of his life, and he had to get it right. "I can promise you three things, Nichole. One, I love you with everything that I am. Two, I will never get drunk again. And, three, I'll never shut you out again."

"I want to believe you, but I'm afraid. I don't ever want to feel that kind of hurt again."

"When a SEAL gives you his word, you can believe him. I'd rather die than hurt you. That's not to say that I won't do things to piss you off, because I'm sure I will. That works both ways. It's how relationships work. We just have to promise each other that we'll always talk things out."

Tears shimmered in her eyes, and he caught one with his thumb when it fell. "I love you like I've never loved another or ever expected to. Please give us a chance."

She stepped away from him. "I don't know if I can."

That wasn't a yes or a no, but seeing her trembling lips, he couldn't bring himself to push her any harder. Because of him, she was close to crying, and that wasn't acceptable.

"I think I should leave," he said. "Take all the time you need to decide if you want to be with me, and when you do, I'll respect your decision, even if it's not the one I'm going to go home, fall down on my knees, and pray for."

"Jack."

Anguish was in her voice when she'd said his name. Damn him for making her afraid to love him. "Whatever you decide, Nichole. All that matters is that you're happy." He brushed his thumb over her quivering bottom lip because he had to touch her, afraid it was going to be for the last time. "I love you, but I won't bother you again. What happens next is your choice."

He left, skirting around her house to his truck before she had a chance to respond. Everything that made him the man he was rebelled at walking away. A SEAL always completed his mission.

*You're not a SEAL anymore.* Okay, there was that, but it wasn't like he could wipe all his discipline and

training from his mind. He sat in his truck for a few
minutes, debating the wisdom of leaving. He'd told her
he wouldn't bother her, that what happened next was her
choice. What if he never heard from her again?

Should he try to talk to her one more time, convince
her that they belonged together? No, she needed time to
come to that on her own. All he could do now was be
patient and hope that she wanted him in her life.

The day Lane Gregory got out of the hospital, however, whether she liked it or not, Jack would be shad-
owing her, making sure she stayed safe. According to
Deke, Gregory was pretty messed up and would be in
the hospital at least another week. Deke promised to
call the minute he learned when Gregory would be released. The day that happened, Jack would pitch a tent
in Nichole's yard if it came to that.

As he drove home, he realized that he'd forgotten to
tell her about his future plans. Would that have made a
difference if she knew he had a plan for his life now?
He thought about it, then decided that wouldn't have
made a difference. Her problem was with his shutting
her out, not whether he had a job or not. Even if he were
unemployed, she would have stood by him if he hadn't
gotten stupid.

If he ended up blessed to have her back in his life, he
made a vow that he would never shut her out again, no
matter how low or angry he might feel. If she couldn't
find her way back to him… He shook his head. He
couldn't bear to think of having to exist without her.
She'd said she loved him, and he would hold on to that.

# Chapter Twenty-Five

Three days after Jack had apologized and then told her he loved her, Nichole's brain and heart were still raging war.

Brain: *You know you can't trust our heart's judgment. Heart has been wrong too many times.*

Heart: *Shut up, stupid brain. I want him.*

She laughed at the conversation going on between those two organs, because, seriously, what else could she do? Cry some more? God, she missed him. Her phone chimed Eric Clapton's "Little Rachel." Just the person she needed to talk to.

"Hey, Rach. You did it again."

"What's that?"

"You knew I needed to talk to you."

Her friend laughed. "You keep assigning magic powers to me. I was simply thinking about you, so decided to give you a call."

"Deny it all you want, but you'll never convince me otherwise. How's the movie going?"

"We're wrapping up tomorrow. Why do you need to talk to me?"

She told Rachel about Jack's visit and what he'd said. "I'm just really confused."

"Do you love him?"

"Yeah, I do." Crazy loved him.

"Then what's the problem? He apologized, explained why he acted like a jerk, and he told you he loves you."

"I've always had a tendency to choose the wrong men, and I don't trust my judgment anymore."

"From what you've told me about him, he's not Lane or like any of the guys you've dated in the past. Does he treat you with respect?"

"Yes."

"Has there ever been any hint that he'd get violent with you?"

"Jack would never hurt me like that." She knew that to the bottom of her heart.

"Does he make you laugh? Look at you like he wants to gobble you up? Make your girly parts tingle?"

"Yes, yes, and oh God, yes."

"I think my work here is done but tell you what. You decide you don't want him, send him my way."

"He's mine!" She grinned when Rachel laughed. Rachel could always cut through her BS.

"You just growled at me."

"Don't be silly." She totally had. It was the first time in her life she'd ever growled over a man or even wanted to.

"So, you've punished him with your absence for three days now. What you gonna do, ghostbuster?"

"Go get my man."

"Atta girl."

"Thank you for helping me get my head on straight. I love you, bestie."

"Ditto, BFF."

After hanging up, she grabbed her earbuds, then

took Rambo out. As soon as he did his business, she'd shower, put on her prettiest sundress, and then she'd go get her man.

Rambo was sniffing a bush when a truck slowly passed, a heavy metal song blaring from the radio so loud she could feel the vibrations. Because she was standing behind a tree, she doubted the driver saw her, but she sure saw his passenger door open and then a small brown ball of fur tossed out.

"Hey!" she yelled as she took off running, pulling out her earbuds and dragging Rambo behind her.

The truck sped up and raced away. When she reached whatever they'd thrown out, she gasped at seeing a cowering puppy. The poor thing shivered as it tried to curl into itself. When it whimpered, Rambo answered with a whine. He plopped down on his belly in front of it, then he licked the little brown face.

Nichole glanced up at the road. "Asswipe."

She picked up the quivering dog. "You poor thing." What kind of people threw out an animal like it was garbage? "You're better off without them, sweetie." But what was she going to do with it? She could barely keep up with Rambo, and she certainly couldn't take two dogs to the River Arts Center with her.

With a peek between the little thing's legs, she saw that it was a girl. The name of the song that had been playing on her iPod when the truck drove by popped into her head. "There's someone I want you to meet, Maggie May."

Jack couldn't have been happier with Trucker's progress. The dog was smart. The Jacobys were taking him home for the night. He wasn't sure that was a good idea yet, but he hadn't been able to say no to Nigel Junior. One night wouldn't do any harm, and even the boy's father had accompanied them this time. Mother and son had visited Trucker twice before without him, which had been worrisome.

He didn't have much experience with those dealing with PTSD, and he didn't want to step wrong. Since meeting Brenda Jacoby and Junior, he'd done a lot of reading on the disorder. In doing so, he'd realized that he suffered from it to a degree, but blessedly not to the extent of Nigel Jacoby.

The man's eyes looked haunted, and he didn't smile. Those troubled eyes softened when Nigel had squatted to scratch Trucker under his chin. That was a positive sign that the dog would help the man to deal with daily life.

Jack sent Brenda and Junior to the backyard with Dakota and her ball. His dog could chase balls for hours on end. Alone with Nigel, he spent twenty minutes with the man on the basics of caring for Trucker and the commands the dog was learning. Nigel didn't say much until Jack ended the session.

"You going back to the sandbox?" Nigel asked.

Jack lifted his arm and eyed it. "Nope. IED ended any chance of that happening."

"You sound disappointed."

"Only that I feel like I've let my team down."

"It's a fucked-up place. I'd put a gun to my head before going back."

Jack tried to think of what to say to that. He met Nigel's gaze. "Promise me one thing. If you ever think that's the answer, call me. Any time of the day or night."

"I'm good… Well, I'm not good, but I'm not that far gone. I only meant I'd do it if I got orders to go back."

"Is there any chance of that happening?"

"No. I'm out for good." He tapped his head. "Too messed up. I'm out on a medical discharge."

"Not trying to pry here, but are you seeing a therapist?"

"Yeah, not that it's doing much good. Still wake up screaming and sweating like I'm baking in the sun of that godforsaken place. Still see my buddy bleed out in my arms." He lowered his gaze to Trucker. "I was against this, getting a stupid dog, but my wife and boy begged me until I agreed to give it a try. Funny thing, working with him now, I forgot to be mad, and when I touch him, that rage inside me gets calmer."

"I get that, man. My dog gave me a reason to get up in the mornings after I got back." Jack debated the next thing he wanted to say but decided to go with it. "I didn't have a wife and child to live for, though. Seems like that would be a pretty damn good reason to want to get better."

"They're my world, but they just don't understand. Not their fault. No one can unless they've been there."

"Copy that, but maybe you could share a little of what daily life there was like. They don't need to hear about the bad shit, but I think it would help your wife and son, and even you, if you let them in a little."

Nigel stared toward the backyard where his wife and son were. "Yeah, I suppose I could do that."

"Good man." He whistled. Dakota raced into view with a laughing Junior running close behind. Mrs. Jacoby followed, her hopeful gaze on her husband. Nigel wasn't healed. Far from it. But Jack believed the man was taking positive steps for a better future. That Jack was playing a part in that gave him enormous satisfaction.

"Don't forget to bring him back in the morning," he told Junior. He squeezed the boy's shoulder. "And no sneaking him people food."

"I won't, Mr. Daniels." Jack handed Junior the end of the leash, and the boy held it out to his father. "Trucker's your dog, Daddy, so you have to take care of him."

The boy just blew Jack's mind with that. One of the things that had worried him was Junior wanting to make Trucker his. Maybe he really did understand that Trucker was a working dog and not a pet.

Long after the Jacobys had left, Jack thought about Nigel, encouraged by the man's comment that his rage calmed when he touched Trucker. Doing what he could to help a brother-in-arms cemented his decision to start a therapy dog foundation for those suffering from PTSD.

His phone buzzed, Clint Alba's name coming up. Mark's game was the only reason Clint would be calling. Hopefully, the news was good.

"Hey, man, what's up?"

"Thought you'd want to know that your boy's game is a winner."

"No kidding? That's great."

"It needs some tweaking, but I've already got some interest in the game. I've got a feeling he'll get some great offers."

Jack grinned, feeling like a proud parent. "Does Mark know yet?"

"That I'm impressed with the game, yes. I have him working on some things to improve it. I'm going to hold off on telling him about the interest until it's more solid. Won't take us long to get it ready to go, and then I'll get serious about shopping it for him."

"Can't thank you enough."

Clint made a snorting noise. "No, man. Thank you. I love finding new talent."

The first thing Jack wanted to do after getting off the phone with Clint was to call Nichole with the news, but he'd promised not to bother her. Three days had passed since he'd seen her, and he was giving up hope that he would hear from her.

He was trying to stay positive, but it was hard. Even Dakota seemed down, and he wished she'd stop watching him with those sad eyes. After getting blown up by a fucking bomb, he hadn't cried. He'd sucked it up like a SEAL should, but he was having trouble sucking up the thought of never seeing Nichole again.

Not being able to call and share the good news about her brother hurt. Not having the right to bring her lunch on her workdays hurt. Not trying to feel her touch when she trailed her fingers over his dead skin hurt.

"I miss her," he told his dog.

Dakota whined, and he took that to mean she missed Nichole, too. He blinked away whatever the hell was burning his eyes. Honest to God's truth, losing Nichole hurt more than a bomb blowing up right in front of his face, hurt worse than everything that had followed.

Maybe Heather could give him solid advice on what he needed to do to get Nichole back. Not that he wanted to share his private life with her, but he would, for Nichole. He was scrolling through his contacts to get to Heather's name when his doorbell rang.

"Who could that be?" he asked Dakota. Probably

someone selling something since he rarely got visitors. That was actually depressing but not surprising given that he'd isolated himself since coming home. With Mark gone and Nichole done with him, the only people showing up lately aside from the Jacobys had been the police kicking his door down.

Dakota stuck her nose in the door crack, sniffed, and then wagged her tail. Okay, it was someone they knew. He tried not to get his hopes up that it was Nichole, but his pulse spiked anyway.

He put his eye to the peephole, his heart stuttering when he saw Nichole. Was it good or bad that she was here? He almost didn't want to open the door. What if she was here to tell him that she'd made her decision, and she was done with him? Not that he would blame her.

Since he couldn't avoid her forever, he inhaled a deep breath, and then opened the door. "Hey," he said, which was the most he was capable of at the moment. There was much more he wanted to say, like *I love you* or *please don't make me face another day without you*. She smiled, and he had trouble breathing. She wouldn't be smiling at him like that if she was here to tell him to go to hell, would she?

Something yipped, and his gaze dropped to the puppy she held against her waist. His observation skills had apparently deserted him. All he'd seen was her face and that heart-stopping smile.

"What's this?" Was she only here to give him a puppy, and if so, why?

"It's a possum, Jack." She rolled her eyes, and then her lips twitched.

Her almost smile and teasing was a good sign, right?

"If that's what it is, then it's the cutest possum I've ever seen. Usually, those things are ugly as sin." He'd spent the last three days imagining their conversation if he ever got to see her again, and he hadn't come close to this.

"So," she said, then glanced down at the puppy. "I hear you train dogs."

That was why she was here, because she wanted him to work with this puppy? Instead of doing what he wanted—kissing her until she forgot her name, until she forgave him—he nodded. "I've trained a few here and there."

Maybe this was a chance to spend time with her again. "If you're wanting this one trained, it's the same deal as before. You have to do it with me." He realized he was holding his breath, waiting for her answer.

"Well, I can't keep it. Someone threw it out of a truck, and I rescued it. I was hoping you'd help me find a good home for it. Can I come in?"

"Of course." She could come in any minute of the day or night. Should he warn her that he might not ever let her leave? As she walked past him, he caught her vanilla and almond scent. He fisted his hands at his sides to keep from pulling her against him and burying his nose in her hair.

Nichole stopped in the middle of his living room, and Dakota sat in front of her, her ears perked up, and her gaze on the puppy. Weird that. He'd never seen her that interested in another dog before, not even Rambo.

"Hey, pretty girl." Nichole leaned over and scratched her muzzle, then glanced up at him. "Will she hurt Maggie May if I put her down?"

"Maggie May, huh? I thought you couldn't keep her."

"I can't. Doesn't mean she doesn't deserve a name."

"Mmm-hmm." Jack swallowed his smile. "Go ahead. Dakota won't hurt her."

Nichole set the puppy on the floor, and Dakota sniffed the little thing from one end to the other. Maggie May froze as if afraid the giant dog might eat her. After a thorough investigation of the puppy's scent, Dakota wrapped her mouth around the back of Maggie May's neck.

"Oh," Nichole said, panic in her voice. She reached for the puppy.

Jack put his hand on her shoulder. "Wait."

He knew Dakota wouldn't hurt Maggie May, but he wanted to see what Dakota was up to. After the dog was secure in her mouth, Dakota carried the puppy to her bed, gently set it down, curled her body around it, and then went about the business of licking it clean.

"I'll be damned." Dakota was sort of friends now with Rambo, but in the beginning, she'd considered Rambo more of an annoying pest. Never would he have expected what he was seeing now.

"I think Maggie May just got adopted." Nichole glanced at him and grinned.

If he could keep her looking at him like that, he'd drag home a hundred puppies. "I think Dakota and I need to have a talk about house rules," he grumbled.

Nichole laughed. "You're a softie. No way you're going to take her new baby away from her."

"Softie, huh?" He liked the way she was eyeing him with that sparkle glinting in her eyes. Like maybe she was ready to forgive him. The hope he'd been trying to squash was bubbling, ready to burst free.

"Yep." She moved to him, stopping in front of him. "I've missed you," she softly said.

"Nichole." Her name was a whisper on his lips. A prayer. Afraid he was misreading her, he opened his arms, willing her to come to him. When she stepped forward, and then rested her head on his chest, he closed his eyes against the burning in them. He wrapped his arms around her, and did what he'd wanted to do from the moment she'd walked in. He buried his face in her hair and breathed in her scent.

*She was back, thank you, God.*

## Chapter Twenty-Six

Nothing in Nichole's life compared to having Jack's arms wrapped around her. They needed to talk, but later. Right now, what she needed, what she wanted was their bodies pressed against each other skin to skin, and his mouth on her.

As if he understood—or maybe he needed what she did—he scooped her up. "Your arm," she said.

"Is fine." He carried her to his bedroom, laid her on the mattress, and then stared down at her. "Tell me I'm not dreaming, Nichole."

"It's not a dream." She smiled at him. "I'm here, right where I want to be."

"And my bed never looked so good." He sat on the edge of the mattress. "I thought I'd lost you."

She reached for his hand, linking their fingers. "You haven't, and we do need to talk, but later."

"Yeah, later." He brought her hand to his lips and kissed her fingers. "Fair warning, babe. I'm going to lick you from head to toe. I'm going to ruin you for any man but me."

"You already have," she whispered. His eyes darkened as they roamed over her, sending heat straight to her center. "But maybe you should ruin me again."

"I think I will." He glanced at her and winked. "Just for insurance purposes. Change of plans, though. I think I'll start with your toes and work my way up." He slid his hand down her leg, leaving goose bumps in his wake. When he reached her feet, he slid one sandal off, and then the other one. They got tossed to the floor.

He toed off his shoes, and then kneeled on the bed between her ankles. His gaze was smoldering as he coasted his hands up her legs. When he reached the hem of her sundress, he pushed it up to her waist.

"Heaven help me." He blew out a breath at seeing she wasn't wearing panties.

"Surprise," she said, giggling.

"Feel free to surprise me like this anytime the urge strikes you."

"Are you going to just sit there and stare at me, or are you going to do something that will put a smile on my face?"

His gaze met hers, and he gave her a sexy smirk. "Forget a smile. I'm going for hearing you scream my name."

"Hmm, we'll see. Take off your shirt."

"Yes, ma'am." He tugged it up and over his head, tossing it behind him. "Now hush and pay attention."

She saluted him, making him laugh. She'd noticed before that not only was he an amazing lover, but that he also made sex fun. That was new and different, and she liked it. A lot. In her experience, most men thought sex was serious business. It certainly was, but Jack also made it fun.

When he stretched out, and his mouth landed on her, and he flicked his tongue over her clit, she moaned her approval. Over and over, he brought her to the edge, then backed off.

"Jack," she said, begging.

"What, Nichole? This?"

"Oh, God. Yes, that," she said when his tongue teased just the right spot. "Jack!" She fisted the sheet as she shattered.

He crawled up her body as she tried to catch her breath. "Told you I'd have you screaming my name."

"Pretty sure of yourself, aren't you?" She laughed. "That's a smug smile if I've ever seen one."

His smile dropped as he stared down at her. "Have I told you how much I love watching your face when you come for me?"

"No."

"Well, I do, and I want to see it again." He moved to the edge of the bed, stood, and then dropped his jeans to the floor. With his gaze locked on hers, he pushed his briefs down.

The man stole her breath. She knew he ran every day for something like ten miles, and that he also worked out. She supposed that as a SEAL he was required to stay in top shape. It showed. Oh, boy, did it ever.

As her gaze traveled over him, he gave her that sexy smirk again. "Like what you see?"

Since she was staring at his impressive erection, she felt herself blush at getting caught. "Huh?" At hearing him chuckle, she jerked her gaze to his. "What?"

He wrapped his hand around his shaft and gave it a stroke. "I asked if you liked what you see?"

How was she supposed to think when he did that? It was the most erotic thing she'd ever witnessed and watching him do it made her feel like the blood travel-ing through her veins was on fire.

"Yes," she finally answered. "I so do."

"Only fair," he said, sliding his gaze over her. "Be-cause I love what I see." He reached into his nightstand, and then dropped a couple of condoms on top of it. "Any more surprises for me under your dress?"

"I thought you were smart enough to figure out by now that I have nothing on under my dress." When she'd dressed to come see him, she had put on a bra and pant-ies, but then she'd considered it, and then she'd removed all her undergarments.

*See how he liked that*, she'd thought. By the way his eyes darkened, it appeared that he did like it.

"Take off your dress and show me."

"Say please."

"No."

Why his refusal excited her, she didn't know. There was just something about the command in his voice and the way he was looking at her—his blue eyes darker than she'd ever seen them—that brought out the vixen in her. Seduction had never been a game before him, and she liked it. She lowered her gaze to his erection, and then slowly licked her tongue across her bottom lip.

"Nichole," he growled.

"Hmm?" She lifted her gaze to his, and just wow. The heat in his eyes was blazing.

"Take. Off. The. Fucking. Dress."

"If you want it off so bad, you take it off."

"You're playing with fire, babe."

"I don't know. Seems like a mere flicker since you're just standing there. Where's the fire?"

Lesson learned… Never dare a man on a mission.

Well, unless you were okay with your dress ripped down the middle. And, dear God, was she ever! She'd unleashed a beast, and the beast was all hers.

Jack had never lost control like that with a woman before, to the point that he'd torn off her dress. "I'll buy you another one," he said, the closest he could come to an apology, because he really wasn't sorry. Besides, she'd as much as pushed him to do it. By the excitement and anticipation gleaming in her eyes, he didn't think she was sorry either.

"This old thing? Don't worry about it."

"What should I worry about then?"

She tapped a finger against her lips. "Let's see. Didn't you say something about making me scream your name?"

"Did that already, but apparently you need a reminder, and I'll be happy to oblige." This woman was perfect. He had a tendency to see the fun side of things, even with sex. Nichole was giving as good she got, and he loved that about her.

"Oh, that wasn't a scream, just a little whimper."

He laughed as he grabbed a condom. "Game on then." After sheathing himself, he stacked pillows against the headboard, then he dropped onto the bed next to her. Sitting up with his back against the pillows, he took her hand.

"Come here." After she was straddled over his lap, he said, "Ride me, Nichole."

The hell but he loved that naughty gleam he could put in her eyes. He groaned when she sank down around him. "Yeah, like that," he said when she lifted up and then back down.

Her breasts were in front of his face and bouncing with her moves. Before he embarrassed himself by drooling, he leaned forward and sucked a nipple into his mouth. She tasted like the vanilla-scented body wash she used. Her eyes slid closed as he played with first one breast and then the other. He leaned away so he could see her face, slid his hands down to her hips, and pressed his fingers into her skin, urging her to go faster. He'd been without her too long, had missed her too much, and he wasn't going to last.

"Come with me, baby." He lifted as she came down on him, needing to impale himself deep inside her.

She bit down on her bottom lip, arched her back, and cried out his name. She hadn't shouted it, but he took it as a win. He kept his eyes on her as he followed her over the edge.

"Jack," she said again, her voice quieter this time.

He wrapped his arms around her and pulled her against him. "I love you so damn much." She was the half that made him whole, the balm that soothed his soul.

It still scared him that he'd almost lost her. Maybe they were meant to be, though. They'd only met because of a twist of fate, because she'd drunk dialed a wrong number. Yeah, meant to be. He liked that.

"Pardon?" he said, his gaze on Nichole.

She was on the floor, playing with the puppy, wearing nothing but one of his T-shirts, and he was having trouble paying attention. The hem of his shirt was bunched up around her thighs, leaving her long legs on display, and all he could think about was those legs wrapped around him while he was deep inside her.

"Where's your mind, Jack?"

"Huh?" He jerked his gaze up to hers.

She rolled her eyes as she laughed. "I asked if you think we can find a good home for Maggie May?"

Maggie May had the end of one of Dakota's tug ropes in her mouth, growling as she tried to steal it away from Nichole. Dakota sat close by, her attention focused on the puppy, reminding him of a mother keeping an eye on her rambunctious child.

"We already have," he said, coming to a decision. At Nichole's raised brows, he shrugged. "I'm keeping her, at least for now. She might make a good therapy dog, and if that doesn't prove true, Dakota can have her."

"Oh, Jack. That's great." She let go of the tug rope, and Maggie May tumbled backward, landing on her butt. Nichole laughed as she leaned over and kissed the puppy's nose. "Silly girl."

"I'm not sure Dakota would let me give her away even if I wanted to."

Nichole pushed up, and then moved to sit on the sofa next to him. She shifted to face him, tucking her legs under her. "So you're going to train therapy dogs? That's just awesome."

"I am." He rested his hand on her knee. "I acted like a jerk when I got the news from the doctor, and I'll say it again, I'm sorry for that. From the time I woke up in the hospital, my one and only goal was to get back to my team. When the doctor told me my arm and shoulder would never get back to normal, I couldn't see my future, and I felt useless. What did I have to offer you? Nothing."

"That's not true."

He smiled. "I know that now. At the time, though, I was feeling pretty sorry for myself, and I got it in my head that you deserved better. I thought I was doing you a favor by driving you away."

"Don't ever do that again." She straddled him, wrapped her arms around his neck, and stared hard at him. "Don't ever shut me out again. If you do, I don't know if I'll be able to forgive you a second time. You get something stupid in your head like that again, you talk to me."

"I promise." It was a promise he would never break since he never wanted to go through life without her by his side. Also, was it too soon to ask her to marry him? "So, what happens now?"

"With what?"

He pointed at her, and then at himself. "You and me. I want to wake up with you every morning."

"I'd like that, too. The problem is that my house is too small for you, me, Rambo, Dakota, and Maggie May, but that's where my studio is, and I work late at night sometimes."

"Did you know SEALs are masters at solving problems?" And this was one he was going to solve fast.

"Are they now?"

He nodded, liking the way she was looking at him, as if she was about to get naughty.

"So, if I told you I had a problem with a little itch I needed scratched, you could—"

"On it!" He carried his laughing girl to his bedroom, the one that would soon be *theirs*.

# Chapter Twenty-Seven

"When's the baby due?"

Nichole blinked at Jack's grandmother. "What baby?"

"The one you're going to give me before I die."

Jack sighed as he poured syrup over his pancakes. "Grammie, you're not going to die. At least, not soon. Besides, she hasn't asked me to marry her yet, so first things first."

Nichole choked on the coffee she was swallowing, getting an amused glance from Jack. Only three days had passed since he'd brought up living together, and they so weren't ready for marriage or babies.

"Well, what are you waiting for, dear? Ask him."

Over pancakes with his Grammie watching? So not happening. "Ah…"

"Next you're going to want to watch us make a baby," Jack said, narrowing his eyes at his grandmother.

"Don't be silly, Jackie. You can just tell me when the deed is done."

Grammie—what she'd ordered Nichole to call her—looked at Nichole and winked. The woman loved messing with her grandson, and it was amusing to see. Nichole grinned. Grammie and her cohorts in crime, especially Mary, were a hoot as long as their attention wasn't on her.

This morning Grammie and Mary had given her and Jack each a copy of the *Kama Sutra*. Nichole had heard of the book detailing sex techniques, and when she'd flipped through it with the two ladies watching, she'd slammed it closed, hoping her cheeks weren't as red as they felt.

"You didn't look inside yours," she'd said to Jack.

He snorted. "Word of advice, never ever open anything those two give you until you're alone."

She'd definitely remember that for all future presents from Grammie and Mary. Embarrassing or not, though, they sure made life interesting. She'd have to learn to take them in stride, or at least pretend to and not turn beet red like she had with the *Kama Sutra* book.

"I can't believe you did this," Nichole said, glancing at Jack, who was wearing a pleased-with-himself-smile. Three weeks had passed since he'd brought up living together, and he hadn't mentioned it since. She'd begun to think he'd changed his mind.

"I want you to live with me, and to do that, you need a studio, so I built you one."

She snapped her fingers. "Just like that?"

"For you, baby, I'll move mountains."

His words made her feel all warm and gooey inside. "Don't mind me. I'm just going to melt in a puddle at your feet."

"I'd rather you stayed a person. Hard to do this to a puddle."

He cupped her face, lowered his mouth to hers, and kissed her with such loving tenderness that she was sure she was going to melt anyway. No man in her life had treated her with so much respect and care before, and she loved him for it.

"I can't believe you built this so fast." The room had been added to the back of his garage and was bigger than her studio. She loved the windows that let in light, which she'd always missed in her garage studio.

"Had some help. Deke and a few of his cop buddies pitched in. He also knew someone that fast-tracked getting a permit." He moved behind her, wrapped his arms around her, and rested his head on hers. "I thought you'd want to decide on where you wanted shelves and stuff, so we didn't do anything to the inside other than the sink and counter."

"Oh, boy." Excited, she clapped her hands. "I'm going to have so much fun doing that. When I set up my garage for a studio, it was when I was first starting, and I really didn't know what I was doing. Now I do."

He chuckled. "I guess I know what we're going to be doing this weekend."

"Hell, yeah!"

"Right after you move in with me," he added.

"I don't remember agreeing to that."

"Then let me remind you." He backed her to the wall, and did he ever remind her.

"I have some news you two are going to like," Deke said.

"Yeah? What's that?" Jack handed his friend a beer.

"Is Nichole around? She needs to hear this, too."

"She's in her studio. She'll want to thank you anyway for helping me get it built."

"Likes it then?" Deke asked as they headed to the studio.

Jack chuckled. "You would've thought I'd given her the moon and stars."

Four days had passed since Nichole had moved in with him. Her studio was set up to her liking, and he was learning the fine art of living with a woman. She accused him of being a neat freak, and he privately thought she was messy, but he knew better than to share his opinion on the shoes left by the door, the pottery magazines piling up in various places in the house, and the ponytail holders all over the place that seemed to multiply by the day.

He wouldn't change a thing.

"We have a visitor, babe." He grinned at seeing the slash of mud on her cheek.

"Oh, hi, Deke," she said.

"Hey." He looked around. "So, this is where the magic happens."

"Yep." She went to the sink and washed her hands. "Thanks for helping Jack get it built. Thank your friends who pitched in, too."

"Will do."

Jack wrapped his arm around her shoulders. "Deke said he has some news for us."

"You'll both be happy to hear that Lane Gregory decided it was in his best interest to leave town. Apparently, he got on the bad side of some dudes you don't want to cross, who are gunning for him."

"The same ones who put him in the hospital?" Jack asked.

"Yes. We'd really like to arrest them, but he refuses to name them or testify against them."

"They must be really scary then. Lane prides himself on not being afraid of anyone," Nichole said.

Deke nodded. "I have my suspicions on who they are, and, if I'm right, Gregory's smart to worry about living another day if he sticks around."

"So we don't have to watch our backs anymore. That is good news." The day Gregory had been released from the hospital, Jack had stuck close to Nichole, taking her to work and picking her up. On her days at the artisan mall, he'd left Dakota with her. Like Jack, his dog would protect Nichole with her life.

"You don't know what a relief it is to know he's gone." Nichole glanced at Deke. "He is gone, right?"

"He left yesterday. I'm meeting Heather for lunch, so I need to go."

After Deke left, Nichole jumped on him, wrapping her legs around his waist. "Well, hello there." He grinned at her. "Someone's happy."

"You have no idea. It feels like a hundred pounds has been lifted from my shoulders knowing he's gone. We need to celebrate."

"And I know just how."

She leaned back so she could see his face, then smirked. "I recognize that look in your eyes."

"Good. Means I don't have to explain what's about to happen."

"If we're going to keep doing this in my studio, I think we need to add another piece of furniture."

Jack groaned when she rubbed her groin against his. "Yeah? What's that?"

"A bed."

"On it," he said, then backed her up against the wall. Even though he was growing fond of this wall, tomorrow she'd have her bed.

Truth, all she had to do was ask, and whatever it

was, he'd do everything in his power to give it to her. And someday, when the timing was right and he was sure she'd say yes, he'd give her the diamond ring he'd bought a few days ago and had hidden away. Then they could get busy making his Grammie happy and give her great-grandbabies to spoil.

# Chapter Twenty-Eight

*Eight months later*

"She's never going to be a therapy dog, at least not the kind I'm training for my military brothers and sisters," Jack told Nichole as they watched the still growing puppy chase Rambo around the backyard while Dakota sat next to him, observing her wards play.

Maggie May was too happy, too exuberant, too needy to get all the love from any person she came in contact with. Besides, he wasn't sure he could give her up. She was a clown with overgrown feet that she kept tripping over. She supplied them with laughs every single day, and he doubted Nichole would be any more willing to let her go than he was.

Maggie May was also dumb as shit. As a therapy dog, she'd shower her owner with love, but that was about it. Even after eight months of working with her, the silly dog couldn't remember her lessons from one day to the next, but he had an idea of a way she could contribute.

"Then we get to keep her?" Nichole asked.

"I figure neither you nor Dakota will speak to me

again if we don't." He could probably include Rambo in that, too. The three dogs had formed a tight family.

She laughed. "You have that right."

"I do think she'd make a good therapy dog in another way. I'd like to try her out on visiting the children's floor at the hospital and making visits to retirement facilities. We could start her out at Grammie's place, get her used to doing something like that."

"That's a great idea! I think she'd be amazing with children and older people."

"You're amazing." He glanced at the woman who'd taught him how to be happy. "You look good enough to eat. If we didn't have to leave in five minutes..." He waggled his eyebrows.

"But we do, so let's get the dogs in." As they herded their fur-kids inside, she said, "Are you nervous?"

"There wasn't a military operation I went out on that made me as nervous as I am now, if that tells you anything." That was a fact. His stomach was doing somersaults, and he was afraid he might lose his lunch.

She grabbed his hands and pulled him to a stop. "Everything is going to be perfect."

"As long as I have you, that's all that matters."

"You will always have me. Now, let's go to the grand opening of Operation K-9 Brothers."

"On it," he said.

Jack hadn't dared to hope that every invitation he'd sent out for the Operation K-9 Brothers grand opening would be accepted, but he couldn't think of a single person on the invite list who was missing, except for his SEAL brothers who were deployed. If they were stateside, he knew every single one of them would be here for him.

He'd taken Nichole to Virginia Beach a few times when the team had been home, and they now considered her their sister. Double D had even sung Sister Sledge's "We are Family" to her.

On their last visit, his team had warned him to treat her right or he'd be hearing from them. That was something they'd never have to worry about, but he loved that his brothers had adopted her.

He glanced over at the tables where all the items for the silent auction were set up. Every potter friend of Nichole's was out in force, their donations to the cause on the tables. Three different caterers had donated food and sodas, a local winery had set up a tasting booth, as had two of Asheville's microbreweries.

The support from his town was humbling.

Dirty Mary's laughter caught his attention. The one table he refused to go near was the one his grandmother's cronies were hosting. It had drawn a large crowd all afternoon, and he shuddered at the thought of what items they'd come up with to sell.

Ron Kitterman, his mentor, who'd helped fast-track Jack's therapy dog certification, slapped a hand over his back. "You should be proud of yourself, son."

Jack scanned the area around him. "Do I sound like I'm bragging to say that I am?"

"Hell no. You worked harder to make this happen in about half the time than I thought possible. Definitely be proud. I have something for you." He handed Jack a check made out to Operation K-9 Brothers.

Jack's eyes widened at seeing the amount. "Damn, I wasn't expecting this."

"You're doing some good for people here, Jack. By giving you this, I get bragging rights that I discovered you."

"No way I'm going to say no to that."

Ron squeezed his shoulder, then melted into the crowd. Jack looked at the check again to make sure he hadn't read the amount wrong. He hadn't. Ron had also worked with him on designing the kennels and training center after Jack had purchased the land. He owed the man big-time.

Other donations were coming in, and he'd already sold two sponsorships. Operation K-9 Brothers' website was amazing thanks to Nichole's brother. And then there was Nichole. She now donated a percentage of all her pottery sales to Operation K-9 Brothers. That meant more to him than he could ever tell her.

How was he going to thank all the people who'd helped make his dream happen? A year ago, he'd thought his life was over, and now he had a new future that excited him as much as being a SEAL had—even more, actually—a woman who loved him in spite of all his faults, a super-smart military-trained dog, a dog that was learning to live up to his name of Rambo, and a dumber-than-dumb dog that he wouldn't have any different.

What more could he ask for?

He stood near the kennels, watching the people check out his dogs. He had eleven in various stages of training and was on the lookout for more.

The Jacobys approached, Trucker walking next to Nigel Senior, and Jack smiled as they neared. "Thank you for coming," he said when the family stopped in front of him.

Nigel offered his hand. "We wanted to be here. I'll admit that I wasn't a believer in what a dog could do for me."

"And now you are?"

"And now I am. I'm not back to where I was before my deployments, but I'm a lot better than I was before Trucker." At hearing his name, the dog peered up, and Nigel scratched his head.

"I want to train dogs like you do when I grow up," Junior said.

Jack smiled down at him. "Tell you what. When you get a little older, if you want, you can volunteer a few hours a week, see how you like it."

Junior glanced at his parents. "Can I? Please. Please."

"If you still want to by then," his father said. "We're going to head out. Just wanted to tell you that you're doing a good thing here. I'll see you Tuesday."

"You bet." Jack had fast-tracked Trucker's training, but the dog still wasn't where he needed to be, so he was working with Nigel and Trucker one-on-one on Tuesday mornings.

After they left, he scanned the area, looking for Nichole. Mark was standing with Deke and Heather. As soon as Mark learned Gregory was gone, he'd returned, and with the mind-boggling money he'd sold his game for, he'd bought Nichole's house. He'd created another game already and was busy fine-tuning it before sending it to Clint Alba, now acting as Mark's agent. Jack was surprised at how much fun he was having, playing the new game with Mark, looking for bugs.

He gave a grunt of satisfaction. All was right in his world…or would be if he could find Nichole. Today was important for more reasons than she knew. The event was winding down, and people were leaving. The time for the next item on his agenda was drawing near. He was nervous as hell.

*  *  *

"Come with me, Nic," Mark said.

"Have you seen Jack?" Everyone was gone, the grounds cleaned up, and her boyfriend was nowhere in sight. Jack's grand opening had been a tremendous success, and she couldn't be prouder of him and what he'd accomplished.

"He's around somewhere." He grabbed her hand. "I need to show you something."

When he stopped in front of the Operation K-9 Brothers sign, she glanced around. "What am I supposed to be looking at?"

"Just stand here and don't move," he said, then walked away.

Okay, this was weird. What was her brother up to? Maybe a minute passed, and then Dakota trotted up to her, carrying a silver gift bag in her mouth. Dakota sat in front of her, and Nichole took the bag.

"What's this?" She reached inside, pulling out a black satin mask with a note attached to it. "'Put this on,'" she read aloud. Weirder and weirder. Well, only one way to find out what was going on. She put on the mask.

As she stood, waiting to find out what was going to happen, she heard rustling, a dog that sounded like Maggie May bark, and then the quick growl that Dakota would give Maggie May when she was misbehaving, and was that Grammie giggling? She was sure it was her brother who shushed her.

Then all was quiet.

"You can take off the mask," Jack said.

"Not sure I want to," she muttered, suddenly nervous and not sure why.

Jack chuckled. "Do it anyway, babe."

The sight in front of her sent her heart into jackhammer mode. Jack was on one knee, holding a black-velvet box open to reveal a beautiful diamond ring. Dakota sat on his right side with Maggie May next to her, and on Jack's left was Rambo.

"Oh," she whispered. *Oh.*

"Nichole Masters, when I was at my darkest, you walked into my life, bringing light. I wasn't expecting you, hadn't planned for you, and probably don't deserve you." He glanced at the velvet box. "I bought this ring eight months ago, knowing even then that I wanted to wake up next to you for the rest of my life."

"Jack." Darn him, he was going to make her cry.

"Hush. I'm not done yet." He gave her his special smile, and if melting into a puddle was a possible thing, she'd be doing it again. "As hard as it was to wait to ask my question, I did because I wanted to make sure you saw that I could make something of myself, that I'm more than what I even thought I could be. That's why you're standing under the sign for my new future… Our new future."

"Oh, Jack," she whispered, falling to her knees in front of him. "I always knew you were more."

"And you made me believe it." He glanced to his right, where his two dogs sat. "Along with me, Dakota and Maggie May are asking you and Rambo to be a part of our lives forever. Will you marry me, Nichole?"

Rambo barked.

Jack winked at her. "He said yes. What do you say?"

Only because she'd spent months with him learning about dogs did she catch his subtle sign telling her dog to bark. "I think you cheated," she said, laughing.

"I'll do whatever it takes to make you mine, Nichole."

"Only if you're also mine, Jack Daniels."

"I wouldn't have it any other way, babe." He slipped the ring on her finger and then kissed the daylights out of her.

"Finally, I'm going to get great-grandbabies," Grammie said from behind them.

Nichole snorted a laugh against his mouth, and then couldn't stop laughing.

"Not right this minute, Grammie," Jack said between kisses as he laughed along with her.

"Who would have thought that one drunken phone call would lead to this?" She held up her hand, admiring the platinum square-cut diamond solitaire ring.

"Babe, you can drunk dial me anytime you feel like it."

She smiled at the beautiful man who'd shown her how love could really be…how it should be. "I might just do that."

# *Epilogue*

Noah Alba leaned against the wall of the nightclub in Virginia Beach, his gaze on the woman in the red dress that hugged every curve. He eyed the fine ass that the dress barely covered. Maybe she could make him forget for a few hours. Nothing else had worked—not the whiskey that was his new best friend since being sent home, and not the shrink his commander ordered him to see.

"You look like you could use a little pickup." Rocky held out his hand, a small dime-size baggie of white powder in his palm.

"What is it?"

"The best kind of candy. This one's on the house." Rocky tucked the baggie into Noah's shirt pocket, then pushed off the wall and walked away.

"On the house, my ass," Noah muttered. It hadn't taken long after Rocky had sidled up to him earlier in the evening and introduced himself to figure out the man was dealing drugs. He hadn't tried to hide the money and baggies changing hands.

Noah knew the reason for the freebie...get him on the hook and then wait for him to come back for more.

He put a finger to the outside of his pocket, feeling the outline of the baggie. Maybe it was the answer to helping him forget.

"Babe, have you seen my wallet?" Jack said. "I thought I left it on the coffee table."

Nichole walked out of the bedroom, and Jack let out a breath, forgetting about his missing wallet. She had on his favorite dress, the black one with the slashes of red that she'd worn on their first date.

He moved next to her, then trailed his hand down her bare back. "As beautiful as you are in this dress, all I'm going to be thinking about tonight is getting you out of it."

She laughed. "You think the same thing when I'm wearing my ratty potter clothes and covered in clay."

"Not my fault you're sexy as hell covered in clay." It was Heather's birthday, so he and Nichole were treating her and Deke to dinner at one of Asheville's finer restaurants. He rested his finger at the low V of the dress, so tantalizingly close to her gorgeous ass. "We could call them and say you're sick, and I have to stay home and take care of you."

"You have a one-track mind, Jack Daniels."

"Not denying it, and it bears repeating… Your fault."

"Well, if I have to be blamed for something, I'll take that one."

And damn if that smile of hers didn't still make his heart twitchy, but he was good now with twitchy. Real good. "I guess since you won't let me call in sick, we should go. I just need to find my wallet."

"Have you checked Maggie May's bed?"

"Right. Should have thought of that." Maggie May

had turned into a master thief and hoarder. Nothing was safe from her thieving. Fortunately, she never chewed things up, just wanted to own them. It was good he had a soft spot in his heart for the idiot dog.

Sure enough, his wallet was in her bed, along with Nichole's Kindle, one of her bras, and a collection of dog toys. He'd cleaned out her bed this morning, and already she'd amassed a hoarder's treasure trove.

Dakota walked up next to him, and Jack glanced at her. "Can't you do something about your kleptomaniac daughter?" All he got from her was a doggy sigh. "I know the feeling," he said.

As he headed back to the living room, his wallet safely in his pocket, his phone rang. He frowned at seeing his former commander's name on the screen. Why would he be calling?

"Sir?" Jack said on answering.

"I need you to come get Double D."

Huh? "Get him from where?" Jack had heard that an operation Noah Alba was on had gone south, but he hadn't heard the details.

"From here. He's in trouble, Jack, and you're the best plan I can think of for saving him."

There was no one Jack respected more than his commander, a man he couldn't say no to. "Maybe you should tell me what's going on."

"He made a mistake that resulted in the team's dog and translator getting killed. He's drowning in an ocean of guilt. I'll brief you when you get here."

Even though Jack was no longer in the military, his former commander was giving him an order, one he wouldn't ignore.

"I'll leave in the morning, sir."

\* \* \*

Noah groaned at the hammering in his head that kept time with whoever was pounding on his fucking door. A full bottle of whiskey might not have been the smartest thing he'd ever done, so why he kept doing it was… whatever. He couldn't follow his own thought process because some asshole was banging in his head!

He stumbled to the door, opened it, and said, "Go away."

"You look like shit, Double D."

Noah blinked until he could make out the man standing in front of him. "Whiskey? What the hell are you doing here?"

"You're my brother. Where else would I be when you're diving into the rabbit hole headfirst?" His former teammate pushed past him, and when he was inside, his gaze went straight to the coffee table. He walked over and picked up the dime-size baggie. "The hell, Noah?"

"That's not mine."

Jack lasered him with a hard look. "That's what they all say."

Eff him. He'd meant to throw that shit away. He couldn't deny he'd considered snorting it in the hopes it would take away the nightmares, but that crap was a one-way ticket to hell. He wasn't so far gone that he didn't recognize that. Not that he owed Jack an explanation. Whiskey could stare at him all he wanted, but since he didn't appreciate the surprise visit, he was feeling ornery enough to let Jack think whatever the hell he wanted.

"Why are you here, Jack?"

"I've come to take you home with me."

\* \* \* \* \*

*Reviews are an invaluable tool when it comes to
spreading the word about great reads.
Please consider leaving an honest review for this or
any of Carina Press's other titles that you've read
on your favorite retailer or review site.
To find out about other books by Sandra Owens or to
be alerted to cover reveals, new releases, and other
fun stuff, sign up for her newsletter at
https://bit.ly/2FVUPKS*

# *Acknowledgments*

You know the saying it takes a village? I've learned how very true that is over the course of my publishing career. I'm blessed to have a fantastic village, which means so many people to thank.

First up is Sandra's Rowdies, my Facebook reader group. When I need encouragement, my Rowdies dump it on me by the truckload. When I need a good laugh, boy do they deliver! Believe me, they are aptly named. So, to Sandra's Rowdies, thank you from the bottom of my heart for being such amazing friends and readers. I love you all and look forward to many years of fun times.

One of my favorite things about becoming an author is the reader friends I've made from all over the world. I love the idea that I have friends not only in America, but in the Netherlands, Australia, Wales, Ireland, Canada, Germany, the Philippines…well, the list is long. It's so cool, and I hope to get to meet some of you in person one day. Thank you all for loving my books, for the reviews, and for recommending them to your friends! Just so you know, my favorite question is, "When's your next book coming out?"

To all the great book bloggers, thank you for reading my books, reviewing them, and talking about them. Y'all rock!!!!

Before I was published, I was in awe of authors. I still am. I never dreamed the day would come when I would have author friends, ones I'd spend time with at conferences, go on writing retreats with, talk on the phone with, and email back and forth with. So, wow on that! I wish I could name them all, but there are three in particular I want to thank. Jenny Holiday, my friend and critique partner, thank you for the years of love and friendship. To Miranda Liasson and A.E. Jones, my Golden Heart sisters, I love you both so much! You have no idea how much I appreciate the plot talks, the encouragement, and for always being only a phone call away when I need you.

Now we come to editors. I wouldn't be half the author I am without my editors. Who else would tell me my favorite scene needs to be cut? When that happens, my first reaction is nooooooo! Those are the best words in the manuscript. How could you think they need to be cut? But then I calm down, consider her reason for daring to think that, and then, you know what? She's almost always right. Or what about when she tells me I need to dig deeper into a character's emotions or the reason he/she did something? My first reaction is a groan with the word "Really?" But again, she's right, so I dig deeper and, look at that, the scene turns out a thousand times better. To my Harlequin/Carina Press developmental editor, thank you Deborah Nemeth for showing me how to put a beautiful shine on my story. To my acquiring editor, Kerri Buckley, thank you for believing in the Operation K-9 Brothers series.

To my agent, Courtney Miller-Callihan, what an

amazing seven years it's been! A huge thank-you for all you've done for me. You're a rock star!!!

And last, to my family, love you Jim, Jeff, and DeAnna. (Jim, a special thanks for never complaining about the burnt dinners when I'm on deadline. *kissy, kissy*)

## About the Author

Bestselling, award-winning author Sandra Owens lives in the beautiful Blue Ridge Mountains of North Carolina. Her family and friends often question her sanity but have ceased being surprised by what she might get up to next. She's jumped out of a plane, flown in an aerobatic plane while the pilot performed death-defying stunts, gotten into laser gunfights in Air Combat, and ridden a Harley motorcycle for years. She regrets nothing.

Sandra is a Romance Writers of America Honor Roll member and a 2013 Golden Heart Finalist for her contemporary romance *Crazy for Her*. In addition to her contemporary romance and romantic suspense novels, she writes Regency stories. Her books have won many awards including The Readers' Choice and The Golden Quill.

Join Sandra's Facebook Reader Group:
https://www.facebook.com/groups/1827166257533001/

Connect with Sandra:
Facebook: https://bit.ly/2ruKKPl
Twitter: https://twitter.com/SandyOwens1

Coming soon from Carina Press and Sandra Owens

Keeping Guard

On medical leave from his SEAL team, all he wants
is a bit of peace. What he gets instead is a runaway
bride in need of a bodyguard.

Read on for a sneak preview of
Keeping Guard,
the next book in author Sandra Owens's
Operation K-9 Brothers series

"He's a stray someone tied to our gate a few nights ago."

Noah Alba, Double D—or sometimes just DD—to his SEAL teammates, stared at the fifty pounds of wiggling mass. "Are you sure it's actually a dog?"

The thing looked more like something put together all wrong. Wiry fur stuck up and out at odd angles and had to be about a dozen different colors. There was more fur on his furiously wagging tail than on his body. The oddest part of the animal were the two different colored eyes, one blue and one brown.

His friend and former teammate laughed. "Actually, no."

A year ago, Jack Daniels—Whiskey to the team—and his dog had come home to Asheville, North Carolina. When he learned that his arm and shoulder were permanently damaged, he'd started Operation K-9 Brothers to train therapy dogs to be companions to their military brothers and sisters who were suffering from PTSD.

Noah was both proud and impressed with what his friend had accomplished, but the last thing he wanted was to be around people and dogs. Former teammates were included. The only reason he didn't do a vanishing act was because his commander had ordered him here. If he left, he'd be AWOL. He'd fucked up his life enough without getting charged with a serious crime.

"He's yours to work with while you're here," Jack said.

"Oh, hell no." The last dog he'd been around was dead because of him.

Jack put his hand on Noah's shoulder. "Yes, and that's an order, DD."

Noah pressed his lips together to keep from telling him what he could do with his order and the dog. What had his commander been thinking by sending him here, and not only that, but also ordering him to report directly to Whiskey? Hell, Jack wasn't even in the navy anymore.

"You'll work with me every day on training him while you're here. You also need to give him a name."

The ever-simmering rage inside him burned hotter. "You're making a mistake trusting me with a dog."

"I disagree."

Noah slipped his hand into the pocket of his jeans, his fingers wrapping around the pair of dice he always carried. They'd belonged to his father, a reminder of everything he refused to be. All he had to do to remind himself that he was not his father was to touch the pair of dice. Throughout his life, he'd touched them thousands of times, and it always worked, always led him to find the calm in his soul that made him not his father. To be the kind of man his mother would have been proud of.

For the first time since he was a boy, his rage didn't go from boiling over back to simmering when he touched them. "I need to go," he said. "Somewhere for a while."

"Take the dog with you."

Noah hated the knowing look in Jack's eyes, like his friend knew he was losing it and understood. Maybe he did. Jack had appeared three nights ago at their home base in Virginia Beach, announcing that he was taking Noah home with him. Noah had told him to go to hell.

"You have two choices," Jack had answered. "Come with me or tell our commander you refused to obey an order. Makes no never mind to me which you pick."

Noah knew his friend and teammate was there to save him, and that made him antsy. He didn't want to need saving, had never expected to be the one his SEAL brothers had to worry about. He had his shit together. Nothing could be as bad as what his boy-self had survived, right? Or so he'd thought until his mistake caused the team's translator and their dog to be blown up.

Noah took the dog with him...as far as his new apartment. The ants weren't just crawling under his skin, they were biting. He couldn't be near a dog right now. Every time he looked at the thing, he saw his team's dog.

After giving the dog time to do his business, Noah took him inside. "Here's the thing, dog. I don't own this place, so don't chew on the furniture or pee on the floor." Unable to think of anything else the dog needed to know, he left the creature to his own devices.

He ended up on the Blue Ridge Parkway, his rental car pointed in the direction of the waterfall Jack had taken him to yesterday. After hiking down to the bottom of the falls, Jack had said, "This is a good place to come when you feel like you're about to lose your shit."

He'd glanced around. "If you let it, you can find a few moments of peace here."

"Speaking from experience?" Noah had asked.

"I've spent quiet time here, especially after I first came home." He smiled. "Before I met Nichole."

That was another thing. Jack had gone and fallen in love. Noah never thought he'd see Whiskey look at a woman with sappy eyes. Nichole was great, and she'd even seemed disappointed when Noah said he was going to find an apartment to rent while he was here.

He didn't think Jack was happy about that either— he'd prefer to have him where he could keep an eye on him. Understandable since Noah had been falling down drunk when Jack arrived to collect him.

After Noah swore there'd be no repeat performance— all the booze he'd poured down his throat hadn't wiped his memory clean, anyway—Jack helped him find a lease-by-the-month one-bedroom furnished apartment. He'd moved in right away, grateful that he hadn't had to sit around with Jack and Nichole last night and pretend he was enjoying himself.

If Noah had to be around people twenty-four seven, he was going to climb out of his skin.


Peyton Sutton wasn't supposed to overhear her fiancé telling his best man that he was only marrying her because her father had promised him a share of her family's brewery. The share that was supposed to be hers.

The rat bastard. She'd only overheard the conversation because she'd gotten last-minute cold feet and wanted to talk to Dalton, needed him to assure her that they were both ready for a lifelong commitment. Turned out he was more committed to her father than to her.

After she graduated from college, her father had dangled a carrot in front of her. Do this and a share in the company will be yours one day. Do that and the entire company will be yours one day. She'd jumped through hoops doing this and that, trying to please him. Like saying yes when Dalton asked her to marry him. Dalton was Elk Antler Brewery's chief financial officer, the son her father had always wanted, and marrying Dalton would make Gerald Sutton happy with her.

Well, to hell with both of them.

She gathered up the skirts of the princess wedding gown her father had chosen, the one she'd gritted her teeth over to keep from telling him how much she hated it. She was done with trying to please her father.

From the time he'd let her hang out at Elk Antler Brewery, she'd been fascinated by the process of making beer. She'd been thirteen the first time he'd brought her there, pointing at the corner where she could do her homework. It was supposed to be punishment for not getting a perfect score on her math test.

That day had been far from punishment and set the course of her life. She spent her afternoons at the brewery, supposedly doing her homework, but any time her father was in a meeting or out of the building, she was learning how to make beer instead. Her father's brewmaster had taken a liking to her, and over the years he'd shared his knowledge, his love of brewing, and his recipes. She could step into his shoes and no one would notice.

She'd returned home with degrees in business and marketing and went to work for her father. Pleasing him was impossible—even with bringing in more business with tours and events—but she'd kept trying anyway.

Until today.

She was over it. He'd made her a promise that he obviously had no intention of keeping. The long hours she'd put in, the heart she put into the brewery, the jumping through hoops for him apparently meant nothing.

"Where is she?"

Peyton stilled at hearing her father's voice. If he found her, he'd convince her to go through with the wedding.

With the voluminous skirts of the gown gathered up, she headed in the opposite direction. She didn't have a plan since it hadn't for a minute occurred to her that she'd sneak out on her own wedding.

Three hundred and twenty-nine guests were seated in the country club ballroom waiting for her to walk down the aisle in a matter of minutes. They were sure going to be in for a surprise when the bride didn't appear. Avoiding the ballroom, she scooted into the banquet hall. The staff setting up for the reception all stopped what they were doing to stare at her. She nodded at the bartender, snatched two bottles of champagne, and almost laughed at his wide eyes.

"You never saw me," she tossed over her shoulder as she headed for the door leading to the parking lot.

Outside, she paused for a moment, and as she breathed in the pine-scented mountain air, the heavy weight that had settled on her shoulders ever since Dalton had put an engagement ring on her finger lifted, carried away by the breeze. As much as she wanted to luxuriate in the feeling of freedom, she needed to go before someone found her. But where to?

Her car wasn't here since she'd arrived with her father in the limo he'd rented. She spied Dalton's silver Mercedes parked near the main entrance and headed for it. Wasn't her fault he'd once shown her where he'd hidden a spare key remote.

She cringed at the Just Married someone had written on the rear window with white shoe polish. Couldn't be helped. She needed a getaway car, and Dalton's was her only choice. After retrieving the key, she unlocked the door, got in, put the champagne bottles on the passenger seat, and then spent minutes she didn't have getting the skirts of the stupid gown inside so she could close the door.

The next time she planned to get married, she was wearing one of those slip wedding dresses. Much easier to escape in if need be. She glanced in the rearview mirror, saw her father and Dalton walk out of the building, and hauled ass.

With no direction in mind, she drove around, and at the entrance to the Blue Ridge Parkway, turned on her blinker. What she really wanted to do was go home, get out of this ridiculous dress, put on her jammies, and then plow her way through the champagne.

Or go to the brewery and make beer. Getting lost in recipes, that was her peace place. Where all her troubles floated away. But she couldn't do either of those things. Home and the brewery were the first places her father and Dalton would look.

She needed to find somewhere she could think, make a plan for where she'd go from here. After her stunt today, she doubted her father would welcome her back to the place she loved above all else. Oh, he probably would if she went back and married Dalton, but that was so not happening.

Peyton blinked away the tears that threatened at the thought of never setting foot in Elk Antler Brewery again. Not good to bawl her eyes out while driving. Along with a place to consider her future, she needed somewhere she could have a good cry in private.

After driving along the Parkway for a while, she saw a sign announcing a waterfall. No other cars were in sight in the parking lot, and she decided it was the perfect place.

She parked in the lot, grabbed the two bottles of champagne, then headed for the trail. She stopped and eyed the steep path down. No way was she going to manage that wearing white satin heels without falling and breaking her neck. She kicked them off. The sheer white stockings the bridal shop consultant said she had to wear soon followed. They were her first ever stockings, and she hated them as much as the dress.

Even barefoot, going down was tricky in a gown consisting of more material than all the clothes in her closet put together. A squirrel clinging upside down to a tall pine tree chattered at her as she passed. "Yeah, yeah, I'm not having a good day either."

She almost slipped when she stepped on a mossy rock, and, forgetting she had a champagne bottle in her hand, she grabbed hold of a rhododendron branch. The bottle rolled and bounced down the trail. Thankfully, it didn't break. She needed that champagne.

"Well, that wasn't a piece of cake," she muttered after finally making it to the waterfall with both bottles intact. Speaking of cake, she should have snatched some of her wedding cake while she was at it since she hadn't eaten anything all day because her stomach had been in knots.

The dress her father had paid a small fortune for was torn and dirt streaked. He wasn't going to be happy about that, but she wasn't happy with him either, so they were even. She headed for a boulder with a flat surface. She tried to climb up it, but that proved impossible when wearing a million yards of…whatever the dress was made of. Fashion and fabrics weren't her thing, the reason her father had chosen the gown. Clothes were a necessity, something she had to put on before she could appear in public. And right now, there was no public, and she wanted on top of that boulder. She deserved to be up there after knowing her actions would cost her the only thing that mattered to her.

So…it was a struggle, but she finally got the hated gown off. Irritated with the stupid thing, she tossed it to the side with more force than she'd intended.

It tumbled down the embankment, landing in the waterfall pool.

"Oops." Who knew a dress that heavy could travel so far?

Free of the gown, she climbed up to the top of the boulder, giving thanks that it wasn't winter, when she'd be freezing her bottom off wearing only a sexy white corset that she *had* wanted to wear. She'd imagined that Dalton would finally look at her with desire in his eyes—something he'd never done—when he saw her in it.

Although brewing beer and creating events that brought beer lovers to Elk Antler Brewery was her jam—or had been—she wanted to experience how it felt to be truly wanted by someone.

She was, as far as she'd gathered, the result of a one-night stand between her parents. The mother she only vaguely remembered had dropped her off at her father's when Peyton was four years old, then had disappeared from her life. Her father had kept her, but she'd never been sure he'd been happy to have her. That uncertainty was the reason she'd spent her life until now trying to please him…so he wouldn't give her away like her mother had.

All good reasons why the champagne should go straight down her throat. She managed to pop the cork on one of the bottles. The cork shot up before arcing and falling into the pool to join her wedding gown.

"Cheers to me." She lifted the bottle to her mouth as tears rolled down her cheeks for what she'd lost today.

There was only one other car parked on the dirt-packed lot at the entrance to the falls, a silver Mercedes with "Just Married" scrawled on the rear window. Shrugging off his curiosity, Noah locked the doors of his rental and headed for the trail going down, hoping Jack was right and a bit of peace awaited him at the bottom that would quiet the ants.

Noah paused at the top of the trail going down, frowning at seeing the white heels, one upright and the other on its side. A pair of white stockings were draped over a nearby bush. He glanced back at the silver Mercedes. Was he going to stumble on a bride and groom, and what the devil were they doing here of all places?

He almost turned around to leave, but curiosity got the better of him. If he discovered them getting it on—a distinct possibility considering the bride was shedding clothing—he'd discreetly disappear. Going down in stealth mode, he reached the bottom of the trail, stopping dead in his tracks when a feminine voice said, "Cheers to me." He blinked and then blinked again.

A woman wearing nothing but a white corset and a veil was perched on a boulder, a champagne bottle held up to her mouth as she chugged the contents. He scanned the area, searching for the groom. Something white floating in the pool caught his eyes, and after staring at it for a minute, he realized it was a wedding dress. The hell?

His gaze returned to the woman. Had she done away with her groom? Was the man in the pool under her dress? He wasn't sure what to do, but one thing was for sure. This woman—whoever she was…a murderer?—had him forgetting his own troubles.

She still hadn't noticed him, and he took the opportunity to observe her. Black hair fell around her shoulders and down her back, and the corset did a mighty fine job of displaying her breasts. Her long, firm legs were splayed apart over the rock as if she had no modesty.

Of course, she thought she was alone, and realizing he was no better than a peeping tom, he debated leaving or making his presence known. But what if she had offed her groom? Was that why she was crying? The last thing he wanted to do was get involved in someone else's mess, so he decided a dead groom wasn't going to be his problem. When he got to the top of the trail, he'd call Jack, tell him what was going on, and let him decide what to do.

Besides, he wasn't fond of brides. He'd almost had one of those once. His had walked out on him the day before their wedding after telling him that he loved his SEAL team more than her. That wasn't true. He'd loved her as much as his teammates. Brides couldn't be trusted, especially a killer bride who chugged champagne to celebrate her groom's demise.

Time to do a disappearing act. He took a step back, but his movement caught her attention before he could slip away. She lowered the champagne bottle and stared at him. Blue eyes the color of the sky above, he inanely thought.

She tilted her head as she studied him. "Are you going to kidnap me?"

"Wasn't planning on it."

"Oh." She sounded disappointed.

"Sorry. I didn't mean to disturb you. I'll be going now."

"You don't have to. Just ignore me."

Like it was possible to ignore a beautiful woman wearing nothing but a corset. "That's okay. Probably best if I go."

She lifted a foot and stared at it. "My feet are dirty."

"I see that." Weirdest conversation ever.

"You want some champagne?" She held up the bottle, showing him the label. "Only the best will do for my father."

"No, thanks." If he stuck around and drank with her, his luck, he'd end up arrested as an accomplice to murder.

"I'm a runaway bride."

He didn't know what to say to that, but he definitely had thoughts. Like, there you go, just more proof that brides can't be trusted. Then another one…at least that meant there wasn't a dead groom under that wedding dress. That one was definitely a relief. And why was she only wearing a corset and veil, and her dress was floating in the pool?

"Do you need some help?" he finally said, hoping she said no.

"Yeah, with this champagne. It's not good to drink alone, you know."

He did know that, not that it stopped him. Why wasn't she afraid of him? She picked up a second, still corked bottle, and held it out to him. "You can even have your own if drinking out of a bottle my mouth has been on bothers you."

His gaze fell to said mouth. Negative. He'd have absolutely no problem putting his mouth anywhere hers had been. *Situation dire!* Time to retreat. He didn't do brides, even ones with sky-blue eyes and lips made for kissing.

"Come on. Don't be a stick in the mud." She waved the bottle like it was a red cape and he was the bull.

Apparently, he was a bull because his feet took him to the edge of the boulder. "Why aren't you afraid of me?"

"Should I be?"

"No, but you can't know that."

She shrugged. "I figure the universe can't be meaner to me today than it already has. And if it is, not sure I have it in me to care anymore." She tipped the bottle up, chugging down more champagne like a pro.

As much as he wanted to leave, knew he needed to put this woman and her problems behind him, he couldn't bring himself to go. Not when tears were pooling in her eyes and her lips trembled. Somehow, he knew she was trying hard not to cry in front of him.

So, as much as he hated brides, crying women, and champagne, he took the already opened bottle from her and brought it to his mouth. She was right. Daddy did go for the best. First time he'd actually liked the taste of champagne.

"You can't stay down there if you're going to drink with me." She patted the space next to her.

Obeying, he pushed himself up. As they passed the bottle back and forth, he tried to imagine telling Jack that he'd spent the afternoon at a waterfall, drinking top-shelf champagne with a runaway bride who was wearing only a corset and veil. His friend would laugh his ass off, not believing a word of it, then say, "Good one, DD."

\*\*\*

*Don't miss*
Keeping Guard *by Sandra Owens*
*Coming soon wherever*
*Carina Press books are sold.*
*www.CarinaPress.com*

# *Love Harlequin romance?*

## DISCOVER.

Be the first to find out about promotions,
news and exclusive content!

**f** Facebook.com/HarlequinBooks

**𝕏** Twitter.com/HarlequinBooks

**◎** Instagram.com/HarlequinBooks

**𝓟** Pinterest.com/HarlequinBooks

**You Tube** YouTube.com/HarlequinBooks

ReaderService.com

## EXPLORE.

Sign up for the Harlequin e-newsletter and
download a free book from any series at
**TryHarlequin.com**

## CONNECT.

Join our Harlequin community to
share your thoughts and connect
with other romance readers!
**Facebook.com/groups/HarlequinConnection**